JORDAN WRIGHT

The Mandala Chronicles

Realm Of Intention

First edition

ISBN: 978-0-6455405-0-5

*This book was professionally typeset on Reedsy.
Find out more at reedsy.com*

For my kids. May you always be able to tap into that incredible power within you.

Contents

Acknowledgement

Every time I spoke to someone about this book it just kept getting better and better. This is the second time I have published it and I am more in love with it now than I was the first time I wrote it. Thankfully, the people who have been with me on this journey since the beginning have fallen more in love with it as well. So thank you to my editor Kate, who has supported every change I've made (and there's been a lot!). Thank you to my friends who kept hassling me about when they would finally be able to read it. And thank you to my kids for pushing me to take a chance on my writing, so I could show you how important it is to pursue the things that bring you joy.

Chapter 1 - Nora

Nora Parker's throat burned as she took in another large gulp of seawater. Waves crashed around her, and all her senses became hyper-aware as she shielded herself from the onslaught of attacks being fired her way.

Each one working harder to knock her under the water.

But still, she didn't fight back.

There were people nearby, and she couldn't risk hurting anyone. This new power she'd been experimenting with… she didn't know what it could do.

She wasn't entirely sure how they got to the beach. One minute he'd discovered her walking home from university, and the next the man had roughly dropped her into the waves of the nearby beach and lifted himself into the air before so much as a drop of salt water splashed on the black and gold tunic he was wearing.

While she sluggishly dodged another attack, Nora realised the man was just toying with her until she grew desperate enough for air that she would retaliate. She wasn't entirely sure what he wanted, but she wasn't giving it to him as her head once again sunk below the surface of the water.

"Whatever it is you want, just take it away from here," Nora called once her head was above the waves once more. She tried not to swallow another mouthful of seawater as she looked up at the man floating above her with a buzzing black energy ball aimed at her face. "Take me with you. Just—please, let's leave here."

The man sneered, ignoring her plea.

That unforgiving black energy was the last thing Nora saw before she went under the water one last time, instinctively creating her own blast of energy so powerful that the salty water surrounding her turned to steam as she tried to keep herself alive.

The man hissed angrily as the hot steam rose so quickly it scalded his skin.

Taking a large gulp of air, Nora knew it hadn't done much, but it was all she could manage.

No one's going to know where I am... she thought to herself. The man furiously dove down to grab her as she laid, exhausted, on the wet sand, as the quickly refilling beach water lapped at her sides and lifted her into the air by her hair.

A large portal appeared in the sky, and both Nora and the man disappeared.

* * *

The library was empty. With everyone having already gone home for the holidays, Nora assumed that no one else would be getting in some extra study time like she was.

Not that she was working on her degree.

She was lucky that she and her brother had both managed to get accepted into the university near their home, because it meant that they were able to come and go as they pleased without needing to rent out one of the dorms. Not that she ever missed a dorm party. Her brother on the other hand ... he was a bit more of an introvert, often choosing to go home and work in his garden.

Running her hands through her wavy, shoulder-length, dirty blonde hair, Nora sighed when she couldn't find the information she was looking for and absently ran her hands over the circular object she had tucked away in her pocket.

"Nora!" a voice shout-whispered across the room, and Nora turned to see her friend mouthing sorry to the librarian who glared at her as she hastily walked towards where Nora was sitting.

Layla Forrest was a force to be reckoned with, and Nora covered her mouth with her hand to stifled a laugh as her friend reached her.

"Nora," Layla whispered, quieter this time, as she slipped into the chair beside her. "I have news."

Nora's face lit up, and she scooted her chair closer, leaning in as Layla pulled something out of her satchel. Nora coughed as a dust cloud wafted up her nose when Layla dropped the huge, brown, tattered old book on the table in front of them.

"Sorry," Layla grinned as Nora downed half a bottle of water to clear her throat.

"No worries, I wanted to be assaulted today," Nora replied, her amber eyes watering from the dust.

Layla shot her a grin before gingerly opening up the thick cover.

"What is it?" Nora asked, leaning forward to get a closer look.

"I'm not sure, but Aunt Simmy had hidden it at the very back of her closet underneath a bunch of old clothes, so she definitely didn't want me finding it."

The two of them sat in silence as Layla began to gingerly flip through the pages.

It looked like a list, but Nora had no idea what for.

3

"I don't know what any of this means," Nora said to her friend, looking up at her as they reached the final entry. "Do you?"

"No," Layla answered honestly, "but maybe you can take it home and see if it'll help with those dreams you've been having."

"No, you take it back with you. Simmy will kill you if she finds out that you took that from her. She doesn't keep much hidden from you, so that book must be important if she hasn't shown it to you yet," Nora said, gently closing the cover to avoid another dust attack.

Layla sighed. "Yeah, that's true. I'll have to make sure she doesn't see me putting it back, otherwise I'll have to help her in another one of her classes, and I'm not mentally prepared to be her assistant again. That was hell."

Nora laughed, watching as Layla carefully slid the book into her satchel and covered it with a cardigan she wasn't going to need in this summer heat. "It can't have been that bad, she's Life Science, isn't she?"

"Yeah, which is something that Simmy's been teaching me since I was a toddler. I seriously thought that I was going to fall asleep!" Layla emphasised, dragging her hand down her face dramatically.

"I think Noah's in that class." Nora replied, trying to remember what her brother was studying. Heck, she couldn't even remember what she was studying half the time.

"Yeah, I saw him sitting up the back with a couple of your other friends. The pretty Indian girl and the red-haired guy."

"Oh, Ashlee and Josh?" Nora asked, packing up her backpack and swinging it over her shoulder.

"Must be." Layla shrugged. She waved goodbye to the librarian as they walked outside, squinting at the bright sun. "Wait," Layla stopped suddenly, placing her hand on Nora's elbow and grinning at the eyebrow Nora raised in silent question. "Isn't Josh the one *you're going on a date with this weekend?"*

Nora sighed and looked at her friend guiltily. "Yeah, but I'm only going because Noah begged me to. I've known Josh since we were kids. He's like a brother to me. I don't want to hurt his feelings."

"Why didn't you just tell him that?" Layla asked.

"Because he's the sweetest guy. I can at least give him a chance, and if I still feel the same way afterwards I'll let him know. He's cool, it won't be a problem if nothing happens."

"Well, we redheads are pretty chill," Layla laughed, flicking her wild fiery hair behind her as she walked, and Nora rolled her eyes and grinned.

"Are you waiting for Simmy tonight, or do you want to walk home together? Noah's already left to go help Dad in the garden," Nora asked.

"I'll wait for Simmy. Hopefully she won't be able to tell I've got her book in my bag." Layla shot Nora a guilty look.

Nora laughed and pulled her friend in for a hug, kissing her on her temple. "Here"—she pulled the circular package from her pocket and handed it to Layla—"in case you need it tonight. I'll see you tomorrow." She waved and walked down the path to exit the campus.

"Thanks, see you tomorrow," Layla called, pocketing the package before walking off in the direction of the staff room.

A gust of strong wind came from behind Nora, blowing her wavy hair into her face. Before she could turn to see what had caused it, a rough hand gripped her elbow, and the next thing she knew she was completely submerged in a body of water, her backpack sinking to the bottom.

* * *

5

Groaning, Nora opened her eyes and rubbed her pounding head.

The surface she was lying on was rough and the pillow was lumpy and damp. Her mouth was dry too. She tried licking her lips, but her tongue felt like sandpaper. Sighing, she tried sitting up instead, but the moment she moved her arms, pain shot through her entire body and she became aware of a pair of electrical cuffs that were bound to her wrists and ankles forced her to lay still.

"You're awake then?" came a gruff voice from the doorway. Nora stiffly turned her head to find the man who had taken her leaning against the doorframe.

The room was so dark that she couldn't see his face properly, so she tried to lift her head for a better look and hissed in pain as the electrical cuffs forced her back down again.

The man slowly walked over, looking her up and down as he did so. Once he reached her side, he gripped her chin painfully in his fingers, forcing her to look at him, taking no notice of the pained expression on her face as the cuffs reacted to her movement.

"You have knowledge about something I've been looking for," he hissed in her ear. "I just don't know *why*."

Nora gritted her teeth as the sharp pain of the cuffs continued to shoot through her body, but she refused to cry out, instead hissing back, "I don't know what you're talking about. And even if I did, I wouldn't help you."

The man laughed cruelly before roughly throwing her head back onto the pillow. "Yes," he said softly, looking her in the eye, "you will."

Nora glared at him, her amber eyes flashing as she watched the man turn on his heel and stalk out of the room, closing the door loudly behind him.

Once she was sure that he was gone, Nora let out a frustrated cry. Tears pooled in her eyes as she pulled against the cuffs with as much strength as she could muster, but the cuffs just got tighter and tighter the more she struggled, shocking her painfully each time she pulled against them.

Finally, when she was sure she couldn't handle any more, Nora took a deep breath in through her nose and out through her mouth to calm down, closed her eyes, and dug deep within herself. There was a power within her that she had only just begun to learn about, and she knew now was the time to tap into it.

Taking another deep breath in and out, Nora opened her eyes, focusing her attention on her hands, willing her amber energy to her fingers.

It took a few tries, but finally she was holding a sphere of energy the size of a tennis ball in both her hands.

"Yes," Nora breathed, a tight smile forming on her lips. She wasn't sure how to use it yet but she knew she needed to get these cuffs off. She closed her eyes and visualised the energy she was holding in her hands expanding over her entire body, matching the vibration of the cuffs, trying to force them off her wrists and ankles.

Keeping her breath steady, Nora focused on her energy, embracing the feeling of it covering her body, and nervously tested whether the cuffs holding her were gone by lifting her hand.

Hissing in pain as it shocked her, Nora gritted her teeth and tried again. And again. And again. Until finally, tears streaming down her cheeks, her wrists and ankles raw, she felt the cuffs fall away.

Gasping, Nora sat up stiffly, rubbing her raw wrists, and looked around the room, trying to see if there was any way out.

She didn't know where the man had taken her though, so even if she *could* escape, she had no idea how to get home.

But she had to try.

Gritting her teeth again, Nora quietly stalked to the closed door and pressed her ear against it.

Not hearing anything, she gingerly tested to see if it would open, relief flooding through her when it did.

The man clearly thought his cuffs were strong enough to hold her, so he hadn't bothered to lock the door.

Slowly turning the handle so she didn't make any noise, Nora pushed it open and was immediately flung back into the room, roughly hitting the wall and sliding onto the bed.

"Interesting," the man said as he walked back into the room. "You might be of more use than I thought."

Chapter 2 - Noah

MISSING GIRL
18 YEARS OF AGE
SHOULDER-LENGTH BLONDE HAIR
AMBER EYES
PICTURE PROVIDED BELOW
PLEASE CONTACT LOCAL AUTHORITIES IF YOU HAVE ANY INFORMATION

Eighteen-year-old Noah Parker watched miserably as the missing person posters were plastered around the small town where he lived.

Picking one up off the ground, Noah stared at the picture of his twin sister.

Apart from the wavy blonde hair and amber eyes, Noah Parker was the polar opposite of his twin sister. He hadn't yet grown into his height and still had the teenage lankiness that made his skinny torso seem overgrown.

Nora, on the other hand, was a bronzed beauty who had filled out early in her teens and always seemed to be laughing. She was the sweetheart of the town, with her fiery amber eyes wreaking havoc with the local boys.

Noah and Nora had been as thick as thieves, but he sometimes felt a twinge in his heart over how easily she made friends and how effortlessly smart she was. He was never the one to stand up to others, it was always Nora who made sure he was alright. She would often tease Noah about his lack of enthusiasm for anything that didn't involve a patch of dirt, some seeds and a watering can. Although she was always the one to remind him of his talent for making them grow - a talent that sometimes surprised even him.

A small, cold hand placed itself at the crook of Noah's arm, which shook him out of his reverie. It led him down a driveway to a cosy-looking house in the middle of the street.

Jen Parker was shorter than Nora, but it was obvious that both twins had taken after her with her kind smile and untamed shoulder-length dirty blonde hair which, at the moment, was trying to free itself from the tight bun on top of her head.

The twins' father Paul, with his jet black hair, looked nothing like the rest of the family except for his piercing amber eyes, today dulled with a crippling sadness at the loss of his baby girl.

Jen opened her mouth to speak, but no words came out, so she closed it, keeping her hand on the crook of Noah's arm.

It had been a week since Nora's disappearance.

Noah, Jen and Paul had done everything within their power to find her. Personally drove to each police station within five hours of their little town to see if anyone had seen or heard anything that could link them to Nora, and to hand out the missing person fliers so that they would know immediately if anyone had spotted her.

Paul, who Noah knew had prided himself on being the rock of the family, was leaning on his wife for support. It was as if he now carried the weight of the world on his shoulders, and needed her to help guide him.

Jen, the silent glue of their family, had always let Paul feel like he was in charge, but Noah saw how she had automatically accepted Paul's need for support and let him share the burden he was carrying with her.

Noah and Jen, with her hand still in the crook of Noah's arm, reached the house first, followed by his father who absently shuffled into the living room and poured himself a glass of scotch.

Saying nothing, Noah gently lifted his mum's hand off his arm and slowly walked to his bedroom, flopping face first on top of the covers. Tears streaming down his face, he fell asleep.

* * *

How long had she been gone? Weeks, even months, could have passed. Noah couldn't tell anymore.

His home, that used to be full of life and laughter, was now dull. A layer of dust had settled over the floor and furniture, and the contents of the fridge wafted a foul odour whenever it was opened.

Daily life was the basics, and sometimes only if prompted. Food was provided by concerned friends and neighbours who let themselves into the house every now and again, otherwise the fridge would have been completely bare. Bathing was perfunctory. Discussions became circular and then talk ended. Sitting gazing at the wall was the standard gap filler.

Then one day, there came a loud knock on the front door.

No one had bothered to knock for ages. They had just let themselves in and allowed the family to wallow in their grief, not wanting to overstep their boundaries.

At the sound, Jen and Paul blinked and looked at each other.

"Who could that be?" rasped Paul, his voice rough from disuse.

Jen shrugged and walked, dreamlike towards the door, passing Noah on the staircase, who had shuffled out of his bedroom and down the stairs. She hesitated for a second before turning the handle of the solid timber door.

Could it be news about Nora? Noah asked himself, staring down the stairs forcing the hope that was rising in his chest back down.

The door swung inward with a slight nudge from the occupant on the front porch. The bright sunlight poured in, and almost vampire-esque, the Parkers shielded their eyes with their hands.

The guest waited patiently for the family to adjust to the new stream of light.

Noah's eyes adjusted first, and he blinked once, twice, as he saw the figure standing in the doorway.

"Ms Johannson?" he asked, with what would have been shock, had he been able to feel emotions anymore, at the sight of his favourite teacher.

The portly woman at the door smiled, her straight teeth and warm brown eyes visible from even where Noah was standing. "Noah Parker. I have missed you in my class," she said. "It's been quite a while."

Jen and Paul's burning eyes had adjusted enough to the light in their doorway to be able to make out a woman with thick dark auburn hair that reached just above her shoulders.

"Simone?" Jen exclaimed. "Wha— What are you doing here?"

For the first time in weeks Jen Parker saw what her house had become and, horrified, indiscreetly started brushing the dust off the vase closest to her onto the layer that coated the shaggy carpet.

Noah became vividly aware that his whole family were wearing dressing gowns and slippers, except for Paul who had only managed to pull on one slipper while the other sat forgotten at the foot of his armchair as he shuffled to meet their visitor. His unbrushed hair was sticking up in the back where his head had been resting.

It was a token of the type of person Simone Johannson was that she didn't mention any of this, but smiled brightly at the three of them and answered Jen with a tone that was extremely kind, but didn't allow any disagreement. "I've come to speak to you all. I've missed seeing Noah in my class, and I also wanted to introduce you all to my niece, Layla Forrest."

Noah, unaware that Ms Johannson had a niece, opened his mouth to exclaim this when a small face surrounded by a lot of wild, bright red hair appeared from behind her.

"Yes, of course," Jen exclaimed. "We—come in! We're so sorry we didn't contact you sooner. Tea? Yes. Come in—of course!" In a flurry, Jen turned to look for some teacups in the living room and seemed confused when she wasn't able to find them.

Ms Johannson held up her hand, her kind smile still upon her lips. "There is no worry at all. The loss of a child and sister is a great tragedy upon any family. We were hoping to catch up with Noah at university to see how he had been coping, but we decided to stop by earlier. I think in times like this we need to stick together, do you agree?"

Still searching for the teacups, Jen nodded furiously while

Paul, who was still standing in the same place at the doorway, was now tapping his bare foot forward and back as if he was contemplating walking but not able to comprehend how to do it.

Ms Johannson spoke again. "May we sit down?" she asked, gesturing to the living room. "And as we are going to become a much closer group in the near future, I must insist that you call me Simmy." Catching Noah's eye, she nodded at him. "You as well Noah, unless of course we are in class, where Ms Johannson will suffice."

By this stage Paul had managed to comprehend walking, and had reached Jen, who was still looking for the missing teacups. He put a hand on her shoulder to stop her search, as they were currently not residing in the living room, but in a cabinet in the kitchen where they had always been. He held out his other hand to Simmy. "We are so sorry we haven't been in contact," he said, nodding his head at the mop of red hair standing beside Simmy in acknowledgement.

Simmy moved forwards into the house and clasped her warm hands around the one Paul had extended her. "Sometimes we need help to bring ourselves back," she said, looking at the Parkers with an expression of such sincere love on her face that Noah's eyes prickled. He noticed a glimmer in Jen's blue eyes and Paul suddenly found something on the carpet extremely interesting.

"We realise that you must be struggling through the suddenness of it all," Simmy said. "If only there was a way for us to predict things such as this, and maybe prevent them from happening. But unfortunately, the path we are given can take us on a turbulent road." With that final comment, Simmy led Layla into the house and they both sat down on a three-seater leather sofa near the fireplace.

Paul and Jen rushed into the kitchen to organise tea for everyone. There was a crash as one of them collided with the wall, a soft tinkle of breaking china and a choice swear word that followed, then, finally, the sound of the kettle boiling and five cups being placed upon saucers.

Noah, who had still been standing on the stairs, made his way to the living room, silently thanking all the people who had provided them with baked goods so they could offer Simmy and Layla something other than dusty tea and awkward company.

"Come and sit down, Noah," Simmy said to him, leaning over and patting the cushion next to Layla.

Noah took his time sliding onto the couch, and sat half on the cushion, half on the armrest, leaving a good few inches between himself and Layla.

Layla's slightly too-far-apart emerald green eyes stared at Noah, and, for a second, Noah could have sworn he saw a look of recognition on her face, but he blinked and it was gone.

Jen and Paul reappeared in the living room. Jen carried the cups and saucers, while Paul carried the kettle and a delicious-looking lemon and coconut slice that Noah had no idea who'd baked for them.

He mentally thanked them as it took Layla's eyes off him, and he turned his head away while attempting to get comfortable.

His mother passed Noah a cup and saucer with a tea bag already inside it, and he tried to wait patiently for his father to pour the water so he could do something with his hands.

Finally, Paul reached him and slowly tipped the water into

his cup until it was full.

Noah preoccupied himself with dipping his tea bag into his water so thoroughly that he only vaguely heard his mother ask, "So do you and Noah know each other, Layla?"

A huskier voice than Noah had been expecting came from beside him. "I believe I'm in a few of his classes this semester, but he hasn't been back yet to confirm it. I helped teach a class with Simmy that he was in earlier this year," Layla replied. "We haven't had a chance to properly meet. I'd only just become friends with Nora recently and she never had the chance to introduce us as we were always so busy."

Paul, who had finished pouring the tea, lifted his cup and took a sip. "Well, it's lovely to meet you, Layla," he said.

"You're welcome around here whenever you like," Jen added.

"Thank you," Layla replied. "Aunt Simmy was fond of Nora as well, so we're going to do everything in our power to find her."

"We're very grateful to you," Jen said, her voice thick.

Simmy smiled, clapped her hands once and stood up. She picked up a slice of the lemon and coconut tart and turned to leave.

Noah, Jen and Paul also stood up with Simmy, Jen and Paul's tea slopping out the sides of their teacups in their haste.

"Well," Simmy said, "I think we will leave it here today. We've trespassed on your company long enough." She rested a hand on Layla's shoulder, indicating that it was time to go. "If you don't mind, Noah, would you please show us to the door?"

Noah nodded, at the same time Jen took a step to see the two women out.

"You two stay here, and have a piece of that delicious slice and relax," Simmy said to both Jen and Paul. "Noah is a very capable young man, I'm sure he knows where the front door is. Thank you for your hospitality today. It was lovely to see you, and I hope to see you again soon."

"Goodbye, thank you for the tea," Layla said, giving Jen and Paul a small wave as she turned to follow Noah and Simmy to the front door.

Simmy turned to Noah. "I want to see you back in my class sometime soon."

Layla then unexpectedly handed a small circular package to Noah. "This was Nora's, she gave it to me to hold onto the day that…" Layla shook her head. "Anyway, she would have wanted you to have it."

A burning sensation in Noah's throat, that had nothing to do with the hot tea, stopped him from thanking Layla straight away.

He swallowed deeply and looked at her in her bright green eyes. "Thank you," he said. A fresh row of tears started to form, and Noah quickly swept them away.

Layla put her hand on his forearm in understanding. "Nora's not gone forever. She's out there somewhere, and we're going to find her sooner rather than later."

Simmy nodded in agreement behind Layla, and Noah turned to her. "I'll come back to school next week. I…I think I should. Nora wouldn't want me moping around forever."

Simmy smiled her bright, warm smile at him and pulled him into a hug. "I'm glad to hear it. I will have a full lesson waiting for you upon your return."

On that note, Simmy gave one final wave, then walked out the door. Layla followed with one last smile at Noah, and they were gone.

17

Noah closed the door behind them and walked back into the hallway. He glanced into the living room and saw his parents chatting, almost like they used to, each had their cup of tea in one hand and a piece of slice in the other.

Not wanting to disturb them, Noah walked up the stairs towards his bedroom, pausing briefly at Nora's bedroom door, then walking on past. He wasn't ready to open it just yet.

There was a little spring in his step as he walked, though. It was the first time in what felt like a lifetime that he'd forgotten to feel sad. Smiling to himself, Noah looked down at the small package in his hand.

It felt strange. It was round, bumpy, and Noah was sure that it had grown warmer as he held onto it.

Intrigued, he reached his bedroom and gently unfolded the paper with one hand while the other hand, palm open, held the package flat for him to see.

Inside was a mandala, the same size as the palm of his hand, with stones that looked like tiny suns weaved throughout the centre of it.

It was beautiful. It reminded Noah of sunny days, blue skies and laughter.

Noah picked the mandala up with his free hand and gasped. He was no longer in his room.

Looking around, Noah could see there were blue skies, a large warm sun shining down on him, and the grass beneath his slippered feet looked soft and gentle. He sat down, closed his eyes and took a deep breath, in through his nose and out through his mouth.

Sitting there, Noah kept his eyes closed and soaked up the warmth that his body desperately needed.

He leant back, laying himself down on the comfortable grass

and, slowly and easily, drifted off to sleep.

As he slept, the mandala slipped through his fingers and onto the grass beside him, and as soon as he'd stopped touching it he was transported back to his bedroom.

The next morning Noah woke up feeling well-rested and refreshed, with the mandala lying innocently next to him on the bed.

Chapter 3 - Layla

L ayla sat down in the back of the study hall, flicking
through the notes she'd kept ever since Nora had
disappeared.

If only I'd walked home with her, she thought to herself,
placing her notebook down and rubbing her eyes with the
palms of her hands.

But it was no use thinking like that. She didn't have the
ability to turn back time. As Simmy often told her, everyone's
path leads them down difficult roads at times. But this wasn't
meant to happen. Not to Nora.

"Layla!"

Someone called her name snapping her out of her reverie.

Straightening up, Layla saw her aunt standing at the doorway, waving her down. Packing up her things, Layla zipped
her satchel and made her way towards the door, trying to
decipher the pinched look on Simmy's face.

"What's up?" Layla asked.

"Class has been finished for fifteen minutes already. I was
wondering where you were. Do you still want to walk home
together?" Simmy asked, concern washing over her face. "It's
been a few weeks since Nora disappeared, are you still fixating
that you didn't walk her home?"

"I'm not fixating," Layla mumbled, but her frustration evaporated as quickly as it came when she saw the worry on her aunt's face. "No—yes—sort of. If I'd gone with her then she'd still be here!"

"You don't know that," Simmy replied softly, pulling Layla into a one-armed hug. "You could both be missing instead."

"I could have helped fight off whoever took her!" Layla insisted, pulling out of her aunt's hug and running her hands over her face. "I'm strong enough."

"We don't know a fight occurred yet," Simmy replied in that same soft tone, although the look on her face made Layla think she knew more about what had happened then she was letting on. "But Nora is powerful too. She hadn't managed to fully tap into it while she was working with us, but I hope she's managed to tap into it now..." Simmy trailed off.

Layla looked at her. "Do you think she'll need to?"

Simmy sighed. "I hope not."

Layla didn't reply, instead she fell into step with her aunt, who had started walking to the exit. Their house was only a short walk from the university, so the two of them often opted for exercise rather than driving. The fresh air helped keep Layla's head clear.

They walked in silence, both trying to make sense of their thoughts.

Layla had met Nora in the library a couple of months ago and knew right away that they were going to be fast friends. There was an energy about Nora that drew her in, and Layla had no trouble opening up to her, telling her things she'd rarely shared with anyone.

Like ever since her parents had died in a car crash when she was still an infant, Layla had been in Simmy's care.

21

Simmy wasn't her aunt by blood, but because she had been friends with her parents before Layla was born she'd taken her in without question. Layla didn't know much about her other blood relatives, but Simmy had been enough. Taking care of her, providing for her, not only the things she needed but also the things she wanted. Alright, Layla was a bit spoiled, she'd admit it. Simmy had never left her wanting.

It wasn't what most people would call a usual childhood, but Layla wouldn't change it for the world. The adventures she'd been on and the experiences she'd had were out of this world.

Literally.

They turned into their driveway, walking up to the small townhouse where the two of them lived. Layla pushed her key into the door, stepped inside and kicked her shoes off at the entrance.

"Make sure you finish your assignments before you get too carried away," she heard Simmy call to her, as she walked down the hall to her bedroom. Layla waved a hand, knowing that Simmy was watching her go.

Turning on her laptop, Layla tapped away absently in case Simmy was listening in to see if Layla was actually doing as she'd asked.

When she figured that she'd faked it long enough, Layla closed her laptop and pulled a circular package from her pocket and placed it on her palm, opening it up to show a mandala, the perfect match to that she'd given Noah.

Simmy hadn't told her why the two mandalas were identical. She was always talking about Divine Timing, and said that when Layla was ready to hear the information she would be told, but she wouldn't hear it beforehand.

It was really frustrating to be honest. Layla wanted to know everything about everything and wanted to know it now. This Divine Timing thing was really grating. Why couldn't she know things before she was meant to?

Layla placed her index finger on the largest nearly translucent, orange sunstone in the middle of the mandala and closed her eyes, anticipating the familiar feeling of being *whooshed* away.

Opening her eyes, Layla looked around at the barren surroundings. She was standing on the top of a hill and there was nothing around her except for a forest of thin, dead trees, a dried up lake and dark, grey clouds covering the sun. The dead grass crunched under her bare feet and she wiggled her toes, trying to soften it so it would become more comfortable.

She knew she couldn't stay here for long. Simmy would notice her using the mandala and would come in to stop her any minute now.

Closing her eyes again, Layla connected with the emerald green energy within her and expelled it from her body, keeping it thin and light so no one would be able to detect it.

She wasn't even sure if this would work, but she had to try. If Nora was here, if she had been taken here because of what she had been working on with her and Simmy, then Layla would never forgive herself if she didn't try everything she could to find her.

It didn't take long for Layla's energy to spread itself so thin that it disappeared completely, evaporating into the thick air surrounding the barren land she was standing in.

Sighing, Layla opened her eyes again and took her finger off the mandala, allowing herself to be transported back to her bedroom, only to find Simmy leaning against her door frame, looking at her through narrowed eyes.

Layla opened her mouth to explain, but Simmy held up a hand, stopping her.

"If you were to disappear as well, what do you think I would be able to do to help you?" she asked, her voice soft.

Layla didn't reply. She knew that Simmy was in a difficult situation right now. She hadn't thought of that when she'd gone to find Nora, she just knew she couldn't sit idly by while her friend may be in danger.

"I'm doing everything I can to find Nora," Simmy continued.

"I know," Layla mumbled, guilt spreading through her chest.

"If we have any chance of helping her, I'm going to need you here with me, not running off every chance you get because you feel like it's your responsibility."

Layla didn't reply.

Simmy's soft footsteps padded on the carpet as she pulled her niece into a hug, leaning her chin on the top of her head as Layla sat in the chair. "I couldn't bear losing you too."

"Sorry," Layla replied, holding onto the arm that was around her.

They stayed like that for a few minutes before Simmy sighed, placed a kiss on top of Layla's head and then let go. "Dinner will be ready in fifteen minutes," she said. "Make sure you get some schoolwork done before then."

"Okay," Layla replied. "Okay!" she said again, at Simmy's pointed look.

When Simmy closed the door behind her, Layla sighed, wrapping her mandala back in its cloth and placed it in her pocket. She'd been carrying it around with her everywhere since she'd met Nora, and if she left it behind she felt lost without its comforting weight.

Opening her laptop again, Layla logged into her student portal and looked at the assignments she had due. Sighing again, she ran her hands through her hair and leant back into her chair.

Assignments were the last thing she wanted to be working on right now, but if there was nothing she could do to help Nora, then she may as well keep busy.

She plucked a thick textbook off her desk and opened it to the tabbed page she'd been using previously, re-reading the information. She definitely wasn't going to get a distinction on this essay, but she could probably manage a pass. *P's get degrees,* she thought to herself as she started typing out the research for her assignment.

* * *

The urge to keep searching for Nora was overwhelming, even haunting Layla in her dreams. She couldn't remember the last time she'd had a decent night's sleep.

Tossing and turning in her bed, Layla decided that it was pointless. *What's another night of no sleep?* she asked herself, so she sat up, turned on the lamp on her bedside table and checked her phone, going through the last messages she and Nora had sent to each other.

She'd already done this a hundred times, but maybe this was the time she found something worthwhile.

Flicking through the messages, Layla paused every now and again to write down a note in the little booklet she always had near her before scrolling on.

When she'd reached the end of the messages she groaned. She wasn't able to find anything substantial. Unless Josh had kidnapped her before their date, she didn't have a single lead.

Dread began to fill her as she imagined the worst, but she quickly shut it down. There wasn't a chance anything she'd imagined actually happened so she wasn't going to think about it.

Lying back down on the bed, Layla reached out and grabbed the book she'd started reading a few weeks ago but hadn't gotten around to finishing. If she needed to keep her mind occupied, then that's what she was going to do.

Unsurprisingly, the book didn't manage to keep every bad thought from flying through her head, but it did keep her entertained enough to make it through to the morning.

Yawning as she dragged herself over to the mirror, she wasn't surprised to see dark rings under her eyes so she dotted on some concealer before making her way to the table for breakfast, not bothering with any other makeup.

Simmy was already awake and making pancakes as Layla poured herself a cup of water and sat at the table. "Thanks," she said as Simmy passed a plate of the hot deliciousness towards her.

Pancakes were her favourite. Simmy never made them anymore, but one glance told Layla that Simmy hadn't slept well last night either, and they both needed some comfort food to help them get through the day.

"I wonder if Noah will turn up to classes today?" Simmy mused out loud.

"It's only been a couple of days since we went to see him," Layla replied. "He said he'd come back next week, so I doubt it."

"Hmm," Simmy hummed in reply, flipping the batch of pancakes she was cooking.

"What?" Layla asked, the bite of pancake she was about to eat paused at her mouth as she looked at her aunt.

"I'm just thinking." Simmy said, but didn't elaborate.

Rolling her eyes and trying not to smile, Layla shoved the pancake into her mouth. Simmy always got like that whenever she had a new idea that she wasn't sure would work out. When she was ready to share it with Layla, she would.

The rest of the meal was eaten in silence with both Simmy and Layla lost in their own thoughts. "I'm going to walk on ahead," Layla said, looking at her aunt, who was still in her pyjamas and dressing gown.

"Get some extra work done on those assignments of yours," Simmy said sternly.

"Yeah, yeah," Layla replied, giving Simmy a kiss on the cheek before walking out the door. "See you soon."

Taking her time, Layla walked to the campus, wishing she was going anywhere but class. She had no interest in her studies right now, not when there was still so much that needed to be done to find Nora.

Swatting away a fly that had started to buzz around her while she walked, Layla took a deep breath. *I need to stay positive,* she thought to herself. She couldn't help Nora if she wasn't in the right frame of mind.

Gritting her teeth in determination, Layla decided to make the most of her day, while also keeping an eye out for any clues that might lead her to Nora. It was all she could do right now, so she was damn well going to do it.

Chapter 4 - Noah

A few days had passed since Noah's dream about being transported to that warm sunny hill, although for some reason he couldn't shake the feeling that it hadn't been a dream at all. So, just in case, he'd tightly wrapped the mandala up again and hidden it in his underwear drawer.

He had noticed, though, that ever since he'd had that dream, the tightness in his chest had lifted. But since it had also been the day that Simmy and Layla had come to visit, he convinced himself that they were the reason he felt so much lighter.

Even his parents were in higher spirits.

The guests that had been popping around since Nora's disappearance, who were expecting the dull forms of the Parker family that had previously greeted them, had been pleasantly surprised to find that the family had started to come alive again.

Simmy had also returned to the house once more to confirm that Noah was returning to school next week, and to provide him with his new timetable.

Glancing down at it, Noah had expected it to be similar to his timetable the previous semester. "Ms Johanns—Simmy," he corrected himself, "I think there's been a mistake on my timetable. It's showing me that every class is a free choice, except for Life Science classes with you every day."

Simmy smiled. "Yes, I wanted to talk to you about that. I believe that we should all be focusing more on the things we love, and because you have had a rough few weeks, I asked the professors who used to teach you if we could make an exception for you this semester to focus on what you enjoy. You need to make sure that you keep a slot free to work in the gardens with the groundskeeper, though. But," Simmy added, seeing the ecstatic expression on Noah's face, "you need to keep your grades up in your other classes, otherwise this privilege will be taken away from you. Understood?"

Noah nodded quickly. "Yes, I understand. Thank you, Ms Johann—Simmy. Thank you, Simmy."

"I've also asked for Layla to join you in most of your classes as well," Simmy said. "The professors are aware and will let her know which classes you choose."

Noah kept nodding, not saying anything. His heart had given a strange, unfamiliar lurch at the mention of Layla.

"If you look at your timetable once more, you will see that you are having specialised classes with me this semester too," Simmy went on.

Noah looked down again, and sure enough every afternoon at three o'clock there was an unspecified class with Simmy. Unsure as to why he needed a special class, and having an inkling that Layla would also be joining them. Noah nodded again.

Looking up from his timetable, Noah saw that Simmy had left his side and was now greeting Jen and Paul in the living room.

Noah's suddenly too-long legs stumbled awkwardly from

his standing position as he followed Simmy, passing his mother his timetable so she could examine his classes.

"What are all these blank periods?" Jen exclaimed. She had always been concerned that Noah hadn't picked up academics as easily as his sister had.

"It's only for this semester," Simmy said, with a wink at Noah. "I believe that it is important for Noah to concentrate on something he is good at and enjoys for the time being, so he's going to choose his own classes while also helping the groundskeeper with the gardens around the campus," she repeated for Jen.

Jen made an indistinguishable noise between a grunt and a cough and turned her eyes back to the piece of paper in front of her.

Paul, on the other hand, who had always enjoyed Noah's love for the outdoors and the endless fruits and veggies he supplied for their table, stood up and thumped Noah on the shoulder, causing Noah's knees to buckle.

Giving a pointed look at his wife, Paul said to Simmy, "I agree, what a great idea. Imagine how much happier we'd be if we could focus on the things we enjoyed all the time."

"Exactly!" Simmy replied. "I believe that this will help Noah's academics in the long run."

Mollified by Simmy's last statement, Jen handed Noah's timetable back to him. "I suppose, yes, but I still want to see you doing well in your other classes," she said sternly to Noah.

Noah grinned, an exercise that made his cheeks hurt as the recently unused muscles contracted. "Thanks Mum, I'll make sure to keep an eye on my grades. Besides, Simmy's already told me that I need to keep on top of everything."

Jen hummed in response, and she went into the kitchen to

boil the kettle.

"Well, I must be off. Lots of work to catch up on, I'm afraid," she said as Paul opened his mouth to offer her a cup of tea.

"Alright," said Paul, walking her to the door as Noah trailed slightly behind them. "Thanks for dropping this off. Noah will be back to classes on Monday."

"Excellent. I look forward to seeing you with us again soon, Noah. Life Science just isn't the same without you," Simmy said warmly, waving at Jen's head that had popped around the kitchen doorway then turning to leave. "Oh," she said, turning back slightly, "Noah, please bring that mandala that Layla gave you to the classes you have with me in the afternoons. It's very important."

Smile faltering slightly, Noah nodded. "Oh, okay. I'll remember it," he said, thinking to himself that it wouldn't matter if he *accidentally* forgot it for the first lesson. He still wasn't confident about picking it up again.

Simmy shot Noah a look, giving him the impression that she knew what he was thinking. "Please do." And with that, she turned on her heel, walked down the driveway and was gone.

Paul closed the front door, then turned to Noah and whispered, "Make sure you *do* keep your grades up, I want you to put what you learn from the groundskeeper into a new garden for winter." He winked as he turned, racing into the kitchen at his wife's call. "Coming, dear!"

Noah laughed, shocked at the sudden show of humour from his dad, and followed him into the kitchen to set the table for lunch.

* * *

Monday came around far too quickly for Noah's liking.

As he pulled on his jeans and shirt, Noah realised with a pang that this would be his first day back at school without Nora. The first day seeing their friends without his sister, outside of when they came to visit, but he'd been in such a fog whenever they'd come over that he could barely remember it.

Suddenly, one sneaker on, Noah didn't want to go anymore. He sat staring at his toes for ten minutes before he heard the shuffle of someone walking on the carpet outside his bedroom door.

Still in their dressing gowns, Noah's parents stood in front of him. His mum held her arms out, offering an understanding hug.

Feeling foolish, Noah accepted his mother's embrace and soon felt his father's arms around him as well.

It reminded Noah of the type of hug his parents used to give him when he was a little kid, and they were protecting him from the monsters hiding under his bed.

When the tightness in Noah's chest eased, the family broke apart. Jen had tear streaks down her face, and Paul was purposely avoiding eye contact with both Noah and his wife.

Noah coughed loudly to clear his thick throat and looked at his parents. "Well, I'd better go. I'll be late otherwise."

Jen nodded and handed him a small wrapped package. "Simmy will be furious if you forget this."

It was the mandala. Noah had taken it out of the drawer that morning and placed it on his mantel.

"Oh shi—ugar... Sugar." Noah hastily corrected himself as his parents narrowed their eyes, "Thanks, Mum."

Noah accepted the package, pulled on his other sneaker and quickly jogged down the stairs to the front door, away from

Jen before she could reprimand him. "Bye Mum, bye Dad," Noah called, running out the door.

The twenty-minute walk to the campus reminded Noah how unfit he had become, and he rubbed a stitch in his side as he walked through the front gates.

Noah glanced awkwardly around. He had been expecting whispers behind his back, but he hadn't been prepared for the blatant staring and obvious conversations about him that ended as soon as he walked into view.

Keeping his head down, he walked as quickly as he could to his first class.

"Morning, Noah," a familiar voice said quietly behind him, causing him to jump a foot in the air.

"Layla," Noah gasped, holding his chest. "What are you doing here?"

"We're in the same class, remember," Layla announced, as she walked between the rows of desks and took her seat.

"We are? Is this part of the new timetable? We have most classes together don't we?" Noah asked, absently fishing for his timetable in his backpack.

"Simmy thought it would be best if we stayed together," Layla replied, and took her seat next to Noah.

Noah just stared at her sitting calmly next to him, until she looked up and pointed her pen to the front of the class indicating that the professor had just walked in.

Noah was half expecting Simmy to be standing behind the teacher's desk, and felt slightly ill when he saw that it was the old Maths Fundamentals professor, Mr Greeves.

Mr Greeves had the air of someone who had been teaching for a very long time, but never truly understood the art of it. He had short grey hair on either side of his head and a large bald patch in the middle, but the most prominent feature of Mr Greeves was that he had an exceptionally small nose, which struggled to hold up his very large tortoiseshell glasses.

Heart sinking, Noah knew that Mr Greeves was going to bring attention to the fact that he was back, and tried, unsuccessfully, to sink under his desk. *Why did I decide to take this class again?* Noah mentally berated himself. *Oh right, it's good to know maths for the gardens. Maybe Dad lied to me when he told me that.*

"Noah Parker!" barked Mr Greeves. "Good to have you back, son. Stand up so everyone can see you."

Noah fidgeted with his hands at the uncomfortable silence that swept over the room as he stood up in front of the class as slowly as possible.

It was times like this he wished he wasn't so tall.

Noah tried not to catch his classmates' expressions, mixed between uncertain smiles of support and blatantly looking in the other direction. Mr Greeves opened his mouth once more.

"Terrible tragedy," Mr Greeves said, and gave a dramatic sigh that made Noah's arm hairs stand on end.

Praying that Mr Greeves would let him sit down soon, Noah merely nodded and avoided the eye contact of a girl with long brown hair pulled back into a braid, who was openly staring at him.

"Now," continued Mr Greeves, who in all his years of teaching had never understood teenagers, "I don't want Noah to be alone in his return back to school. I want a buddy system. Who wants to buddy up with Noah?" he looked around the room, expecting every hand to shoot up in the air.

"I will, sir," said a voice next to Noah.

"Who said that?" asked Mr Greeves, eagerly looking for the owner of the voice.

"I did, sir," said Layla, standing up on her chair so her little frame could be seen next to Noah's tall one.

"Very good, Leanne!" Mr Greeves said importantly, completely ignorant to the fact he'd gotten Layla's name wrong.

Noah turned to look at her.

Meeting his eye, Layla shrugged and whispered, "We're in the same classes, and Mr Greeves wouldn't have let it go until you had a buddy for the day, so I thought I'd step in for you."

Noah stared at Layla without saying anything.

"I hope you'll all take a leaf out of Leanne's book," Mr Greeves said, looking at the students in his class who were all suddenly very occupied with their own books or fingernails. "Stepping up for a fellow classmate."

Noah fought a grin in spite of himself at the justice Mr Greeves was trying to inflict upon the rest of the class.

Thankfully, they were all saved as Mr Greeves finally let Noah and Layla sit down, and the lesson started.

It was one of the most boring classes Noah had ever had to sit through, but he had to be honest with himself, he knew he'd be able to implement some of the things he learnt in his garden.

Finally, the class was over, and the sound of students chattering was deafening as people scrambled from the room before Mr Greeves could call them aside.

"We'd better get going," Layla said, glancing at her timetable. "We have Simmy next, and she's not going to appreciate it if we're late to her class."

Glancing at his own timetable, and seeing that he did indeed have Life Science next, Noah followed Layla out of the classroom.

They both walked together in silence until they reached the science block.

Simmy's classroom did not look like a usual science lab.

The students were greeted with a dark classroom filled with crystals, salt lamps and an extraordinarily large mandala draped over the ceiling, embedded with hundreds of tiny luminescent, milky-white moonstones.

Entranced by the mandala, Noah hadn't heard Simmy greet the class and tell them to take their seats until Layla swung her notebook at his head and knocked him out of his reverie.

Looking sheepishly at Simmy, Noah took his seat, allowing her to begin her class.

Simmy cleared her throat and smiled her big, warm smile. "Welcome back, everyone. You may have noticed a change in decorations over the weekend." She paused as the students murmured at her statement. Some of the class looked around the room, while others tried to adjust their eyes to the darkness.

"As you know, this semester we are learning about the human body. Last week we finished learning about the science of the physical body, the biology of our body, our organs and physical attributes,"Simmy said as the class nodded. "This week we are starting our studies on the science behind the human mind."

The class all looked at Simmy. Some were confused, some excited, and some were flicking through their notebooks to start writing down what she was saying.

Simmy walked up the hall, talking in a low, enchanting voice, keeping her students hanging onto her every word. "Our mind is the most underrated tool we have at our disposal.

Now, I'm not talking about your brain. Your brain, yes, is extremely powerful and very, very important. But your mind..." Simmy paused, causing the class to shift to the edge of their seats in anticipation, "your mind determines everything. Your thoughts become things. You all need to remember this. Your thoughts become things."

The class looked confused again.

"Let me explain." Simmy began walking amongst the students. "I am sure that most of you, if not all of you, can tell me a story of when something was on your mind—something that you were thinking about constantly—that came into fruition. For example, you were going to be late to school and you kept thinking, *'I don't want to be late, I don't want to be late, I don't want to be late,'* and then, lo and behold, you got caught in traffic, or there were an endless amount of slow walkers in front of you, or you left an important book at home and needed to go back and get it, and the whole time you kept thinking, *'I don't want to be late.'* You see, the way the mind works is that it focuses on what you're thinking. You might be thinking now, *'But wait! I was thinking that I 'didn't' want to be late to school,'* and you're right, you *were* thinking that, but you were concentrating on the *being late* part, so that's what happened. Your thoughts were so powerful, and were so concentrated on being late to school that that's what happened."

Simmy paused and looked around the classroom. Noah took this chance to look at his classmates as well. Some of them were just staring at Simmy, others had their mouths slightly agape, and one girl with long brown hair, the girl who had been staring at Noah in Mr Greeves' class, was writing down everything Simmy was saying so furiously that he was concerned her notebook would catch on fire.

"Now," Simmy continued, "if you had been thinking, *'I will get to school on time,'* it would have been different. You would have been focusing on *getting to school on time,* and so, more often than not, you would have found yourself having an easy trip to school."

Noah watched as Simmy made her way back to the front of the classroom and stared out into the sea of faces.

"What you must be wary of is that little voice in the back of your head," Simmy started to explain.

What little voice? Noah thought.

"You know, the little voice that just asked *'what little voice?'"* Simmy smiled.

The class laughed. All of them had heard it.

Simmy held up her hands to settle the class once more. "That voice will be your undoing if you let it. It is both everything you dislike about yourself, and so overconfident that it will give you unrealistic expectations. For example, it can make you believe that you aren't smart enough, pretty enough or talented enough to accomplish what you're aiming for. But, at the same time, it will try to make you believe that you are too smart, too pretty and too talented to need to aim for what you're trying to accomplish. It will try and sabotage you and your goals in one way or another. We call this voice your Ego."

BEEP! BEEP! BEEP!

Someone's alarm rang and a student at the front of the class hastily turned it off.

"Goodness, that class flew by," Simmy exclaimed with a clap of her hands. "Homework. I want you to keep a diary, and write down the time of day that you find yourself thinking negative thoughts. Don't lie. There is no right or wrong here, it just is. I also want you to say three things you are grateful for before you go to bed each night. Class dismissed."

The sound of scraping chairs filled Noah's ears as he packed his books into his bag. He stole a glance at Layla, who was writing down the homework into her planner, and he thought that she looked awfully calm for having been bombarded with so much information at once. But then he remembered that Simmy was Layla's aunt, and Layla had probably been taught all of this before.

Waiting for Layla to finish packing her bag so they could walk to their next class together, Noah looked up at Simmy and saw her surrounded by students full of questions about the lesson. The same brown-haired girl who had been writing down everything so furiously was now speaking rapidly, firing question after question at Simmy, her long braid flicking from side to side as she ducked to write down Simmy's answers. "Ms Johannson, what happens when you think all positive thoughts?", "Ms Johansson, is it possible for your Ego to take over completely?", "Ms Johansson, are we able to will *anything* into existence?"

Not sticking around long enough to hear Simmy's answers, Noah ducked out of the classroom, Layla by his side as they headed off to their next lesson.

"That was a very interesting class," Layla said, stuffing her timetable back inside the pocket of her black skirt.

"Yeah," Noah replied, half glad to chat about it and half wanting to keep his thoughts to himself. "It makes sense though, doesn't it. I mean, the voice in your head and everything..." Noah trailed off.

Layla didn't press him and instead guided him to their

next classroom, where they were once again greeted by Mr Greeves, who nodded at them knowingly as they walked into the class together. He must have been filling in for their normal teacher for the lesson.

Noah nodded back, knowing that if he didn't acknowledge him, Mr Greeves would begin to ask a million questions that Noah didn't need. His mind was still reeling from their previous class, as were the minds of the rest of the students who had just come from Simmy's Life Science lesson. Throughout the class, Noah could hear the odd whisper of *'Ego'* or *'Ms Johannson'*. The girl with the long brown braid had an annoyingly smug look on her face, like she had some secret knowledge that the rest of the class weren't privy to.

The time in Mr Greeves' class ticked by a lot slower than Simmy's, and Noah found himself doodling in the margin of his notebook, not paying any attention to what Mr Greeves was saying. The class had been learning something while he was away, so he was prepared to use ignorance as an excuse should he be called upon.

Thankfully he wasn't, and finally it was time for his first break of the day. Mr Greeves called out the homework, "Finish off all unanswered questions and start on page one fifty-two of your problem-solving tasks in your textbook," to an uninterested class, aching to escape.

Noah packed his bag once more and turned to Layla, who was chatting with the girl with the long brown braid.

Catching Noah's eye, the girl stopped her conversation with Layla and walked over to him.

"I was sorry to hear about your sister. We were in the same maths and drama classes. I'd like to think we were close friends," the girl said to him.

Not expecting this abrupt statement, Noah gaped at the girl for a few seconds and then, fidgeting with the strap on his bag, replied, "Oh... uhhh... thanks."

The girl held out her hand to Noah. "My name is Abigail. Abigail Thomas."

Awkwardly glancing at Layla, whose face gave away nothing, Noah shook Abigail's hand.

"I was just inviting Layla to sit with me during her break. I'd love to hear what Ms Johannson has taught her. I know that she's your aunt," Abigail said, turning to look at Layla for that last part.

"And I was just about to say that I can't sit with you this break, unfortunately," Layla replied. "I've been asked to catch Noah up on the classes that he's missed in the past few weeks." Noah didn't think that Layla thought it was an unfortunate situation at all. She wasn't looking the least bit sorry that she'd have to miss being bombarded with questions by Abigail.

Frowning slightly, Abigail sighed, "Oh really? That's a shame. Well, I guess I'll check online and see if I can find out more about it. It's really interesting, you know. How powerful our thoughts can be."

"Yes, it's very interesting. And the library is a great idea," Layla said, not allowing Abigail to sneak in any questions regarding the subject. "Well, I'll see you in art class, Abigail." Layla grabbed Noah by the elbow and lead him towards a secluded, sunny area of the campus grounds.

Noah looked back at Abigail as he was being pulled away and saw that the frustrated look was still on her face, but, resigned to finding out the information herself, she took off in the direction of the library.

Turning back, Noah caught a look at his group of friends

41

that he'd known since he was a kid. He hadn't really spoken with them since Nora's disappearance, and he wasn't sure he was ready to either. He gave them a small smile, a wave and a shrug as he mildly over-dramatised the force with which Layla was dragging him.

His friends smiled back at him but didn't move to chase him, which Noah was grateful for.

Finally, Noah and Layla reached their destination. Noah sat down, and then immediately jumped up as if he had been burned. "What are we doing *here*?" he hissed to Layla. "This is where couples come when they want to make out without being disturbed!"

For the first time since Noah had met her, Layla laughed. "I know," she said.

Noah looked flabbergasted. Had Layla brought him here to... here to...? He immediately imagined an image of Layla leaning forwards, her slightly too-far-apart green eyes closing...

"Oh calm down." Layla interrupted Noah's train of thought. He could feel his cheeks start to heat at what he'd just been envisioning. "I just don't want us to be disturbed."

"Oh," said Noah, not sure if he was disappointed or not. "Of course. Yeah... Erm, why don't we want to be disturbed?"

Layla was only half-listening as she fished around her school bag, and Noah couldn't help but think that she was a tiny bit crazy.

Finally, Layla found what she was looking for. She pulled out her lunch box, ripped it open and shoved a cheese and tomato sandwich into her mouth with one hand, pulling out a familiar looking wrapped package in the other.

Layla swallowed her mouthful and looked at Noah. "Did

you remember to bring yours?"

Noah, who had also fished out his lunchbox, took a bite of his apple and nodded, reaching into the front pocket of his backpack and pulling out the wrapped mandala.

"Excellent, Simmy wants to work with these in our class this afternoon. You saw the massive one hanging on her ceiling, didn't you?" Layla asked, talking in between bites.

"Yeah," Noah said, picturing the moonstones he'd struggled to take his eyes off. "How could I miss it?"

"Good," Layla said. "Make sure you keep your mandala on you at all times. You've got two free periods next, don't you?"

"Uhh, yeah, I think so," Noah replied, searching his bag for his timetable once more.

"Great, make sure you use that time to clear your mind and really enjoy yourself while you're working. You're going to struggle in our class with Simmy if you don't," Layla announced, standing as she turned to leave their secluded area.

"Oh, okay, yeah I will. Thanks Layla," Noah said, standing to leave their lunch spot as well. "Well, I guess I'll see you this afternoon then?"

Layla smiled at Noah, nodded, and then ran to catch up with some other girls who must have been in her art class, brushing off their smug grins with a wave of her hand, dismissing any ideas they'd been sharing about where she'd just been sitting and who she'd been with.

Noah, also catching the eye of some giggling girls he recognised, felt the blood rushing to his face, and he quickly averted his eyes to the floor, racing towards the groundskeeper's hut.

Chapter 5 - Noah

The groundskeeper's hut was a long walk away from the main campus. Noah wished that he was allowed to zoom around in the little golf buggy the groundskeeper had. This walk was killing him. Sweat dripped down his brow, and Noah was panting as he finally reached the three steps leading up to the hut.

"You're Noah Parker?" a gruff voice called to him from inside.

Squinting, Noah could see a large silhouette in the doorway at the top of the stairs. "Yes," he replied hesitantly.

"Glad to see you made it here, mate," the shape said. "My name is Mr Reynolds, but you can call me Geoff." He stepped out into the sunlight, and Noah stared at the face of a man who looked like life had tossed him around a few times.

There was a scar down his left eye, and a chunk of skin under his chin was missing. His light brown crew cut was speckled with grey hairs, which somehow made his deep brown eyes appear brighter, and his five o'clock shadow was slightly overgrown.

Noah shook Geoff's hand and instantly noticed the tight grip. His dad had always told him that it was rude to shake someone's hand with a loose grip.

Geoff released Noah, picked up an old pair of overalls from the small table that was on the deck, and threw them to him. "Put these on," he said. "Your clothes are going to get dirty otherwise."

Pulling the overalls over his outfit, Noah watched as Geoff gathered the tools they needed for the day's tasks.

"We've got a decent two hours," Geoff said to Noah as he packed the golf buggy, "so we're going to head on over to the campus entrance and tend to the plants that need some loving out there."

Geoff's gruff voice and the word *loving* sounded weird to Noah, but he didn't dare mention that to him.

"What are we planting today?" Noah asked, jumping into the passenger side of the buggy.

Starting the engine up with a loud rev, Geoff reversed out the driveway and started the journey to the entrance of the campus. "Nothing yet. The hibiscus flowers are looking sick after the heat we've been experiencing these past couple of weeks. They thrive in temperatures between sixteen and thirty-two degrees Celsius, but with temperatures rising up to thirty-eight and over, the flowers are starting to wilt, so we're going to create some shade for them."

"Well that explains the shade sail we've brought along," Noah said.

"Exactly," replied Geoff. "How handy are you with a hammer?"

Noah grinned. "I've built a few veggie gardens in my time."

Geoff gave a crooked smile in return and was silent for the rest of the trip.

At the gardens, Geoff handed Noah the tools he'd need for the task, gave him a quick rundown of what needed to be done, and then left him to his own devices.

Noah embraced the independence and thrived under the warm sun, his skin soaking up the rays. He'd missed the familiar prickle of it after all those weeks locked away in his room.

Every so often Geoff would walk past to check that Noah was okay, and even praised him for clipping the dead flowers off the hibiscus plants to make room for new ones to grow.

By the end of the two hours Noah was filthy, but his spirits were high.

"You did well today," Geoff said to him when they arrived back at the hut, handing him a large glass of iced water.

Noah gulped the water down gratefully. "Thanks, I enjoyed working outside again. I've missed being in the garden."

"Well, you're going to be working a lot more around these grounds," Geoff said, "so bring a spare change of clothes with you next time. The ones you're wearing now are all sweaty."

Geoff was right. Noah's jeans and shirt were drenched with sweat, and he could feel it starting to dry against his skin. "Yeah, I'll definitely bring a change of clothes tomorrow," Noah said, holding his arms out to try and air-dry his shirt.

Grunting, Geoff threw him an aerosol deodorant. "Put that on before your next class, you'll stink the room out."

Noah thanked him and sprayed his whole body.

"Get in," Geoff said, walking towards the golf buggy. "I'll give you a lift."

Gratefully, Noah jumped in and relished in the cool air rushing through his hair as they drove. He would have to remember to thank Simmy for organising this for him.

Layla was already inside the classroom when Noah arrived that afternoon. Simmy was chatting to her in a low voice about something Noah couldn't hear. It must have been private though, because as soon as he walked inside Simmy stopped talking abruptly and smiled at him.

"Welcome to the first of our private sessions," she said happily.

"What are we learning?" Noah asked, curiosity finally getting the better of him. "Are we the only ones in this class?"

Layla and Simmy stole a glance at each other.

Simmy's warm smile faded slightly, and she walked over to Noah, guiding him and Layla to a corner of the room where a few squishy black beanbags were placed. The only light came from a couple of glowing moonstones that were sporadically stuck to the wall, and Noah was once again entranced by the ethereal glow they were producing.

Sinking into one of the beanbags, Noah let out a long breath, his muscles aching from his work with Geoff. There was something about the way Simmy and Layla kept glancing at each other that made him think they were hiding something.

Simmy cleared her throat softly and pulled a smaller version of the moonstone mandala that was hanging from the ceiling out of her pocket.

Layla followed suit, taking her mandala out as well and placing it on the floor next to her. Noah noticed, as he pulled his own mandala from his backpack, that while Simmy's mandala was completely uncovered, Layla's was wrapped in similar packaging as his.

Noah opened his wrappings, making sure not to touch the mandala with his bare hands. He was still hesitant about the dream he'd had when he'd touched it that first time.

Layla was doing the same, taking the same caution as Noah not to touch her mandala with her bare skin.

When Layla unwrapped her package, Noah realised they both had identical mandalas, right down to the sizing and placement of the sunstones.

Not knowing whether this was common or not, Noah decided to keep his questions to himself until Simmy had explained what they were doing here.

"In class today, Noah," Simmy said, "we started learning about the science of the mind. The power of thoughts and how they determine a lot of what happens in our lives."

Layla was listening intently to what Simmy was saying, although Noah was sure that she'd heard this all before.

Simmy continued. "We also briefly touched on what happens when our Ego, or the little voice in our head, starts to take over our thoughts. This is very important to understand, Noah, as our Egos will try and take over our whole thought process, especially when we are going through a tough time."

Noah's heart gave a sickening twinge as the smiling picture of Nora on the missing person posters popped up in his mind. He lowered his gaze to the floor.

Simmy looked at Noah. "This is why we're here today. There is a lot for you to learn when it comes to keeping a clear mind. We are always comparing ourselves to others, thinking we're better than others or thinking that others are better than us. We often think that we have done something wrong, or that someone has done something wrong by us. We have so many blocks to fix and mindsets to change. It can be a very difficult journey, and you need to be completely on board if you want to become a part of it."

There was an urgency in Simmy's voice.

"Noah, have you touched the mandala that Layla gave you with your bare hands?" Simmy asked.

Hoping this would help explain his dream last week, Noah replied. "Yes, I have."

"And what happened when you touched it?"

Noah hesitated slightly, but felt no inclination to lie to Simmy. "Well, I was sitting on my bed when I unwrapped it, and when I touched the mandala I must have fallen asleep, because I blinked and all of a sudden I was in a large green field of grass. I'd never been to a place like that before. It made me feel really... calm," Noah finished sheepishly, looking from Layla to Simmy.

"That wasn't a dream, Noah," Simmy said. "That's a real place. It's a place that is powered by the thoughts and dreams of the people here on Earth, and it is directly related to what we have been learning about in class. Thoughts become things, remember?"

Confused, Noah nodded slowly.

"That place is called the Realm of Intention. This Realm provides a guide for humans when we need advice, and it is from this guidance that our great lightbulb—or *aha*—moments come from. Those moments create the ideas that we know we need to follow through with. It thrives on positive thoughts, gratitude, and love, and rewards those who project gratitude and love with positivity and happiness in return. It guides what people are visualising towards them," Simmy explained. "This is where *'thoughts become things'* plays a very important role. Because if you are visualising positive things—success, guidance and happiness—and not allowing your Ego to take control of your thoughts, then this is what will be projected back to you. But, if you are thinking negative thoughts—expecting bills, expecting people to cancel on you, expecting to have car troubles, expecting to be late to school

49

or appointments—and not sending out love and gratitude, then this is what will be projected back to you.

"You see, negativity is very powerful. It is much easier to think a negative thought than to think a positive one on this Earth, and that is because we are inundated with negativity every day, whether that be from watching the news, reading stories in the newspaper, or being exposed to people complaining or sharing negative experiences online. We are conditioned to expect bad news and we accept it readily. We are less conditioned to accept positive news. And when we do hear positive news, instead of feeling happy for the person who has shared it, we often feel jealous, which is very easy to do, but doing so makes it very easy for our Ego to take control of our thoughts and lead us down a spiral of negativity."

Simmy finished her explanation with a deep breath in. "So, you were taken to a section of the Realm that still had a lot of good to give. There are still people who are projecting gratitude and love, which allows that part of the Realm to flourish. With these mandalas that the two of you have you are able to travel to and from the Realm at will. I will explain why at a later time, but I will say this—make sure that you are feeling happy when you travel to the Realm. Otherwise you may end up in a dangerous place. The Realm does not judge, and it does not feel emotions. It just is. It feeds off what is given to it and gives back when it needs to. Emotions are a very human trait, we often let them get the better of us and forget that love and gratitude are what's necessary to live a happy life."

Noah didn't know what to think. This was a lot of information for him to take in. Another Realm? A Realm that feeds off the emotions that humans provide? None of this sounded real. But there was no reason for Simmy to lie to him. There was no reason for him to believe that she was making any of this up. There was a reason she was telling him this though, a reason that they had given him the mandala.

"Nora?" Noah asked. "Nora knew all of this?"

Layla answered in Simmy's place. "Yes, Nora knew all of this. You know that the mandala you have originally belonged to her. Nora spent a lot of time in the Realm. She was really passionate about helping people become the best, most positive versions of themselves, and when she discovered the Realm a few months ago she was determined to find out everything she could so that she could teach others."

Layla's voice cracked as she spoke, and it dawned on Noah how close Layla and Nora had actually been.

"There's something you need to know, Noah," Simmy said hesitantly.

Noah looked up at her, not sure if he wanted to hear what she had to say.

"The Realm is in trouble and it is affecting the lives of the people here on Earth. Nora was on a mission to find out what was causing all these changes."

"Why didn't you go to the Realm and try and find out for yourself?" Noah asked, trying to keep his voice as polite as possible.

"Well…" Simmy sounded like she was choosing her words very carefully. "I, personally, am unable to travel to the Realm right now."

"Why?"

"Simmy has some… history with the Realm," Layla replied, in Simmy's stead. "I'm not entirely sure what it is exactly…" she trailed off, glancing at Simmy, who nodded at her.

Noah watched the exchange, waiting for one of them to continue the story.

"Nora and I became friends about six months ago," Layla went on. "We were both in the library and I saw her reading a book on the power of positivity. She was so engrossed in it that she didn't even realise I was there at first, But then we got talking and we shared our experiences, and I knew that she needed to know about the Realm. So I invited her over to our place that afternoon and I introduced her to Simmy. I asked Simmy if she could give Nora our other mandala so that we could introduce her to the Realm. Simmy was hesitant at first; she didn't want to put anyone in danger, but as soon as Simmy got to know Nora, she knew that we needed her. So we spent that whole afternoon introducing Nora to the Realm, giving her all the information we knew about it and coaching her through the skills she needed to learn in order to use the mandala to its full potential."

Noah wasn't sure what this had to do with him, but he was becoming so invested in the project Nora had been working on before she disappeared that he didn't dare interrupt Layla.

"When we met Nora my mandala was immediately attracted to her, which was why I asked Simmy to give her its twin. We used the power of Simmy's mandala to bring light back into Nora's and the positive response the mandala had to Nora was immediate. This meant that we needed to educate Nora as quickly, and as efficiently, as possible so that she could wield the mandala in order to fight against the darkness that has started to take over the Realm."

Noah looked down at the mandala sitting on the floor next to him, still lying on the packaging that it was given to him in.

"This is why we've given the mandala to you, Noah," Layla

said, looking him in the eye. "We need someone to pick up where Nora left off, and we feel like the best person for this job is you."

"Is the only reason you've chosen me because I'm Nora's twin?" He didn't want to ask it, but the question blurted out of his mouth before he could stop it.

Layla, her large green eyes showing nothing but honesty, said, "No. There wouldn't have been any benefit in choosing you purely because you're related to Nora. We need someone who has a kind soul, is willing to help others, and feels a pull to save the Realm. You may not know it yet, but this is you."

"How do you know that, though? You barely know me!" frustration overwhelmed Noah. He'd just been told that Nora, at only eighteen years old, was planning on saving humanity. Noah had barely thought about what he was going to do once he graduated.

"Nora," Layla said simply.

That stopped Noah short. "What?"

"Nora spoke about you all the time. She spoke very highly of you as well. You may not realise that you have all the qualities that we're looking for, but you do, and we want to help you realise that for yourself."

Noah wasn't expecting that. All of this information was way too overwhelming for his first day back at school, although he realised that the two of them must know more about Nora's disappearance than they were letting on.

Simmy, having listened to Layla's explanation, decided to address Noah herself. "Noah," she said gently, "we know that this is a lot to take in. We wouldn't have mentioned this to you if the situation wasn't as dire as it is. But we also understand that this is your decision. If you would like to learn the skills of mastering your mandala and travelling between the Realm of Intention and Earth, then we would love to teach you. But if you don't feel up to the job, or if you simply don't want to do this, then that is completely fine as well. We are not here to judge, and we are not here to push you into doing anything you don't want to do."

"Can I see it?" Noah asked after a pause.

"See it?" Simmy questioned.

"The Realm of Intention. Please," he added as an afterthought.

Simmy and Layla glanced at each other. Layla opened her mouth to disagree, but Simmy quickly cut her off.

"Yes," she said. "Yes, I think that's probably a good idea."

Layla looked miffed. "You didn't show me the Realm until I had had *years* of training!" she protested.

Simmy looked at Layla apologetically. "I know, but you were much younger than Noah is now, and Noah is a very hands-on learner. He's someone who needs to be able to see what he is working with. Also, he's already been to the Realm. It's best that we show him this now before he tries to go by himself. Now, take Noah's hand. Noah, I won't be able to transport you, but I will guide you both there."

Layla, not happy with Simmy's response, didn't argue, but resignedly took the hand Simmy had offered her, holding her other hand out for Noah. "You're going to need to take my hand if you want to see the Realm, Noah," Layla said when he hesitated.

Noah looked at the hand Layla offered him and suddenly realised that he was nervous, especially now he'd been told Simmy couldn't travel with them.

He tentatively grabbed Layla's hand, and Simmy gave

Noah's arm a reassuring squeeze.

He closed his eyes, felt a warm sensation flow through him, and when he opened his eyes once more, he gasped.

The landscape in front of him was vastly different to what he'd seen last time.

Instead of endless green plains and a wide blue sky, there were dark clouds, no leaves on any of the trees, and large patches of black dirt replacing the grass.

Noah shivered. This place felt...heavy.

His chest felt tight. He clasped at it, his breathing became ragged.

Falling to his knees, Noah groaned, and his eyes widened as a dark shadowy figure pulled itself out of his chest.

It looked down at Noah on the ground, its lanky figure flickering as it gave Noah a nasty, sharp-toothed smile.

He felt Layla next to him, mumbling something in his ear, but he couldn't hear what she was saying. His chest felt empty and there was a ringing in his ears as he stared back at the shadowy figure.

Noah took another shaky breath and watched as the figure turned and stalked away. He tried to call out and stop it, feeling like a part of himself was being ripped away, but before he could he felt that warm sensation flooding through his veins once more, and was transported back to Simmy's classroom.

As soon as his knees hit the ground, both Simmy and Layla were fussing over him, covering him in blankets and making sure he was okay.

"Thanks," Noah said to them as his breathing evened out. He rolled over to sit down in one of the squishy black beanbags. "So, just a question. What was that dark... thing that came out of my chest?"

Simmy sighed. "That was your Ego, Noah. It was ripped out of you and became a Shadow Being. Because of the grief you have been feeling for Nora, it was easy for it to escape you when you got to such a negative part of the Realm. I didn't realise that would happen, I never would have let you go if I knew..." she berated herself.

Noah looked up at Simmy and Layla from his position on the floor, feeling torn between his desire to help their mission and the doubts about whether he would be able to. So much had happened today that he didn't know what to think.

"There is no need to give us an answer now, Noah," Simmy said kindly. "I would like to continue to work together this semester though, regardless of your answer."

Noah nodded and stood up on shaky legs, picking up his bag.

On his walk home his mind was full of unanswered questions, and blurry images of him fighting large, shadowy monsters.

Chapter 6 - Layla

Simmy took longer than usual getting her things ready to head home, so Layla sat on the squishy black beanbag that Noah vacated and absently scrolled through the messages Nora had sent her before she disappeared.

There wasn't anything left to try and decipher from them anymore, it was just her new comfort habit.

Glancing up at Simmy, who was hunched over her desk grabbing the papers she needed for the night, Layla noticed that she was moving a lot slower than normal. "Are you okay?" she called from her seat.

"Yeah," Simmy replied, her voice breathless. "Just a little tired."

Layla frowned. It wasn't like Simmy to get tired from their lessons. "Tired from what?"

"I didn't think it would be so draining to anchor both of you to Earth while you travelled to the Realm."

Layla stood up and walked over to Simmy. "We didn't even move from where we landed though. Noah's Ego ripped out of him as soon as we got there, and then he was pretty much hunched over from that point on. We couldn't have moved even if we wanted to."

Simmy shrugged and pulled her large handbag that was full of papers over her shoulder. "It felt like you two were trying to pull free."

"Maybe it was your side? Maybe you've spent so much time away from the Realm that you're losing your connection with it," Layla said, steadying Simmy as she swayed a little under the weight of her handbag.

"Maybe," Simmy replied, and Layla saw a flicker of fear in Simmy's brown eyes.

Deciding not to press her anymore, Layla picked her satchel up off the floor and took Simmy's handbag from her, shot her a glare when Simmy tried to protest and slinging it over her shoulder, Layla clicked a confirmation on her phone. "Our ride's going to be ready for us out the front in five minutes."

"Our ride?" Simmy looked at her incredulously. "We can just walk home."

Layla snorted and tilted her head to the side. "No, *I* could walk home. *You* would need to crawl home."

Simmy opened her mouth to argue, but Layla stopped her, holding up her hand. "For someone who goes on and on about the importance of listening to your body, you sure don't like taking your own advice."

Shutting her mouth, Simmy shot her niece an exasperated look before sighing in defeat. "You're right," she said. "Thank you for organising a lift."

Layla smiled at her aunt, wrapped an arm around her shoulders and kissed her on the top of her head. "Where would you be without me?" she joked.

* * *

It didn't take long for Simmy to get to sleep that night. After a quick takeaway dinner where she'd had to force her eyes to stay open, Layla had ordered her aunt to bed. Simmy didn't even have the energy to argue that she was fine before allowing Layla to guide her to her bedroom and snuggle her up under the blankets.

Layla watched her for a couple of minutes before deciding that her aunt would be okay after a good night's sleep. As she walked to her own bedroom, she pulled out her phone and sent a message:

You free?

She waited a minute before her phone buzzed in reply.

Sorry, busy tonight.

Tomorrow?

Sighing, Layla didn't bother to reply, instead throwing her phone down on her doona and flopping back onto the pillow. It was too early for her to go to sleep, but she figured she may as well try, otherwise she'd be tempted to head back to Realm by herself and search for Nora again. She knew that Simmy would be furious if she did that. And, truthfully, it wasn't worth the risk of getting stuck there. Simmy had been right before, her mission at the moment was here, on Earth, and she needed to see it through. She didn't know what was happening, but there was a vibe surrounding her that she couldn't shake that made her feel like something big was going on.

Deciding to go for a shower to fill in some time, Layla stripped off and wrapped a towel around herself before padding to the bathroom. Flicking on the light and turning on the hot water, she let it run until the room filled with steam before adding the tiniest amount of cold water, just to make

59

sure she wouldn't give herself third-degree burns.

When she stepped inside, she let out a contented sigh as the warmth relaxed her muscles. She tilted her head back, allowing it to run over her curly hair and face, washing away the day.

She hadn't known how the lesson with Noah was going to go, but she'd been anxious about it nonetheless.

All things considered, he took the information pretty well. She'd half expected him to run screaming from the room calling for a witch hunt.

Maybe she'd underestimated him.

Grabbing her strawberry scented body wash and lathering herself, Layla tossed any more thoughts of Noah from her mind, deciding that thinking about him while she was in the shower wasn't something she particularly wanted to do, and instead focused on her breathing. One deep breath in through her nose, one deep breath out through her mouth, calming her mind and allowing any stray messages to come through from her guides in the Realm.

Nothing came to her.

She sighed again. "Of course not," Layla mumbled, turning the shower off and wrapping one towel around her torso and a smaller one around her wet hair.

It was usually easy for her to receive guidance, but ever since Nora had disappeared she'd been left to fend for herself. She didn't know if it was because her guides were busy searching for Nora while she couldn't or whether they just plain weren't allowed to point her in the right direction.

Layla had a sneaking suspicion that it was the latter, and she walked to her room much more aggressively than usual before throwing herself on the bed in only her towels.

Wiping a stray droplet of water before it reached her ear, Layla stared absently at the ceiling. She hated not knowing which direction she should be taking. Her head was telling her that she needed to be searching for Nora, that Nora was imperative to their plans to help the Realm, but there was another, calmer, deep-seated part of herself that was telling her to stay where she was, that she was exactly where she needed to be.

This was really irritating. Layla didn't want to sit still and pretend to be interested in her classes, she wanted to be out there, doing something.

But there was nothing she could do right now, so she just had to wait it out.

* * *

The night had dragged. Any more sleepless nights for Layla and she wouldn't be able to function.

Yawning, she padded her way into the kitchen and noticed that Simmy wasn't awake yet.

It was only six in the morning, and with how exhausted Simmy had been the day before, Layla wasn't surprised.

Opening the fridge and pulling out a piece of leftover pizza from last night, Layla dropped into a chair at the kitchen table and rested her head heavily on her hand, chewing slowly as she tried to keep her eyes open.

There was so much going on that she'd barely been able to keep track of it all.

The Realm had always been a place Layla had gone to when she needed to unwind. When she needed to clear her head and open herself up to truly appreciating everything she had in her life. And now it was tainted. Now it was becoming a source of anxiety.

Layla was sure that Simmy knew more than she was letting on, but Simmy had always told her everything when she was able to. There had never been secrets between the two of them. Well, not when it came to the important things anyway.

Simmy was the only family Layla had, and the Realm was such an integral part of her that, after seeing how exhausted Simmy had been yesterday, Layla was beginning to worry that everything happening in the Realm was affecting Simmy more than she knew.

Well, actually, she probably knew.

Sighing, Layla took another slow bite of pizza, willing motivation into her bones. If she didn't have Noah to keep an eye on she'd have just skipped school for the day, but she did. Nora would kill her if she left Noah to his own devices.

A laugh tried to rise out of her throat, to Layla's surprise.

Yup, Nora would have given her a full instruction manual on what her brother needed while she wasn't here, if she could.

Rolling her shoulders, Layla shovelled the last of the pizza in her mouth and padded back to her room.

It was time to get dressed and take on the day.

Chapter 7 - Nora

S he didn't know how long she'd been stuck in this little room, but Nora knew that if she didn't try to get out, she'd be stuck here forever.

Ever since her attempt at escaping last time, the old man had kept checking up on her. If he saw her doing anything more than sitting on her bed, he would shoot a thin ring of black energy at her, forcing her arms to her side and locking her legs together for hours at a time.

It was beyond frustrating.

Nora knew that she wasn't powerful enough to beat him, but she'd been practising controlling her energies by herself. The blast she'd created in the water when the man had come for her had been unintentional, but it had been enough to distract him from everyone else around her and decide that he needed to get out of the area quickly.

She really didn't want to be here. She wanted to be back on campus, learning with Layla and Simmy. But unfortunately for her, it just wasn't meant to be. Simmy would probably tell her that this was part of her path, but maybe she didn't want this path anymore. Maybe she wanted to create her own path.

And Noah... Nora's heart panged at the thought of Noah. She hadn't clued him in on anything that she'd been doing, and unless Layla and Simmy had reached out to him, he probably thought she was dead.

Scrunching her nose and clenching her fists, Nora tried to push the thought from her mind. She had to do something—anything—to get out of here.

Suddenly there was a soft noise at her doorway, and Nora turned her head slowly to see what it was. Letting out a breath of relief when she saw that it wasn't the old man, she stood up and walked towards the noise, bracing herself just in case she was about to be attacked again.

There was a wispy shadow standing at her doorway, staring at her.

How shadows could stare, Nora didn't know, but this one was definitely looking right at her.

And Nora was drawn to it too.

There was something about it that seemed… familiar.

Hesitantly, Nora looked at the large room outside hers, checking to see if the man was nearby. She couldn't see him, so she quickly took the final steps to the doorway, reaching the shadow.

"Who are you?" Nora whispered to it. "Are you here to help me?"

The shadow didn't reply, but Nora didn't think it would. Why would the shadow be able to talk? Instead, it reached a dark, wispy finger out towards Nora.

"Do you want me to touch you?" Nora whispered as she hesitantly lifted her finger, reaching out towards the shadow.

Her warm hand touched the cold, surprisingly solid finger of the shadow, for a second before she was thrown back into the room by a blast of air that came out of nowhere.

Gasping in pain as her back hit the side of her bed, Nora

covered her face from the blast with her arms and pulled her knees up to her chest, as the few belongings she had in her room were flung towards her.

Then, as suddenly as it started, the air stopped. Nora lifted her head, breathing heavily.

A solid black being now stood where the wispy shadow had been. It was still a shadow, but instead of flickering, this being was humanoid... almost.

"Ahh, thanks for that," the Shadow Being said to Nora in a scratchy, high pitched tone. "This body is so much better."

Nora stared at the Shadow Being from her place on the ground, not daring to stand up just yet. "Who are you?"

"The name's Tick," it replied, stretching its neck and reaching its arms above its head, and Nora could have sworn its figure was feminine. "I'd say you'd recognise me, but you were unconscious when you were brought here, and I was ripped out of you."

Nora let Tick's words sink in before her eyes widened, and she clenched a fist angrily. "I'm in the Realm?"

Tick let out a mocking laugh. "Where did you think you were?"

"I don't know," Nora admitted. And she really didn't. She'd been so exhausted and battered from being constantly alert and abused that she hadn't given any thought that she could have been taken to the Realm. Although it made sense. Not many people were able to solidify their energy enough to physically attack someone on Earth like the man had been doing to her regularly here. The toll it took on your body was never worth the risk.

"Well, isn't this interesting," a drawling voice said from the doorway, and Nora's head snapped to the new arrival so fast she got whiplash.

Gritting her teeth in pain, Nora stared at the man with contempt.

"What do we have here?" the man continued, acting as if he hadn't seen Nora at all, instead opting to walk around Tick with interest.

Tick stood still, allowing the man to investigate her, and didn't make a sound when he prodded her between her yellow eyes with one of his old, crooked fingers.

"How did you make this?" The man, with impossible speed, darted to Nora, gripping her by her neck and lifting her into the air.

"She came to me," Nora gasped, trying to pry the man's fingers from her throat, but his grip was vice-like.

"Don't lie to me," the man hissed, his eyes narrowing.

"I'm not!" Nora spit out, meeting his eyes with her furious ones.

The man threw her against the wall roughly before stalking back towards Tick. "Do you have a name?"

"Tick," she replied immediately.

"What can you do?"

"Anything you want me to."

The man gave her a cruel smile. "Correct." He turned back to Nora for a brief second, saw that her crumpled form was still breathing, and turned on his heel. "Come with me."

Tick strode after him, keeping to his heels like a lapdog, letting him know that she was ready to be used in whatever way he needed, and sneering as the man created a red energy barrier over Nora's doorway so she couldn't escape.

Nora coughed once they had gone, tasting blood in her mouth. She was sure that something was broken, and she had to force down a scream as her back and leg protested against even the smallest movements.

She was sick of this. What was the point of her being here?

As soon as she thought that, something snapped within her. Her resolve hardened, and she managed to push herself to her feet.

She didn't care that she was hunched over and in agony, she was still standing.

No more, she thought to herself. *No more.*

She wasn't going to just sit here any longer.

Amber electricity sparked from her fingers and she threw it at the wall behind her, ignoring the pain that shot through her body as she did.

Crawling into her bed, Nora pulled her aching body on top of it, holding back furious tears. There *had* to be more going on. There *had* to be a reason she was here now. The Realm needed her for something, so she was going to figure out what it was, and take that man down while she was at it.

Chapter 8 - Noah

A couple of days had passed since Noah's first day back at school, and while he was slowly finding his rhythm, it was still surreal not having Nora by his side.

He picked up his mandala and tentatively unwrapped the packaging, staring at the warm sunstones. He thought of Nora and her journey with the mandala and touched the largest one in the middle. Suddenly his bedroom disappeared, and Noah was being shown images that appeared in front of him like an old movie.

An image of Nora was projected, and he shouted out to her, but she showed no signs of hearing him.

Resigning himself to the mandala, Noah watched what it wanted to show him.

Simmy had just taught Nora a simple breathing technique to help calm herself down. She'd been getting frustrated that she wasn't learning everything she wanted to quick enough. Just take one deep breath in through her nose, and out of her mouth, and repeat the process until her mind is at ease.

Nora didn't know why this worked, but it always did. Without fail, the little voice in the back of her head became much less prominent, and she was able to focus.

In the few weeks that she'd been spending with Layla and Simmy, Nora was acutely aware that she hadn't been spending any time with her brother, and she knew that Noah was aware of it too.

"Sorry Noah!" Nora shouted as she ran out the door. "I'm off to my friend's place again. We'll watch that movie next weekend!"

Repeating what she had said to him every weekend for the past month.

The scene changed.

Nora and Layla appeared. There was something about Layla that really made Nora sit back and think about everything she'd been taught as a child. There was no judgement in this girl. She said things how they were and wasn't afraid to stand up for herself and her beliefs.

Nora arrived at Layla's house, and as usual, the living room had been darkened, and there were candles lit. The faint smell of musky lavender filled Nora's nose.

Nora pulled her mandala from her pocket and smiled down at it. She felt like she had a connection with the Realm now. She truly believed that she could use the skills she was learning to help other people.

She couldn't wait to tell Noah about what she was doing because she knew that he would be an amazing asset to their mission. Nora had told Layla and Simmy her thoughts on this as well, that the next person to bring into their mission should be Noah.

Nora sank into the comfortable seat on the couch next to Layla and placed her sunstone mandala on the table in front of her. Layla placed her identical mandala next to Nora's and took her hand in her own.

"You're in charge today," Layla said, squeezing Nora's hand reassuringly. Nora took a deep breath in, closed her amber eyes and concentrated on visualising the location they normally transported

to.

Noah blinked as the scene went dark for a moment, and once it lit up the girls were in the Realm. But it was a place that had been overrun by Shadow Beings.

Nora gasped, and Layla quickly stifled any more noise by tightly placing her hand over Nora's mouth.

"Shh," Layla whispered in her ear, pulling Nora to the edge of a forest filled with thin, dying trees.

Eyes wide, Nora did as she was told and kept herself quiet. Layla pointed into the distance towards a tall figure that appeared to be giving the Shadow Beings orders.

All of a sudden, the two of them found themselves being forced back to Earth, a livid Simmy looking down at them as they shuffled uncomfortably on the couch.

The images in front of Noah flickered as he frantically bent to catch the mandala that had slipped from his fingers as he watched, entranced at the scenes before him. Noah tried to focus back on the scenes, but it was too late.

The images cleared, and Noah was back in his bedroom with a thousand questions running through his head.

Rolling onto his side, Noah looked at the time flashing next to him.

23:35

Closing his eyes, Noah realised that he had a lot to ask Simmy and Layla, but thought he'd better get Layla by herself first. He wanted as much information as possible, and he knew that Layla wouldn't want to tell him everything in front of Simmy.

* * *

The next morning, as Noah got dressed, there was an uneasiness in the pit of his stomach. He'd made the decision to ask Layla everything that had gone on with Nora and their trips to the Realm. If he was going to take Nora's place on this mission, then he needed to know what she had been involved in.

Noah didn't want to be a new Nora. He wanted to be himself, and he didn't want to be joining this mission for the wrong reasons.

Starting his trek to the campus, Noah used the time to clear his head.

He was so lost in his thoughts that he didn't notice a girl quietly slip into step beside him until he was interrupted by a mat of wild red hair out of the corner of his eye.

"Hey," Layla said to him once she saw Noah had noticed her.

"Hey…" he replied. He wasn't sure which question to ask Layla first, so he purposely avoided her eye contact as they walked to try and deter her from asking anything he didn't want to answer. Unfortunately for him, Layla saw right through him.

"Simmy wanted me to make sure that you had your mandala with you for our session this afternoon. She's going to be in a staff meeting, so she's left me in charge," Layla said, eyeing him out of the corner of her eye.

Noah looked pointedly at a particularly crunchy looking leaf on the ground. "Oh, right, yup, that's fine. I have my mandala with me," he replied.

Starting to walk a little faster so that he wasn't in Layla's direct line of sight, Noah felt his calf muscles start to burn. For someone so small, Layla easily kept up with his long strides.

To Noah's relief, apart from the occasional side-eye, Layla didn't push him about his behaviour, and with ten minutes to spare, they made it to the campus entrance.

"Layla!" a tall, muscular boy with cropped brown hair Noah hadn't seen before called out, and both Noah and Layla turned to the voice.

"James, hey," Layla replied with a wave.

The boy, panting, caught up to where Noah and Layla were standing and turned, a little awkwardly, to Noah. "Umm, I just wanted to have a word with Layla," he said, his cheeks going pink.

"Oh, sure," Noah said, equally as awkward. "I'll see you in class," he said to Layla before walking towards Mr Greeves' classroom.

As he turned the corner, Noah stole a glance back and saw Layla laughing and James, his face much redder than before, kicking a rock on the ground in front of him.

Noah ignored the flips his stomach started doing at the sight and scuffled into the classroom, taking his seat.

Class had already begun by the time Layla took her seat behind Noah, but being so small, she managed to slip into her seat unnoticed.

"Make sure that you're putting in your best efforts this year," Mr Greeves droned on, the students only half listening to what he was saying.

The lesson seemed to go on forever. Noah didn't retain a word of what was being taught and was grateful when Mr Greeves dismissed them.

"I'll see you later," he said to Layla, who was packing everything back inside her satchel. He pulled on his backpack, walked to meet Geoff at the side of the maths building and climbed into the golf buggy.

"Morning Geoff," Noah said to the large man.

"Morning kid. We're repainting the track lines on the oval today," Geoff replied as they drove around the grounds.

Noah turned in his seat to see the large paint tank sitting in the tray.

"You won't need to get changed," Geoff continued. "We only have one tank, and I'm more qualified to do the work."

Disappointed that he wouldn't be needed this period, Noah ran his fingers through his dirty blond hair and cracked his back. He may as well take this time to chat to Geoff some more. They had spent a fair bit of time together over the last week and had struck up an unlikely friendship.

"Last time you were telling me how you lost a friend in the army," Noah began. "Did you fight together?"

Geoff didn't reply straight away, taking his time unloading the buggy and setting up the tank to paint the field. "We fought together for a couple of months," he started. "I got hit with some shrapnel before I could really be of much use though. Was sent home because of issues with my sight."

Noah looked at the scar running down Geoff's face, never having considered that it was hiding a blind eye.

Not elaborating any further, Geoff started his work, and Noah sat in the buggy, running the conversation he wanted to have with Layla through his mind over and over again.

Then, all too quickly, it was the next period, and Noah waited patiently for Geoff to drive him back up to the school. He was looking forward to this class. Simmy had mentioned during their last lesson that she was going to spice things up a bit by teaching them about something they all did on a daily basis.

They reached the classroom, and he waved goodbye to Geoff before grabbing a seat inside and waiting for Simmy to arrive. The brunette girl, Abigail, was eagerly bouncing in her chair, ready for the class to begin.

Simmy opened the classroom door just as Layla slipped silently next to Noah.

"Good morning, class," Simmy called out cheerfully.

"Good morning, Ms Johannson," the class chimed back.

"As you all know, we have been working on the science of the mind. I've taught you some simple breathing techniques to help keep your mind clear and to relax when you notice yourself thinking negative thoughts. One deep breath in through your nose, one deep breath out through your mouth, and then deep breaths in and out of your nose until you have calmed down."

Simmy was walking around the classroom as she talked, taking note of the students who were paying attention. Abigail, as always, was furiously writing down Simmy's every word, while Layla and Noah, who had been taught this by Simmy in their private sessions, were content to listen to her teach the others.

"But," Simmy continued, after a pause which gained all of her students' attention, "what I've noticed, and this happens to everyone, is that when we are working on these techniques, or really when we work on anything, we are always looking out of the corner of our eyes trying to catch glimpses of what everyone else is doing."

The class gave a low chuckle. It was true.

This was something Noah was especially guilty of. Even as he thought this, his eyes had swung towards Layla to see her reaction to Simmy's statement.

Layla had a knowing smile on her face, and her eyes locked with Noah's as he glanced at her.

Noah gave a quick smile in return and refocused his eyes back onto his notebook, listening even more intently to Simmy.

"We are always comparing ourselves to others. Always trying to see if someone is better than us, if we're better than someone else, if we look ridiculous doing something, if someone else is laughing, smiling, crying or anything else. We are brought up this way. It takes a long time to be able to control these urges that tell you to compare yourself to others." Simmy told the class and smiled at the students she caught eye contact with. "There is a very simple technique to ensure that you stop doing this. Do you know what it could be?"

Everyone shook their heads.

"Closing your eyes," she whispered.

Noah almost laughed out loud.

A smile crossed Simmy's face again. "Closing your eyes," she said, louder, the smile evident in her voice. "If you want to stop comparing yourself to others, to stop watching what they're doing, and wondering if you're doing the right thing, just close your eyes."

Some of the students in the class laughed while others breathed a silent breath of relief. This was something that they could all do.

"Now, we're going to try those breathing techniques I've taught you, but this time we're all going to do it with our eyes closed," Simmy told everyone.

There was an awkward shuffle in the class as some students closed their eyes immediately, while others glanced at their classmates to see whether they were actually doing it.

Eventually the class settled down, and everyone closed their eyes as Simmy counted them into their first breath.

Noah, who had been one of the people to check to see whether the rest of the class were closing their eyes, relaxed into his breath and felt instantly lighter. He didn't try to not think, and he also didn't try to think about anything in particular. He just let his mind wander where it wanted to, and if he needed to readjust his thoughts he counted from one to ten.

All too soon, the class ended and Noah reluctantly opened his eyes.

Simmy was standing back at the front of the classroom. The vibe that embraced everyone was calm and positive, and Simmy was smiling.

"Thank you for cooperating with me today, class. Homework is to take twenty minutes out every day, close your eyes and practise your breathing techniques," Simmy called as they all pulled out their student diaries.

The class, in a dazed and relaxed state, wrote down their homework and trundled out of the classroom in silence after packing away their notebooks.

Noah and Layla were two of the last students to leave, and with a wave to Simmy, who was once again being bombarded with questions by Abigail, they set off towards their next class.

Chapter 9 - Noah

The rest of the day flew by and, before he knew it, Noah was on his way to another private session with Layla and Simmy.

Although during this lesson, Simmy had a staff meeting, so it was just going to be himself and Layla. This afternoon would be the perfect time for him to chat to her about what the mandala had shown him over the weekend.

The sight of the tall figure giving orders to the Shadow Beings plagued Noah's mind, and he knew that there was more going on in the Realm than Layla and Simmy had shared with him. That there was more than just an overrun of Shadow Beings.

Noah's thoughts were all over the place. He hadn't had a chance to compose himself before he arrived at Simmy's classroom. The door had been left open, so Noah let himself inside and found that Layla had already arrived. She was sitting cross-legged on the floor with her eyes closed, the pile of squishy black beanbags arranged in a circle around her, and her mandala sitting by her feet.

Not wanting to disturb her, Noah quietly folded himself into one of the beanbags as well and closed his amber eyes.

As soon as he took his first breath, he was inundated with

images of Nora and Layla hiding behind a dead tree, watching the tall figure pointing a long finger, giving orders to the Shadow Beings.

Layla coughed lightly, and Noah's eyes snapped open. As soon as he saw Layla looking at him with a raised eyebrow, he quickly averted his eyes again, opting to look at his feet. *How do I even bring this up?* he asked himself.

"Has the mandala shown you the past?" Layla broke through Noah's train of thought bluntly.

Noah turned to her in surprise. "What?"

"When I first started learning how to use the mandala, it showed me visions of Simmy and what she'd been doing while she was in the Realm," replied Layla. "It somehow knew that she hadn't yet told me about her time there and felt that it was something I needed to know."

Noah looked at Layla for a few seconds in silence.

"What did the mandala show you?"

Noah swallowed. "Erm, well, it started off showing me Nora and when she first met you and Simmy, and some of your journeys to the Realm."

Noah's eyes slowly turned to look at Layla, who nodded but didn't interrupt him. He had a feeling that Layla knew where his story was heading. "In the last journey, it showed me a tall person who appeared to be giving the Shadow Beings orders," Noah said. "It looked to me like it was in charge of them."

Layla pulled her lip into her mouth and bit it, tugging Noah's train of thought away from the visions for the briefest second.

"I can imagine that that was hard to watch," Layla said.

"You imagine right," Noah replied, forcing himself to look at his feet instead of Layla's lips.

"I'm not sure who that figure is," Layla said. If she'd

78

noticed Noah's lack of eye contact, she didn't mention it. She continued, plopping down into one of the beanbags beside him. "I've asked Simmy a few times but she's told me that I didn't need to know yet. That in due time I would find out. But you're right," she said to Noah. "It appears that... person... is the ringmaster, using the Shadow Beings as its cronies."

"I wonder if Simmy knows who it is," Noah pondered. "You said she couldn't travel to the Realm at the moment. I wonder if this person started attacking the Realm after she'd left?"

"I'm sure she knows," said Layla. "Simmy hasn't been to the Realm for a long time, but she knows everything that's happening there. There's no way something like that could be causing so much trouble without Simmy knowing."

Noah rubbed the bridge of his nose with his thumb and forefinger, frowning. "I guess we'll have to trust that Simmy knows what she's doing and that she'll tell us when we're ready."

"Waiting is such a pain!" groaned Layla, running her hands through her hair. "I've been learning these skills for years! Surely I'm at a point where I can be of use now."

Noah silently agreed. He wanted to know more about what was going on too. "Well, I'm not at the same level as you, but anything that will help bring me closer to finding Nora is important to me. We'll probably want to go back to being ignorant about it all once we're actually in the know, though." He gave a weak smile.

Layla gave a half-hearted chuckle in reply, flopping back onto the beanbag behind her. "You're probably right."

There was a brief silence before Noah asked his next question. "So, you're the friend that Nora was spending so much time with before she disappeared?"

"Yeah," replied Layla softly.

"Do you have any idea as to where she could be?" Noah asked, trying to keep his voice as casual as possible.

"No, I'm sorry, I don't," Layla replied, sitting back up again. "Simmy and I have searched everywhere we could, both in the Realm and on Earth, but she's nowhere to be found."

Noah tried to keep the disappointment from showing on his face.

"I know that Simmy's always on the lookout for clues though," Layla continued. "She's never once stopped looking for her. I think Simmy reckons that it has something to do with the Realm, so she feels responsible for getting Nora back."

"Was Nora happy when she was working with you guys?" Noah asked.

"Yeah, really happy," replied Layla. "She was always laughing. She missed you though, and felt guilty that she wasn't spending as much time with you."

"I missed her too."

Stretching his arms above his head, Noah stood up and paced around the room, taking in all the different gemstones that Simmy had scattered about.

"What did that guy want this morning?" Noah found himself asking before he could help himself.

"He wanted to know if I still wanted to catch up tonight," Layla replied, her lips twitching into a grin.

"Do you?" Noah could have kicked himself. "Sorry, that's none of my business," he quickly corrected.

Layla gave him a sly chuckle and turned to look at him through her lashes, purring, "If you want to know more about what I do in my private time, Noah, you're going to have to become a part of it."

The air rushed out of Noah's lungs, and he felt his tongue stick to the roof of his mouth as he let out a strange gurgle in response.

Layla's grin became slyer, and she laughed. "I'm just kidding."

Noah, finally loosening his tongue, let out an awkward laugh.

"Or am I?" Layla fluttered her lashes at him, before standing up and stretching her arms above her head.

Noah briefly saw her shirt ride up, showing a small sliver of her stomach, before he flung himself over to his backpack, hastily pulled it over his shoulder and stood up as he escaped for the door.

Chapter 10 - Layla

Simmy was out, working late on a project that Layla knew she wouldn't tell her about until absolutely necessary. The university was great for Simmy because it allowed her to put up the ruse of marking papers when she'd really be working on her own thing. Layla knew she was still trying to figure out where Nora had gone and was using this time out of the house to keep away from prying eyes.

Like hers.

While she knew that Simmy trusted her, it frustrated Layla knowing that there were still things she kept from her. That there was nothing she could do to help her friend, or her friend's brother.

Sighing, Layla looked down at her phone:

My parents are out. You can come round
if you'd like.

James had cornered her today at school and told her that he was alone at his place tonight. To be fair, after she'd messaged him yesterday, she couldn't blame him for putting the offer out there. But she really wasn't in the mood. Thoughts of Nora overwhelmed her, as they'd started to do more frequently as she got to know Noah better.

The similarities between the two of them were becoming more apparent. Her heart ached as she thought about what her friend might be going through and the impact her disappearance would be having on Noah. Not that he'd shared much with her yet.

Nora had opened up about her life and Noah every now and again, but she was always so focused on her mission with the Realm that they'd never chatted much about their family. Layla used to see Noah walking around campus with his friends all the time. They always seemed to be in each other's pockets, but now... now he was always either alone or with her.

The pain of being with those friends must be too much for him to bear right now. He puts up a brave front, but I'm sure that he's dealing with a lot, Layla thought to herself as she absently played with a strand of curly red hair that had fallen in front of her face.

She was so young when her parents died that Layla didn't know what the proper process of grieving was, if there was one. She knew that it had impacted her relationships a lot. She'd never really had substantial friendships, always choosing to keep people at arm's length in case they left her, like her parents had. Even though Simmy had always been a stable constant in her life, she still had trouble trusting people.

That was until she met Nora anyway. They clicked immediately.

The same thing had happened with Noah. There was something about him that made her want to be there for him, and to allow him to be there for her when she needed him. She knew that it wasn't something that would happen overnight, especially with him still having so much to process, but she hoped that one day they would be able to be close friends like she and Nora had been.

Were.

Like she and Nora *were*.

Looking at the message James had sent her once more, Layla sighed and threw her phone on the bed, grabbing her favourite book off the shelf and opting for a long, hot bath instead.

Padding her way to the bathroom, Layla turned on the water, tipped in some rose scented bubble bath and lit her favourite musky incense to help her relax. Simmy wouldn't be home for ages, so she had time to have a proper unwind.

Layla sighed as her tight muscles loosened once they hit the hot water, giving her body time to adjust to the temperature before allowing herself to really sink into the tub, reclining until only the top of her head and her knees were showing above the bubbles.

Closing her eyes, she took in a deep breath through her nose and then released it, feeling the bubbles that surrounded her face be pushed away by the force of it. Then, submerging herself completely below the water, she rinsed her hair before resurfacing and playing with the ends of it as it straightened out.

The only time her hair was ever semi-straight was when it was completely drenched.

Tugging on it behind her back, absently playing with the long strands, Layla let her mind wander, grabbing a bar of soap, rinsing off the day.

She smirked to herself as she remembered Noah's shocked expression when she'd invited him into her private life. She had to hold back a laugh at how innocent he was. She'd known that Nora had played around a little bit, but from what she'd been told, Noah was still as innocent as they come. Nora said that Noah had always felt awkward about his body, how he felt he'd never fully grown into his height.

Layla didn't know why though. He was a babe.

Wait...

What?

Layla let the soap fall to the bottom of the tub as she sat bolt upright. She splashed water over the edges onto the tiled floor, but she didn't care. Did she just think of Noah Parker as a babe?

No... no, no-no-no. Nope, double nope, definitely not.

She wasn't going there.

Now was *not* the time to be entertaining a crush.

Maybe I should hit up James after all... she thought to herself, all ideas of relaxation gone as she ripped the soap from the bottom of the tub and relentlessly scrubbed at her skin.

She hadn't brought her phone in the bathroom with her, so she quickly dunked herself under the water to wash off any residual bubbles, haphazardly wrapped towels around her body and hair and emptied the water from the tub.

Grabbing the book she didn't read, Layla sped back to her room and launched herself at her phone.

Simmy will be out for longer - come
here instead.

Less than a second later the reply came through.

Be there in 5

Grinning, Layla pulled the towel off her head and rubbed the rest of her hair dry, leaving the other towel on, not bothering to put on clothes. They'd just be coming straight off anyway.

She heard a light tap on her window and tiptoed over to

85

it out of habit. Even though Simmy wasn't home, James had done this so many times that sneaking around at the house was second nature to her.

"I didn't think you were going to reply," James said breathlessly, a cheeky grin spreading over his face as he eyed her attire.

"I wasn't," Layla replied, raking her eyes over him as well.

With dark brown hair, freckles and vivid brown eyes, Layla appreciated James's face, but it was his lean, muscular build that really caught her breath.

Effortlessly, James jumped through the window, scooped her up in his arms, *'accidentally'* dropping the towel covering her body onto the floor as he did so. She laughed as he threw her on the bed and quickly stripped himself of his own clothes.

Reaching out to cup his face as his lips crashed into hers, Layla wrapped her legs around James' waist as he moved to position them on the bed.

He knew exactly what she wanted, and she let him take control, enjoying the attention he was giving her.

Sighing happily, Layla let herself be completely consumed by the moment.

Yes, she thought to herself as James worked his way down her abdomen, *the best way to get over any wanton thoughts regarding a certain tall, blond individual is to completely immerse myself in someone else.*

Chapter 11 - Nora

Nora still didn't know how long she'd been here. She'd been told she was in the Realm, but every time she tried to focus her energy, something blocked it. This made her second guess what Tick had told her and made her think she was still on Earth because of how restricted her powers were.

Gritting her teeth in frustration, Nora tried creating an energy ball in the palm of her hand once again. But, like all the other times, all she could produce was an unstable glow with no shape, which wouldn't do her any good if she had to fight for her life.

Huffing out a breath, Nora stalked back to her bed and flopped down on it as gently as possible. It was too hard for her to be able to throw herself on it like she really wanted to. But if she banged her fists on that bed, it would hurt her more than help her.

Resting her arm over her face, Nora took a couple of deep breaths in through her nose and out through her mouth to calm herself down. If she let her frustrations get the better of her, then there was seriously no chance of her finding a way out of here.

As she was on her last breath, a noise coming from outside

her room caught Nora's attention, and she paused, lifting her arm a little so she wasn't covering her ear.

Squinting to hear better, Nora pulled her arm off her head completely and sat up on her elbows, looking out into the room beyond her door.

She was never allowed to have her door shut, but even so, the energetic barrier that surrounded the doorway made it almost impossible to see what was happening beyond her prison.

Not being able to stand it anymore, Nora tiptoed to the door and tried to peer out of it, but thanks to the barrier, everything was red and fuzzy. Nora groaned, throwing her hand at the barrier, annoyed. Turning around to stalk back to the bed, the sound of a clearer voice made her pause and look back.

Where she'd hit the barrier, there was now a small, hand-sized hole that was slowly repairing itself. Gasping, Nora jumped back to her doorway, peering through the hole like her life depended on it.

She'd never seen into the room outside before. Eleven statues in thrones and one throne by itself were taking up most of the centre of the room. Crouched down next to the statue closest to her was a very attractive man, with jet-black hair and piercing blue eyes, talking softly to the statue, which was the sound that she'd been able to hear from her room. He couldn't have been any older than his mid-twenties. Nora's breath caught in her throat. *Maybe he's here to help me.*

Before she could call out to him, another sound from a room beyond her line of sight echoed, and the man quickly stood, brushing his hand over his face, and was immediately transformed into a Shadow Being. But not just any Shadow

Being. He was solid, and his energy crackled from his fingertips in the same way Tick's did.

Every time Tick came to visit Nora, she threw a black energy ball her way just for the fun of it, trying to see if Nora was quick enough to dodge it.

Sometimes she was, sometimes she wasn't.

Nora rubbed the fading bruises on her ribs where Tick's blasts had hit her and frowned at the Shadow Being where the man had stood before. The hole in the barrier was so small now as it repaired itself that she was only able to peer through with one eye.

"There you are," Nora heard Tick's voice purr as she swished into the room. "Scratch, are you listening to me?"

Tick clicked her shadowy claws in the other Shadow Being's face, who appeared to be ignoring her.

"Scratch!" Tick screeched again, this time whacking him over his head with a bat of black energy. "You've been summoned. It's time for you to fulfil your duties."

"Well, why didn't you just say so?" Scratch drawled at Tick, lazily rubbing his head where she had hit him and sauntering out of the room.

He looked back to see Tick, seething at him in the same spot she was before, and clicked his claws at her. "C'mon now, you don't want to keep Master waiting."

Tick hissed at him before teleporting away. Nora assumed that she had gone to their Master, who, again Nora assumed, was the man who'd brought her here.

As soon as she was gone, Scratch looked around the room, his eyes drifting back to the statue he was talking to before and narrowing as they passed over her prison. "I'll be back," he whispered before quickly walking out the door, a stark change to the relaxed air he'd had around him while Tick was here.

Was he talking to me? Nora asked herself. *Who else could he be talking to? Maybe he really is here to help me.*

The hole that she had created in the barrier finally sealed itself shut, and Nora took step after step backwards until her calves hit the bed and she collapsed onto it.

Gritting her teeth, she set her mind. "I'm not alone. I'll do whatever it takes to get out of here," she said quietly to herself, standing up.

There were now two things she was certain of. One, she needed to gain the Master's trust so that she could get some more freedom to see if that new Shadow Being—man—person was really here to help her.

And two, she needed to get in touch with Noah.

Nora looked from the barrier keeping her in her room to her hands, an idea forming. Maybe... maybe she had been going about this the wrong way. Maybe instead of trying to force her way into her powers, she just needed to relax into them instead.

Laying back on her bed, Nora took a deep breath in and allowed her mind to wander, thinking of all the good times she'd shared with Noah, allowing the ache in her chest to guide her to him.

Please, this has to work.

Chapter 12 - Noah

Dark, leafless trees surrounded the narrow pathway that Noah found himself walking along. There was something eerie about this place, and he shuddered as a cool night breeze prickled his skin.

Someone was calling him.

He needed to hurry.

Squinting, Noah saw a small ball of light flickering in the distance. Hoping that this was what was calling to him, he quickened his pace, but the ball never got any closer. It was guiding him towards something.

Making sure not to lose sight of it, Noah pushed himself into a run, fighting against his legs that were struggling to move. All of a sudden, the ball of light stopped. Reaching out his hand, Noah wrapped his fingers around the warm globe and was instantly teleported.

Hitting the ground hard on his hands and knees, Noah gasped for air, his lungs constricting at the sudden movement. Still grasping the ball of light, Noah focused his eyes. Looking around at his surroundings, he saw that he was in some sort of temple, hidden behind a large pillar decorated in red and gold trimmings.

Something didn't feel right about this place and, as Noah

peered out, he saw a large room filled with twelve stone thrones.

Eleven of those thrones were occupied by intricate statues of people who, Noah assumed, lived in the Realm.

All of the statues wore long gowns with large, decorative headpieces adorning their regal heads. But it wasn't the unusual clothing that caught Noah's eye. It was their faces. It looked like they had been carved to show surprise... and fear.

Noah rubbed at the goosebumps on his arm, which had nothing to do with the temperature, and tried to study each of the faces individually from his hiding spot.

Suddenly, a noise came from a room that Noah hadn't noticed behind the thrones, and he prayed that he wouldn't be seen as he flattened himself against the pillar, giving himself just enough space to peer into the room in front of him. He squinted, not daring to show himself in case he was wrong, but he was sure that there was someone over there.

He didn't have the chance to investigate though, because as soon as he decided to try and make a run for it and see, someone else walked into the room.

"I still cannot find her," an old, thin man with long grey hair and a long wiry grey beard hissed angrily to himself as he walked over towards the twelve thrones. "I know you know where she is, and until I get some answers, you will all stay like this."

Noah's eyes darted around for whoever the man was talking to, but there was no one there.

The man started to circle the room. He was extremely agile for someone his age. "The sooner I find her, the sooner your bodies will be restored, *Guardians of the Realm*," the man sneered. "I know that you are all desperate to stretch your legs. To feel the sunshine on your skin. To eat and drink like you used to."

A prickling sensation made Noah's skin itch as he realised who the man was talking to. There *were* people here, there were eleven of them. Eleven people who had been turned to stone and were forced to sit and watch as the land they loved died before their eyes.

As soon as he'd realised this, a loud male voice boomed around the room. "We know what you have done to our Realm," it said. "Our place is here, guarding our sister whom you seek."

The old man, furious, summoned a gold cane from thin air and swiped at the nearest throne. "You will tell me where she is!" he screamed.

The shriek echoed around the temple chambers causing Noah's ears to throb, and in an attempt to protect himself, Noah dropped the globe of light and covered his ears with both of his hands.

Everything went quiet.

Noah was in his bed.

Slowly he opened his eyes and saw that he was back in his bedroom. His sheets were barely wrinkled, which meant that he hadn't moved at all since he had fallen asleep that evening.

It was a dream... he thought to himself.

Noah shivered. He would have to chat to Layla and Simmy about it. He let out a long, exhausted breath, rolled over and fell back to sleep.

Chapter 13 - Nora

Nora groaned as she lay in her bed, stiff from overexerting her energy.

She'd managed to get a hold of Noah, but she hadn't been able to bring him to her directly, only to the temple itself.

At least he had seen her captor, though. And the statues of the Guardians. She couldn't believe it hadn't already crossed her mind that these were the eleven Guardians that Simmy had told her about.

Nora had watched Noah as he'd investigated them, hoping that he would know who they were, before she'd made as much noise as possible in her room to bring his attention to her. Which hadn't worked as Noah had disappeared instead.

Nora didn't even know what the man holding her here's real name was. She was certain it wasn't just '*Master*', although he exuded enough arrogance for her to think that he'd like to be called that all the time. He still didn't trust her enough to give away any information about himself. Even though she'd been brown-nosing him as much as possible lately, she hadn't been given any more freedom than before.

Even the new Shadow Being, Scratch, hadn't come in to see her. The only other person she'd seen was Tick. She didn't even know why Tick came to visit her. All Tick did was antagonise her and blast her with energy balls that she couldn't always dodge.

One of them had been so big that it had thrown Nora back against the wall of her room, and Nora was sure she'd felt something snap.

It had taken all of her concentration to relax into the pain and allow herself to try and heal the injury. It wasn't as good as if she'd had full access to her powers, but whatever had broken was semi-fixed. The bruising would have to stay, but that was okay. The bruising would heal more easily than a broken bone.

Rubbing her hands over her face, Nora sat up in the bed. She hadn't had access to a mirror or even a proper shower since she'd been here. She was only ever given a lukewarm sponge and some soap to wash herself in the little sink in her room once a day, so she didn't even want to think about what her bed hair looked like right now.

"You look like crap."

Nora paused, swallowing a snide remark as she turned towards the voice. "Scratch, was it?"

Scratch paused, raising a shadowy eyebrow at her. "Now, how did you know that?"

A shiver ran down Nora's spine. "I have my ways," she huffed, pulling her feet off the bed, hoping she looked more menacing than she felt.

Scratch looked at her for a few more moments before shrugging and throwing a bag at her, which hit Nora in the chest with an "Oomph."

"Oi, asshole, what is it with people throwing things at me in here?" she growled, before opening the bag and finding a fluffy white towel, shampoo, conditioner, body wash and a change of clothes.

"I can take it back, if that's what you'd like," Scratch drawled, holding out his hand.

Nora just scowled at him, clutching the bag of goodies closer to her chest.

"You can't present yourself to the Master looking like a trash rat," Scratch continued, closing his fist and pulling his hand back to his chest. "So, you need to wash…" he slowly raked his gaze up and down Nora, scrunching his nose, and Nora fought the urge to punch him in his smug shadowy face.

When Scratch didn't say anything more, Nora threw the bag over her shoulder and stalked closer to him. "Are you going to show me the way, or what?"

"You're going to need to wear this so you can't see where we're going," Scratch said, holding out a black silk blindfold.

Nora took it from him and tied it tightly over her eyes. "You didn't strike me as the bondage type." She grinned when she heard Scratch gag.

Taking her hand, Scratch pulled Nora behind him at record speed, forcing her to lose her bearings. Even if she had been trying to keep a record of where they were heading, there was no way she'd know where she was now.

"Wash," Scratch instructed, pushing her into a warm room, pulling the blindfold off her as she tumbled forward, and closing the door behind her. "Someone will be in to collect you shortly."

Not too shortly, Nora thought to herself as she looked around the bathroom, taking in the giant tub and waterfall of a shower. *I'll take my time anyway. It'll be their problem if they walk in on me mid-wash.* She grinned again, thinking of the look of horror that Scratch would have if it was him. *Visiting Master. Huh, maybe all that brown-nosing had paid off after all.*

Nora shivered despite the warmth of the water flowing over her. *Hopefully it will be a good visit.*

Chapter 14 - Noah

Aweek passed before Noah decided it was finally time to tell Layla and Simmy about the dream. Every day he was determined he would tell them, but would always change his mind at the last minute, deciding instead to wait to see whether he'd have another one.

But now, a week later, with no sign of another dream coming his way, he decided that Layla and Simmy needed to know. He'd tell them tomorrow during their private session.

Noah scratched the back of his head and sighed, deciding that he'd better head upstairs and do the homework he'd been neglecting.

Quickly thanking his mum for the lemonade and lamingtons, Noah avoided Jen's new favourite topic of how he was spending an awful lot of time with Layla by pulling up his email on his phone, pointing the screen at her and commenting on how far behind on schoolwork he was.

Noah leapt up the stairs three at a time, threw his phone on the doona and flopped face-first onto his bed.

Closing his eyes and throwing his backpack on the floor in front of him, Noah buried his face in his hands and took a deep breath. He was going to be even further behind with his work, but he really wasn't in the mood to use his brain right now. A shower and bed were what he wanted.

After five more deep breaths, Noah convinced himself. *Five more breaths, and then I'll get up and do my homework.*

Noah took a deep breath in through his nose and exhaled loudly through his mouth. His mind was already starting to feel clearer. *One,* He counted in his head.

Another deep breath in, and again, Noah exhaled loudly through his mouth, relaxing even more. *Two.*

* * *

Noah was walking down a narrow path surrounded by tall, leafless trees. There was a globe of light shimmering in the distance, and Noah started to run so that he could catch it before it disappeared.

Grasping the globe in his hand, Noah was transported to the Throne Room, hidden behind the pillar once again. The tall thin man was back and was pacing around the room, this time with a triumphant smile on his face.

"Your resistance has been for nothing. Do you see what's becoming of your precious Realm? The people of Earth are starting to reject it and turning it into a wasteland. Before long, I will have collected all twelve of you Guardians for myself. You were never able to win against me." The man whacked his golden cane on the back of the nearest throne to him. "I will rule this Realm and control the people of Earth. I will create a new Realm. A Realm where no one needs to choose their own fate, as I will choose it for them." The man gave a loud, barking laugh and sank down into the largest throne in the room.

"Where there is evil, there will always be good," a voice

echoed. It was a female voice this time.

Noah didn't get a chance to see the thin man's reaction as the globe's light dimmed, and he was transported back to his bedroom.

Falling onto his bed, Noah looked at his clock. A large *01:14* beamed back at him through the darkness of the night. Noah rubbed his eyes and sighed. He hadn't gotten any homework done again.

Pulling off the day's clothes and changing into his pyjamas, Noah made the decision to tell Layla and Simmy about his dreams tomorrow. He couldn't put it off anymore. Whatever this man was planning, Noah knew that it would be bad news for the Realm if he found the woman he was searching for.

* * *

Life Science class took its time to roll around the following day, and Noah was itching to find out about the vision boards that Simmy had planned to teach them. Maybe he could use them to help find Nora.

"You're not concentrating," Geoff said gruffly to Noah, taking the packet of carrot seeds from his hands and gently placing them in the correct veggie patch.

"Sorry," Noah replied, pulling his gardening gloves off his hands and rubbing his eyes. "I haven't been sleeping well."

Geoff didn't reply. Instead, he pulled a bottle of water from his rucksack and passed it to Noah.

Grateful, Noah accepted the water and guzzled it down.

"You're not taking care of yourself properly," Geoff observed, opening his own water bottle and downing half of it in one swig. "You need to make sure you're eating, drinking and sleeping well if you're going to be of any use to me."

Noah hummed in response. "Yeah, I'm not really doing any of that," he mumbled.

"Your head's all over the place," Geoff said. "You're not helping anyone if your head's not in the game."

"What do you do when you're not sleeping well?" Noah asked, taking another sip of water.

Geoff finished his water and crushed the bottle in his hand. "I talk to someone who can help me figure out what's keeping me awake. You should do the same."

Noah downed the rest of his water, plucked Geoff's scrunched up bottle out of his hand, and walked towards the bin. He knew Geoff was right. He had to chat to Simmy about his dreams.

Geoff finished planting the last of the carrots and jumped into the golf buggy. "It's time for your next class, kid," he said, patting the seat next to him. Noah climbed in, thankful to avoid walking in this heat as Geoff drove him to his next class.

Thanking Geoff for the lift, Noah swung his backpack over his shoulder and headed towards Simmy's classroom.

"Vision boards today," Layla said, appearing out of nowhere.

Noah grinned at her. "Yeah, I'm keen to learn what they're about. I need as much help as I can get right now."

Layla smiled at him as they took their usual seats at the back of the classroom and unpacked their notebooks.

"You can put your notebooks away, students. I have provided the utensils for you today. Abigail, could you please hand these out to the rest of the class?" Simmy asked from the front of the classroom, handing Abigail a large container filled with something Noah couldn't see.

Slowly Abigail made her way to where Noah and Layla were

sitting and passed them both a corkboard, a small bag of tacks and a ziplock bag filled with different cut-out images that Simmy had printed off.

It didn't take Noah long to realise the literal meaning behind the term 'vision board', and he almost laughed to himself. It was so simple.

He went to open his ziplock bag with the printed images inside, but Simmy's voice stopped him.

"Before you all start your projects today, I want to give you some background information on the importance of a vision board," she said to the class.

The chatter stopped abruptly.

Simmy looked around the classroom to make sure that she had everyone's attention before starting to speak again. "Vision boards are an extremely powerful manifesting tool. The history of the vision board can be dated back to the caveman era, where hunters would paint their upcoming hunts on cave walls and envision how they wanted it to go."

The class murmured in interest.

"Vision boards have been around for that long?" Noah whispered under his breath to Layla.

Layla shook her head. "Vision boards like we are making today have only been around for a short amount of time," she explained, "but the practice of using images to visualise something that you want has been around for thousands of years."

"The reason that we are working on vision boards today," Simmy continued, "is because I want you all to focus on something that you desire. Something that you want to achieve or improve upon. So I have provided you all with a wide variety of images that I will let you peruse at your leisure."

"Remember," Noah heard Simmy say, "your vision boards can change whenever you feel like your objectives have changed, or if what you've been working towards has already been accomplished. These corkboards are extremely handy because, unlike the walls of a cave, you can reuse them as many times as you need." Simmy smiled and held her hands out to the class. "Alright, I've talked your ears off for long enough. Time to get started."

Immediately the sound of students chatting and the rustle of plastic ziplock bags being opened flooded the classroom.

Noah opened his own little bag filled with the images that Simmy had chosen and spread them out on his desk.

There were over thirty different images to choose from. Some were images of fit-looking men and women who were exercising and competing in sports. Noah realised that these images were for those classmates who wanted to improve their fitness or improve in a sport they competed in.

Some images had positive affirmations and phrases to uplift the mood, making them feel better about their day and what they were working towards.

Noah shuffled the pictures around some more and saw images of white sandy beaches, musical instruments, knitting needles, exam papers with passing scores, and different types of houses. There were images of people getting their dream jobs and pictures of people travelling the world.

Right now, Noah's goal was creating a vision board that depicted his desire to find his sister and to cleanse the Realm of Intention from the Shadow Beings and the evil man who had been showing up in his dreams.

Noah searched through the images that Simmy had provided for them until he found the ones that felt like they belonged on his board, before packing up the remaining images in the ziplock bag and placing them inside his science notebook so that he wouldn't lose them. He was going to keep them so that he could use them another time.

Pleased with how his board looked—a picture of a smiling family, some inspirational quotes, a photo of his sister that he had found in his wallet and 'I CAN DO THIS' written across the top—Noah smiled.

There was still more to add, but he would do that when he got home and choose the images for himself. Noah wanted to put up pictures of his family and friends on the board as well.

Looking up, Noah saw that Layla was packing away the last of her images and placing them in the front pocket of her backpack.

She smiled at Noah once she noticed that he was looking in her direction and pointed to the front of the classroom.

Abigail, who had finished her vision board very quickly, was standing next to Simmy's desk, asking her questions at a mile a minute about how the process worked and what would be the best way to go about manifesting her desires quickly.

Simmy very patiently looked at Abigail and said, "There is no way to be able to manifest your desires in a specific time limit. As long as you focus on your vision board, say thank you for what you receive and give back as often as you can. Then your desires, if they are meant for you, will come to you when you are ready to receive them."

"What do you mean, 'If they're meant for me?' Isn't everything we ask for meant for us?" Abigail asked, sounding frustrated. Her tone of voice gave Noah the impression that she wanted something that she knew she wasn't allowed.

"No," Simmy replied as the rest of the class packed up their boards. "I will teach you more about that in the next lesson we have together."

"Alright class," Simmy called over the hustle and bustle. "Pack up your things, and remember, there is no right or wrong way to create a vision board. As long as you feel happy and content when you look at your board, then you have created a healthy intention. If you don't feel happy and content when you look at your board, then you need to ask yourself what it is you truly want and adjust your board accordingly." Simmy gave a smile at Abigail's frustrated face when she said this, and turned to pack up her own belongings.

Noah and Layla took their time gathering their things, then started to head towards their usual lunch spot.

"Noah!" a girl called suddenly. "Hey, Noah!"

Noah turned and saw a very pretty, tall Indian girl with long wavy brown hair pulled into a messy ponytail at the top of her head running towards him.

"Ashlee, hey," Noah said, his face warming at the sight of her. He'd been friends with Ashlee since they were in primary school, but he'd barely chatted to any of his old friends since Nora disappeared. They had all hung out together, and he wasn't ready to do that again yet.

Ashlee reached Noah and Layla and smiled at them. "Can I have a word?"

"Sure," replied Noah, pulling his backpack higher up on his shoulder.

"Oh, umm... alone?" Ashlee mumbled, shooting Layla a guilty expression.

"Oh, erm..." Noah paused and looked at Layla.

"No worries, I'll see you later," Layla said to them, and she turned on her heel and walked off to where Abigail and a bunch of other girls were sitting.

Noah watched her leave and then turned his attention back to Ashlee. "What's up?"

Ashlee looked at him firmly, pulling his hand in hers. Noah's heart gave a little jump at the contact. "We miss you," she said to him, gesturing to where the rest of their friends were sitting in silence, watching the interaction.

Noah sighed and gently pulled his hand free. "I miss you guys too," he said, rubbing the back of his neck, "but, being with you all, knowing that Nora isn't there with me too, it's too much."

Especially because I don't have any answers to help find her yet, he thought to himself.

"We know," Ashlee said kindly. "None of us, all your friends, we're not going anywhere. So when you're ready to rejoin our group, we're all going to be here for you."

Noah felt a prickle behind his eyes, and he hastily looked towards the floor. "Thanks," he replied thickly.

"I'll see you later then?" Ashlee asked him.

"Yeah, later, for sure," Noah replied, not giving a definitive time, but knowing that he couldn't avoid his friends forever. Plus, he really did miss them. He just wanted to get some more answers first because he knew they would all be on board in helping to look for her.

Ashlee grinned and gave him a swift kiss on the cheek before running off in the direction of the group, who all waved at Noah as she reached them.

Waving back, Noah smiled before pulling his backpack further up his shoulder and finding a quiet place to eat.

Chapter 15 - Noah

Noah woke up with a start. He'd been transported to the Realm again while he slept. The dreams were becoming more and more realistic, and Noah was desperately trying to figure out who the woman was that the old man was looking for.

She must play an important role in his plan to take over the Realm and, judging from Noah's latest dream, the man was becoming impatient.

No putting it off anymore. It really was time to tell Simmy about all of this. He couldn't keep it to himself, not while he had a strong gut feeling that the information he was receiving would help their mission.

He'd put off telling Simmy about the dreams, even after he'd made the decision to tell her yesterday, because he wanted to keep having them. He kept thinking that they may give him a clue as to where Nora was, although he knew that Simmy wouldn't be pleased that he was travelling to the Realm at night without her, even if it was only in his dreams.

Noah sighed and pulled the covers up under his chin. It was still dark outside, so he knew that there was time before his alarm went off.

Closing his eyes, Noah counted to ten and relaxed. There

was no point in stressing about the dreams. Simmy was asleep, and she wouldn't be able to help him right now.

But still, even as Noah thought this, there was a niggling feeling in his chest that made him wonder if there was something he was missing.

He picked his phone up off his bedside table and typed in his passcode, then hesitated.

He'd been thinking that he could talk to Layla about it all, but he doubted she'd be awake.

Noah opened his recent messages and clicked on Layla's.

Are you awake?

After a couple of seconds deciding whether he should send it or not, Noah pressed send and clicked the lock on his phone.

Minutes passed, and Noah put his phone back on the bedside table and rolled over. Layla was sleeping, as he should be doing as well.

He closed his eyes and just let his thoughts wander as they wanted to.

BRIIIIIIIING!

Noah's eyes snapped open and he jolted awake, sitting up in fright.

It was morning.

With a groan, Noah flopped back onto his pillow, grabbed his phone and turned off his alarm.

He'd fallen back to sleep.

Feeling more tired now than he did when he'd woken up earlier that morning, Noah wondered, as he pulled his doona back over the top of his head, what the chances were of his parents letting him skip university for the day to catch up on sleep.

A faint knock on the front door shook Noah's focus for a

second while he hid under the covers, but he ignored it. *It's probably the mailman*, he thought to himself.

Not even a minute after the thought crossed Noah's mind, his bedroom door flung open and the doona was ripped off his head.

A pair of emerald green eyes met amber ones, and Noah let out a high pitched squeal, pulling what little doona he was still holding onto up under his chin.

Layla rolled her eyes and sat down on the bed.

"What are you doing here?" Noah asked, his voice still several octaves higher than normal.

"You sent me a text at half-past one this morning," Layla replied. "I was worried you were being attacked or something."

"Well I'm not!" Noah replied with a huff. He'd been so comfortable under his covers. "Now, if you don't mind," he gestured towards the door, "I need to get dressed."

Layla rolled her eyes again and walked over towards Noah's wardrobe, pulling out a clean pair of jeans and a t-shirt and throwing them at him. She then walked over to his drawers and opened them one by one until she found his underwear.

Noah, mouth agape, watched her as she pulled out an old, holey, grey pair of boxers and put them back in the drawer, then pulled out a pair of never-before-worn black boxer briefs and threw them in Noah's direction, folding her arms.

Noah caught the underwear and closed his mouth.

"May I please get dressed now?" he asked. "*Alone?*" he emphasised when Layla didn't move.

"Well hurry up then, we need to get going. We're meeting Simmy before classes start this morning," Layla said as she walked outside into the hallway and half-closed the door behind her.

Noah stomped over to the door, clicked it closed purposefully behind her, took a full deep breath in through his nose, and a full deep breath out of his mouth, then picked up the clothes that had been chosen for him.

"Barging into my room like that," Noah muttered to himself as he changed. "I was so comfortable too. Never should have sent that message."

Looking at himself in the mirror, Noah smoothed down his messy blond bed hair and tried, unsuccessfully, to make the top of it lay flat.

Sighing, he looked longingly at his bed, then opened the bedroom door to meet Layla.

She was standing on the opposite side of the wall, and, as soon as Noah opened the door, she thrust his toothbrush into his hands and pushed him towards the bathroom.

"Brush, brush!" she said hastily, making shooing motions with her hands. "Simmy's waiting for us."

Noah grabbed his toothbrush out of Layla's hand and shoved it in his mouth as he walked to the bathroom. "Bruth, bruth," he mimicked as he scrubbed his teeth.

Layla followed Noah to the bathroom and filled a cup of water for him to rinse his mouth.

"Fanks," Noah said, spitting his toothpaste into the sink and taking a large mouthful of water.

"Finished?" Layla asked.

Noah nodded, wiping his mouth on a towel and then chasing after Layla as she raced down the stairs.

"Why are you in such a rush this morning?" he asked as he grabbed his backpack from the front door, calling goodbye to his parents as they ran from the house.

"We're meeting Simmy, I've already told you," Layla explained impatiently.

"But we'll see her on campus," Noah whined.

"We're not going to campus," Layla replied. "We're meeting Simmy at our place."

Finally, after racing past the first block, Layla slowed to a steady walking pace and Noah, puffing, matched her steps, rubbing at a stitch in his side. It was too early in the morning for this type of athletics.

"So, we're going to yours and Simmy's place and... what are we doing there?" Noah asked between breaths.

She looked at him as they neared her house. Noah had forgotten that Simmy and Layla lived so close to him.

"You've been having dreams, haven't you?" Layla asked him.

Noah gaped at her. "How did you know?"

"My mandala gave me a vision last night, when I was unwrapping it, of you running towards a light and then disappearing," Layla replied, her eyes never leaving Noah's face.

"Oh," Noah said sheepishly. "Well, erm, yeah. I've been having dreams."

"You need to tell Simmy what you've been dreaming about and how long you've been having them. You should have told her about them as soon as they started," Layla scolded.

Noah scrunched up his nose. Layla was right. He was frustrated with himself that he hadn't told Simmy about the dreams sooner, but he'd been so focused on getting as much information as possible from them that he'd forgotten that they were supposed to be working as a team.

Simmy flung the front door open before Noah and Layla had reached it and ushered them inside.

"Tell me everything," she said, thrusting a cup of tea into one of Noah's hands and a large plate of buttered toast into the other.

Noah took a big bite of toast and thought about where to start.

"Well," Noah began, a little piece of toast flying from his mouth as he spoke. Layla flinched at the toast spittle while Simmy pretended not to have noticed. "I started getting dreams shortly after the lesson that Layla and I had without you, Simmy," he said.

Simmy nodded. "You are having dreams about the Realm?"

"Yeah," Noah replied. "They only happen sporadically, though."

"And where are you in the dreams?" Simmy asked in a voice that sounded like she was trying to appear calm, but was really very anxious.

"I'm in a temple, always hiding behind a pillar. There's a room with twelve thrones that are occupied by eleven statues. They were called the '*Guardians of the Realm*' if I remember correctly, and they've all been petrified."

"Is there anyone else in the room with the Guardians?" Simmy asked quickly.

"There's an old, thin man with a grey beard and a long golden cane. He's looking for a woman, and the Guardians aren't helping him. I don't know who he's looking for though, or why."

Layla and Simmy stole anxious looks at each other, and Noah placed his now empty teacup on the coffee table in front of him.

"What's wrong?" Noah asked the both of them. "These dreams are just... dreams, aren't they?"

Layla shook her head. "No, these are events that are physically happening in the Realm."

"You mean this is what's causing the Shadow Beings to come out from the darkness?" Noah exclaimed. "Those Guardians of the Realm have been captured?"

Simmy nodded. "That is part of the reason why, but I believe that the Shadow Beings had started to stir even before the Guardians were captured, and that that man in your dream is the ringleader."

Layla looked at Simmy. "Have you been trying to deal with this on your own?"

Simmy's gaze dropped to the floor. "Yes," she replied, "but it hasn't worked. My limitations with the Realm have prevented me from finding the information I need."

"Can someone please explain to me what this means!" Noah burst out. He was the one who'd been having the dreams, yet he was the only one who didn't know what was going on.

"There is a lot to explain," Layla said to him, walking over to the long couch and sitting next to him. "Nora was working with a lot of Realm energy before she was taken, so we need to make sure you haven't been letting off any signals that can guide her captor to you as well."

"Well," Simmy rebutted, "we're not one hundred percent sure that's what happened. I don't believe that Nora was giving off anything excessive."

Layla's lips drew together in a line as she stood and walked up the hall to what, Noah assumed, was her bedroom.

Layla slammed the door, and Simmy looked sadly in her direction. "She's determined to try and blame herself for the work Nora was doing before she disappeared. She feels like Nora was doing more than she needed to, and if she, Layla, could have taken on some of the burden, then Nora would still be here." Simmy patted Noah's hand and met his gaze. "I need you to tell me everything you can remember from your dreams. Even the things you deem unnecessary."

Noah opened his mouth, questions burning on the tip of his tongue, but Simmy held her hand up to stop him. "Tell me everything you can remember, and I will answer all of your questions once we have finished."

"Alright," Noah reluctantly agreed.

"Thank you," Simmy replied. She pulled a brand new notebook from a drawer in the coffee table and opened it to a blank page. "Start from the beginning."

Noah recounted his dreams, sharing every detail he could remember, ignoring the scratch of Simmy's pen as she hastily wrote down everything he said.

After what felt like hours of endless questions—*Where were you standing exactly? What did the statues look like? What did the man with the cane's voice sound like? Were you warm or cold in the dream?'*—Noah felt drained.

He wasn't sure how anything he'd relayed could be helpful, but Simmy hushed him as soon as he voiced his hesitations.

"You've helped our mission more than you realise," she said to him.

Noah grunted in reply. He didn't understand how, which led him to believe that he still didn't have all the information regarding their mission.

Noah stood up, mentioning something to Simmy about going to the bathroom. Simmy, absorbed in her notes, merely nodded and waved him away.

Not at all interested in going to the bathroom, Noah walked down the hallway to the room he'd seen Layla enter earlier on and hesitantly knocked on the door.

"It's Noah," he called. "Can I come in?"

A muffled shuffling could be heard from the bedroom, and Noah imagined Layla tossing off her doona.

The door opened slightly, and Layla peered her head out, looking to see if Simmy was still poring over her notes.

Appeased, she opened the door wider, pulling Noah inside before quietly closing it behind him.

Layla flopped down on her bed while Noah walked over to a desk in the corner of the room, pulled out the chair and rolled it in front of the bed before sitting down.

"Well?" Layla asked sharply.

Noah paused. "Well?"

"Tell me about your dreams!" Layla shot back, like it was the most obvious thing in the world.

"What?" Noah hissed. "If you wanted to hear about the dreams, why didn't you stay in the living room so you could hear me the first time?"

Layla sighed a long, dramatic sigh that made Noah grit his teeth in frustration. "I couldn't stay out there.".

"And why the hell not?" Noah shot back.

"Simmy doesn't take me seriously. She's determined to find out what happened on her own and doesn't let me in on what she's doing." Layla said, looking at Noah so that she could read his reaction. "And besides, I'm sick of arguing with her about it."

Noah's frustration subsided. He could understand where Layla was coming from. In fact, he could understand it very well. Finding out what had happened to Nora was quickly taking over his thoughts. Taking a deep breath, Noah prepared to relay his dreams again.

115

"Well," Noah began, "I was in a large room, and there were eleven Guardians of the Realm who had been petrified all sitting in chairs, but the second chair was empty, and the man who Simmy said was the ringleader kept on telling the petrified Guardians to tell him where their sister was. He'd been asking this for a while. It seemed like he couldn't move further with his plans until he found her."

"Uh-huh," Layla said slowly, her eyes closed in thought.

Noah looked over at her, and he saw that she was sitting cross-legged on the bed, leaning towards him with her elbows on her knees and her forehead in her hands.

"I believe that woman is Nora," Layla said slowly.

"What?" Noah replied, jumping up from the chair so fast that it wheeled away from him and hit the bedroom door. "Why would you think that? Nora's a girl! The man said he was looking for a woman!"

"An eighteen-year-old can be classed as a woman," Layla defended.

Noah waved her comment away. "Nora's a girl. I'm certain that the woman the man is looking for isn't Nora."

"But how can you be so sure? We don't know that the man hasn't been taking over the Realm for hundreds of years and that the woman he's looking for wasn't reincarnated as Nora." Layla's frustration threatened to spill over in tears. "Nora's disappearance isn't for nothing! I know that there is a link between these dreams and Nora! I can *feel* it!"

"You're right," a quiet voice said from the doorway. "Nora's disappearance isn't for nothing."

Noah and Layla both turned quickly to see Simmy standing against the door frame, the notes she had taken with Noah in her hands and an unreadable expression on her face.

"But how are you so sure that Nora's not the woman that man is looking for?" Layla begged for her theory to be heard.

Simmy pushed Noah's forgotten desk chair further into the bedroom so she could come in. "I'm certain that Nora is not the woman that the man is looking for, because the woman he is searching for is me," she said softly.

Noah and Layla's mouths dropped open as they stared at Simmy in shocked silence.

Simmy sighed, closed her tired brown eyes and rubbed her temples with her fingers. "Come, sit in the living room with me. It's time I told both of you the truth."

Chapter 16 - Noah

Noah sat down next to Layla on an old squishy couch, staring at Simmy as she patted her long brown skirt out of habit.

Finally, Simmy looked up at Noah and Layla. "First things first, I want you both to keep an open mind when you hear my story, and please know that it was never my intention for the Realm to turn into what it has."

Noah nodded, and he heard Layla give an impatient grunt next to him. She was waiting for Simmy to get to the point.

"Another thing you need to know is that I have been alive for almost the length of humanity," Simmy continued, somewhat hesitantly.

"What?" Noah and Layla both exclaimed.

"How is that possible?" Layla demanded.

"You two know that the Realm of Intention is there to guide the people of Earth, to help them reach their goals and to pass to the other side peacefully, yes?" Simmy asked the two of them.

Noah and Layla nodded.

"The Realm guides people towards a more positive way of living," Simmy continued. "Promoting gratitude while also helping people accept the faults in themselves and others. The

Realm came into existence through the will of many people. The 'Universe' is what many people call the Realm. The 'Will Of The Universe', 'Fate', and 'Luck' are also other ways that the Realm has been described over the years, and we twelve Guardians were created to assist the people of Earth and ensure that the Realm flourished."

She paused and waited for a response from Noah and Layla. When none came, she continued her story.

"My siblings and I were created not long after the Realm came into existence," Simmy went on.

Noah was dumbfounded. Simmy looked no older than forty-five. "How have you stayed so young?" he asked.

"Well, I'm not entirely human, you see. All twelve of us go through a life cycle where we are born, age—albeit slower than humans—and then we die. A life cycle for us can last over two hundred years, and then we go through what's called the rebirth process, where we die in a sacred space, turn into dust and are brought back to life anew," Simmy explained.

Noah and Layla gaped wordlessly at Simmy.

"We also choose our genders, names and, depending on how long we undergo the rebirth for, we can also decide whether we want to keep our memories from our previous life cycle before we are reborn," Simmy continued.

"If you have all been alive for so long and have been guarding the Realm since its inception, how is it that your siblings have all been turned to stone?" Layla demanded, standing up and pacing around the room. "How is it that the Shadow Beings are causing so much trouble?"

"We got complacent. We were too confident in our abilities. We were so sure that the Realm was safe that we stopped being as diligent in our duties. It was purely our neglect that

119

has caused the Realm to become what it has," Simmy replied, her voice thick.

Noah wanted to walk over to her, give her a big hug and tell her that it wasn't her fault, but there was a part of him that didn't fully believe it. There was still more information he needed to find out. "Who is that man with the cane that I've been seeing in my dreams?"

"His name is Garvan. He was once a Guardian of the Realm himself, and he is my brother," Simmy said regretfully.

"What?" Layla exclaimed.

Simmy nodded slowly. "There were once thirteen Guardians. Garvan is the youngest of us."

"What happened to him?" Noah asked. "What's his plan for the Realm? Does he have anything to do with Nora's disappearance?"

"Why is Noah seeing him in his dreams?" Layla insisted, running her hands through her hair.

Simmy looked from Noah to Layla, deciding which question to answer first. "I don't believe Garvan has realised that Noah is seeing him in his dreams yet, but that doesn't mean he won't find out if you keep on having them," she said, looking at Noah sternly.

Layla opened her mouth impatiently, but Simmy put her hand up to silence her. "Garvan was created and praised as a miracle, as we had always believed that there would only be twelve of us. We always knew that Garvan had extraordinary powers. The original twelve Guardians each had a month where our powers were the strongest. All of us took it in turns to protect the Realm for one month of the year, and then, once our month was over, we would watch the Realm from a distance and guide the current Guardian, letting them know of any issues or good deeds that needed to be fixed or rewarded," Simmy explained. "My month was February. It is the shortest month of the year, but it is a month with very high energies. It is a month of such lovely energy that I always enjoyed my time as the Primary Guardian while I was working with it."

"What about Garvan?" Layla asked. "If there were twelve Guardians for the twelve months of the year, what was Garvan created for?"

Simmy smiled sadly. "Well, as the years went on and the population increased, the amount of energy also increased. People were starting to become selfish. Visualising their success but not putting in any other effort to receive their intentions. They were becoming less and less interested in the Realm and what we could provide for them. Humans stopped meditating, stopped praying, stopped trying to do good deeds for the planet and for themselves and we were put under a lot of strain. The Primary Guardian for the month was using up more energy than normal and had to rest for a lot longer before they could assist the next Guardian. So, once this had gone on too long, Garvan was created. He had the same powers as us but at an alarmingly higher rate. Instead of guiding the Earth for a month, he was able to guide the Earth for a full year."

Noah gaped. "What amazing power," he said and looked at Layla, who sat wordlessly next to him.

"Yes. It was such a blessing to us siblings that we had him available to us. But as the years went on, we started to rely on him too much. We started to neglect our duties because we knew that Garvan would pick up our slack." Simmy continued, her expression regretful. "What we didn't know was that Garvan was frustrated with being a Guardian. He knew he had tremendous power, and, growing up as he did being loved, cherished and adored as a special being, he felt that he was destined for more than just being a Guardian of the Realm. He wanted to be more than our backup."

"He started to turn against you?" Layla asked softly.

"Not at first. First, he came to me and asked me what I felt the true potential of the Realm was. He asked me if I wanted to change the Realm so that we Guardians held more power, so that we could control the occupants of the Realm and the people of Earth... so that, instead of guiding them to create a life they loved and can cherish themselves, we would be telling them how to live their lives."

Noah grimaced.

"I just laughed at first. *'We are here to guide the people of Earth to live their best lives as kind, loving people. We are needed here to keep the Realm a happy place so that when they pass they have a safe place to reside,'* I replied to him. We were originally created to cleanse the people who came to the Realm of the sins they committed on Earth so that they could pass peacefully and watch over their loved ones as they resided in the Realm. But as the inhabitants of the Realm grew and the Earth became a more complex place, we needed more help to cleanse their sins and to keep the energy in the Realm pure. Which is why, when Garvan came along and had such immense power, we original twelve Guardians felt we could relax. We believed that, eventually, Garvan would be the Primary Guardian permanently and we would all support him."

Layla gave a cold laugh. "Well that didn't exactly go to plan, did it."

"Layla," Noah said softly, "this isn't Simmy's fault."

"I know that! I don't blame her!" She turned to Simmy. "I don't blame you. I'm just trying to figure this all out. How did Garvan overpower you all?"

Simmy was silent for a moment. Then she stood up, paced the length of the living room a couple of times and then sat back down again, her auburn hair bobbing from the movement. "Garvan was... always much more powerful than us original twelve siblings," she explained. "Which was something that we all saw as a blessing in the beginning. As Garvan gained experience with the dealings of the Realm, my siblings and I started to back off to give Garvan more control over his Guardianship."

Layla nodded at Simmy, urging her to explain further.

"I should have known when Garvan came to me asking about changing the Realm that something was wrong, but I was so blinded by the idea of having Garvan as the Primary Guardian that I forced my concerns to the back of my mind. Then, by the time I realised what was going on, it was too late. Garvan had already started his plan to take over the Realm." Simmy clenched her fists on her lap.

"What happened when you found out? How are you here with us and not petrified like your siblings?" Noah asked her, a feeling of unease sinking in the pit of his stomach.

"Well, it was the end of my Guarding month. The twenty-eighth of February. Garvan would never attack a Guardian during their Guarding month. It was too dangerous as the Realm would become too unstable. Instead, he reduced the amount of power he gave during the month, meaning that it was putting a lot more strain on my body, especially because I wasn't used to exerting so much power during those last days. That was when I knew something was wrong. I felt much

123

weaker, and I knew the only reason that could be was because Garvan wasn't fulfilling his role during the month, but by the time I was able to warn the other Guardians, Garvan had already petrified them. He had taken them out all at once. I knew that I would be next, so I gathered as much strength within me as I could during those last few hours, then, as midnight came on the last day of February, I transported myself to Earth," Simmy said, a shiver running through her at the memory.

"What happened to the Realm?" Noah whispered.

"It crumbled," replied Simmy. "I left my post early."

"What do you mean it crumbled?" Layla asked. "We've been there, it still exists."

"What you've been to is the remnant of what was once a beautiful place," Simmy said. "When I left my post, Garvan had already petrified the other Guardians, so their magic was no longer available to the Realm. Garvan had stopped his guidance days earlier to exhaust my power, so once I transported myself to Earth and my guiding powers were also removed from the Realm, there was nothing to stop the negative energies from Earth rising up to the Realm. And since there was no one there to purify the people who were arriving in the Realm, the beautiful place that we all used to live turned into a dark, gloomy, miserable place that fed off Garvan's lust for control."

"Is that where the Shadow Beings came from?" Noah asked.

"In a way. The Shadow Beings that are walking around the Realm now are those humans that have come to the Realm to be purified of their sins from Earth, only to find that the Realm is no longer a happy, loving place to spend the rest of their days. A Shadow Being is all the negativity that a human has brought with them from Earth, that has taken over their body and is roaming free, doing as Garvan wills because they too believe they deserve more than what they got," Simmy explained.

"Okay," Layla said slowly, "so Garvan has taken over the Realm, petrified the other eleven Guardians who are unable to use their magic, created a breeding ground for the Shadow Beings and is…what? Looking for more power? Why is he looking for you?"

"Essentially, yes, that's the situation in the Realm right now. I am not entirely sure what Garvan's endgame is yet. I can only guess. But he is looking for me because I currently still hold some power over the Realm. Even though I am located on Earth, I never fully completed my Guarding month so I am still technically the Primary Guardian of the Realm. I never handed the Guidance over to anyone else," Simmy replied.

"You still have power over the Realm?" Noah repeated.

"Yes. Garvan is looking for me because he wants to cut all ties from me to the Realm. He wants to be the Primary Guardian."

Layla laughed loudly. "So as long as you stay here on Earth, the Realm will be fine!"

"In an ideal world, yes, that would work," Simmy replied to Layla, "but my power is dwindling. I have been away from the Realm for such a long time that I am slowly starting to lose my control and it is taking a toll on my body."

"What does that mean?" Noah asked. "Will Garvan gain control once you lose your hold?"

"If I completely lose touch with the Realm, then yes, Garvan will gain control, and I will be automatically transported back to the Realm," Simmy replied.

"We can't let that happen!" Noah and Layla both exclaimed at the same time.

"No, we can't, and we won't. You see, the only reason I am the Primary Guardian is because I haven't handed over the Realm to another Guardian yet," Simmy said. "But, if I have another Guardian of the Realm to guide, then we will be able to create a stronger hold once again."

"But all the other Guardians are petrified. You said they weren't able to access their powers," Layla rebutted, rubbing her face in her hands.

"That is correct," Simmy said, looking from Layla to Noah as she spoke, "but that doesn't mean we can't train another Guardian. Someone who has a connection with the Realm. Someone who truly believes they can make a difference to the world."

"Where are we going to find someone who can become a Guardian?" Layla replied, now running her hands through her bushy red hair in frustration.

"Nora," Noah said softly, looking at Simmy.

"Yes," Simmy replied. "I was training Nora to become the fourteenth Guardian of the Realm."

Layla gaped at Simmy, and Noah nodded his head slowly.

"It makes sense. She was so passionate about the universe and helping others," Noah muttered, mostly to himself. "But she's gone. You weren't able to pass her the Primary Guardianship."

"There's more to the reason why I chose her to become the next Guardian, but I can't share that information with you yet" replied Simmy. Noah thought he saw a flicker of frustration in her eyes. "And no, I wasn't able to pass on the Primary Guardianship. Before we were to complete the transfer, she disappeared."

"Do you…" Noah began. "Do you still believe that Nora's disappearance was a coincidence? That it may not have anything to do with the Realm?"

"No," Simmy answered quietly. "No, I never believed that Nora's disappearance was unrelated to our mission, even if I don't exactly know why she's now gone."

Layla let out a choking cry while Noah nodded. He had half expected that answer. He had also never believed that Nora's disappearance was for no reason, he also just never knew why. The tightness in his stomach loosened slightly. It was as if pieces of a puzzle were falling into place, and he was finally beginning to understand.

"You need a new Guardian," Noah said firmly.

"Yes," Simmy said, looking at Noah.

"You should train Layla," Noah replied, even more firmly.

"Wha—?" Layla exclaimed. "Me? But you're Nora's twin. Surely you'd be the next candidate to be the Guardian."

"No. I'm not ready. I don't have nearly as much experience as Nora had, or you have, for that matter. And you knew Nora just as well as I did before she disappeared. You're the right candidate."

"I agree with Noah," Simmy said while looking at Noah. "While, genetically, Noah would be the obvious choice, he is not yet ready. He wouldn't be able to handle the power. He still needs to train his mind. Layla," Simmy now looked at her, "while you let your emotions get the better of you sometimes, you have a strong mind, and you know what is best for the Realm."

Layla's face had gone white causing her green eyes to stand out even more.

"Don't worry, you won't be alone. I will still be here with you. We will guide the Realm, from Earth, together," Simmy said to her niece, placing a warm hand on hers.

Layla took a deep breath. "Okay. What do I need to do?"

"Well," Simmy smiled, "being my niece, you have already been exposed to the power of the Realm almost your whole life, so this will be easy for you. But before we complete the transfer, your task is to guide Noah and help him understand the powers he has inside of him.

"Okay," Layla replied. "When do we start?"

"First, I think you both deserve a rest after what I've told you today," Simmy said. "I will call your parents, Noah, and let them know that you will be here tonight. Now both of you, go and eat some breakfast, and then choose a book from the shelf. We have a lot of information to learn in a short amount of time, and we need to get started as soon as we can."

Layla and Noah nodded at Simmy and left the living room, chatting intently about what Simmy had just told them.

The feeling of unease still sitting in the pit of Noah's stomach told him that there was more to the story, but he trusted that Simmy would tell them about it when the time was right.

Chapter 17 - Simmy

Simmy smiled after the two of them as they walked out of the living room and then sat on the couch, exhausted, placing her face in her hands.

'You shared a lot today. More than you were planning to,' a voice spoke softly to Simmy.

"I know," Simmy replied.

'But, you still didn't tell them everything.'

Simmy sighed and rubbed her eyes. "You know that I couldn't."

'They will find out everything eventually.'

"When it's time," Simmy answered back.

Chapter 18 - Layla

"What a mind spin," Layla said to Noah as they both flopped down on the bed in her room. "I didn't see that coming. Do you reckon I should have?" she asked, pushing herself up onto her elbow and looking at Noah, who was resting his hands over his face.

"Should have what?" Noah mumbled, his voice muffled by his hands.

"Should have known that Simmy was hiding from the Realm."

"Why should you have known that?" Noah asked, lifting his hands from his face so he could look at Layla, who shrugged, flopping back onto the bed.

"I dunno. I knew she couldn't go to the Realm because of her history with it. I should have questioned it more. Then I would've been able to find out about Garvan earlier and have been able to start investigating him to see if he was the one who took Nora," Layla explained. "I mean, it seems really likely that she's with him."

"Yeah," Noah sighed, exhausted. "It does, but that's probably why Simmy never told you. If Garvan was able to overpower eleven of the strongest beings in the Realm without anyone noticing what he was doing, then what would you be able to do?"

Layla shot him a glare but didn't argue. He was right. There was nothing she'd be able to do right now. She'd been with Simmy her whole life! Why wasn't she able to do more? What had stopped Simmy from training her properly so that she was the obvious choice to be the next Guardian, and not a last resort because the one Simmy had wanted was kidnapped.

Letting out a huff, Layla threw her pillow at the wall and rolled onto her stomach, hiding her head under her arms.

After a moment, she felt Noah lifting her arm up and saw him peer under her armpit, forcing her to look at him. "I don't know what Simmy's plans are, but from what I've seen, she's always going to put your best interests first, even if it's not what you want."

Layla didn't reply.

Noah let her arm fall back down, and Layla rolled to her right slightly when he stood up.

"I'm going to head home. I'll just tell my parents that I wasn't feeling well. You and Simmy should talk," he said.

Layla didn't reply again, just tightening the hold she had over her head, not removing her arms until she heard Noah close the front door behind him as he left.

Sighing, Layla untangled her arms from her head and sat up. *I'll have to apologise to him later,* she thought to herself. *It's not his fault I'm only finding this stuff out now.*

A soft knock on her door snapped Layla out of her reverie, and she glared at it, willing the person behind it to go away. But, alas, she had no such luck, as Simmy's head peered inside when Layla didn't answer.

"I'm guessing you have some questions for me," Simmy said, opening the door a little wider so she could step through it.

"Questions, frustrations, amongst a few other things," Layla replied, narrowing her eyes.

Simmy opened the door to its fullest and stepped one foot into the room, testing the waters. When Layla didn't outwardly object, Simmy walked over to the bed, sat next to her and pulled her into a hug. "I'm sorry I didn't tell you any of this sooner," she said. "I wanted to, but I knew that if I told you what was going on that you would fight for the Realm, would fight for me, and this isn't a fight you can win. Yet," she added hastily at Layla's scowl.

"I still deserved to know," Layla said, pulling herself out of Simmy's grip.

"You're right," Simmy replied. "I'm sorry for not telling you earlier."

"You knew what had happened to Nora when she disappeared," Layla accused. "You knew and you still left Noah and me in the dark. And not just us, Jen and Paul as well! Nora's parents deserve to know where she is."

"I wasn't certain," Simmy replied. "I'm still not completely certain that Garvan took Nora, but it is looking more and more likely every day. Those dreams that Noah's having, it sounds like Nora is trying to reach out to him, but instead of reaching him, she's only able to show him snippets of where she is."

"Is there anything we can do for Nora now?" Layla asked, standing up and pacing her room. "I know that I'm going to be training to become the next Guardian, but how long is that going to take? There must be something that we can do to let her know that we're coming to help her."

Simmy looked at Layla sadly. "We can't risk it," she said, and held her hand up as Layla opened her mouth to furiously object. "We don't know what state Nora's in. Noah hasn't seen her in his dreams, and there is no way of contacting her without risking Garvan finding out and finding me. Nora's health and safety is my utmost priority, but as the Primary Guardian of the Realm, it is my duty to ensure that the Realm doesn't fall into any more chaos. I physically can't do anything that will jeopardise that. That's why I wasn't able to tell you anything about this earlier, because if you knew you would fly into the Realm, guns blazing, and that would lead Garvan straight to me. I'm restricted until situations change and allow me to open up to you about this knowledge. I genuinely can't share more than you need to know with you."

"Well, that's crap," Layla replied, softening her expression and dropping back onto the bed next to her aunt. "I didn't know."

"I know," Simmy said. "I know you've been frustrated with me. Heck, I've been frustrated with myself too."

Layla coughed out a laugh. "Did you just say heck?"

Simmy grinned, "Sometimes we need to let out a curse when the situation calls for it."

Layla laughed again and pulled Simmy into a hug. "We're going to win this," she said. "I'm going to work my ass off to become the best Guardian there ever was."

"I never doubted it for a minute," Simmy replied, squeezing Layla back.

Chapter 19 - Noah

Layla and Noah spent hours the next day learning as much as Simmy was able to share with them about the Realm as possible. From the Guardians, to the Shadow Beings, to what the Realm had looked like in its peak, and how it helped both the people of Earth and those who had passed over to the other side.

And even though they were mentally drained afterwards, they hadn't even scratched the surface.

Every time Noah thought he'd learnt as much as his brain could handle, more questions would pop up, and he'd need to know the answer. He had opened Pandora's box when it came to the Realm, and now he needed to learn everything he could about it.

"I'm exhausted," Noah groaned, gently laying back on a black beanbag in Simmy's classroom and rubbing his temples gingerly.

Layla slumped down into the beanbag she'd been standing next to and rubbed her tired eyes with the palms of her hands. "Same."

Noah ran his hands through his hair and looked at Layla. "There's just no end to everything we can learn. I mean, I *need* to know everything, but I don't see how all of this information is going to help us find Nora."

Layla sighed a long, slow breath out.

"What?" Noah asked.

"I know that Simmy physically has to do what's best for the Realm," she started, pausing as Noah shifted into a more comfortable position. "I'm just wondering what that means for us."

"What do you mean?"

"I mean, we're both in the middle of this right now," Layla explained. "I wonder why *now* is the right time for us to be thrown into everything."

Noah looked at her, confused, and Layla let out a huff. "What if it means something bad has happened to Nora, or that something bad is *going* to happen?"

"Something worse than being kidnapped by some crazed magical Guardian and being kept as his prisoner?" Noah deadpanned, and Layla let out a small laugh.

"I suppose that it's already gotten pretty bad," she replied.

"Look," Noah said, leaning forward on his knees, "I don't know what's going to happen, but I have to believe that Nora is okay. I have to believe we're going to be able to save her."

"Yeah, you're right. And help free the Realm at the same time," Layla said, shifting forwards and resting her head on his shoulder.

Noah's heart did an odd somersault, which he pretended he didn't feel.

"I should get home," Layla said after a moment, lifting her head. Noah grinned awkwardly, forcing his heart to stop its audition for the local circus.

Layla stood, dusted off her skirt and picked up her satchel, slinging it over her shoulder. "I'm glad we're in this together,"

135

she said before shooting him a smile and a wave as she walked out the door.

"Me too," Noah said quietly as she disappeared. He sighed, rubbing his face with his hands as he collected his own belongings and took his time leaving the campus.

"Hey! Noah, wait up!"

Noah turned around and saw his friend Ashlee running up to him, her wavy brown hair in a long braid down her back.

"Ashlee, hey," Noah said as she caught up to him. "What's up?"

Ashlee caught up with him and Noah fell into step with her. "How are you? I've been chatting with the others a lot about you lately. We're all missing you and want to be there for you, but we're just not sure how... I know that it must be hard seeing all of us. It's not the same without Nora in our group."

Noah nodded. He knew that he'd been hiding himself away from his friends. He thought about them, now, remembering how close they'd all been before Nora's disappearance.

Josh Western, a short, stocky boy with red hair and freckles, was one of the nicest people Noah had ever met. They'd hit it off right away in the playground when they were only five years old, and they'd been friends ever since. He was supposed to go on a date with Nora the day she'd disappeared. He'd been gutted when he thought she'd stood him up, and even more upset when he'd heard what had actually happened.

Mia Weir was a tall, sporty girl who spent all of her time outside. She had short sandy-blonde hair that was always tied up in a ponytail. Noah met her for the first time when he went to Josh's house one day. She'd just moved in next door, and they were dying to try out her trampoline. Her parents made them homemade lemonade that Noah spilt everywhere while trying to drink and jump on the trampoline at the same time.

Ashlee Singh, had met Nora one day at a gymnastics class, and they had been best friends ever since. Noah couldn't remember a time when Ash hadn't been around. Noah blushed as he remembered that Ash had been his first kiss when they had gone to a party in the fifth grade and played a game of spin the bottle.

And finally, there was Max Taylor. Max was the oldest one in the group at nineteen years old. His mum had died when he was only six, and his dad decided to take him out of school for the remainder of the year, and then start him up again the following year so that the family could be together during the tough time. Most people found Max to be really good looking with his dark skin, dark hair that was styled in short dreadlocks, piercing brown eyes and a lopsided grin.

Noah stopped reminiscing and looked at Ashlee. "I've missed you guys too."

"We're still here for you," Ash said earnestly. "Mia's been trying to think of ways to corner you after class, but she didn't want to force you into anything you weren't comfortable with."

"I needed time," Noah said. "Nora was—is such an integral part of me. I feel like I've lost my right arm."

Ash pulled Noah into a tight hug, which made Noah's brain go fuzzy for a second as it flashed back to the party in the fifth grade.

"I understand," Ash said softly as she pulled away just a little.

They were so close that Noah was able to see flecks of gold in her brown eyes.

Time seemed to hit a standstill.

Noah wasn't sure what to do. Did he stay still? Pull away? …Move closer?

Noah's heart did a funny jump as the last thought crossed his mind.

Did he even want to move closer?

What was Ash to him?

A loud motorbike revving past them pulled Noah out of his reverie, and he quickly patted Ash on the back as a return embrace and awkwardly pulled away.

Ash's eyes were brighter than usual as she also pulled herself back to reality. "I should go," she said quickly. "I need to hurry home. My mum needs me to help with dinner. Um… bye." She waved and quickly raced off in the direction of her house.

Ash had turned on her heel and sprinted away before Noah had a chance to reply, so he awkwardly stood on the pathway, watching Ash's retreating figure for a few seconds before stiffly turning back to the direction of his house. He should really get home too.

Chapter 20 - Noah

"Don't forget you have a lot to catch up on, Mr Parker." Noah groaned inwardly and tried to focus all of his intentions on the old Agriculture Studies hag Mrs Henry bursting into flames, along with the encyclopaedia of homework she had given him that morning.

"Your extended leave from class, albeit understandable, does not help with your studies in the long run. I expect you to work twice as hard to catch up on everything you have missed out on, and I will personally be checking your notebooks to make sure. While I'm sure you are still adjusting to your new routine, it is important to keep your mind active. You will not look back on this time and regret that you took the time to study hard. Run along now."

"Miserable old—"

"Not talking about Mrs Henry I hope, Noah," Simmy's cheerful voice cut into Noah's mumbling, and he jumped in shock.

"Ms Johansson," Noah exclaimed, his eyes widening as he saw her standing next to him with crossed arms. "I didn't see you there."

"Clearly," Simmy replied. "You know, your professors are just looking out for you. They want you to get the best education you can."

"Yeah, yeah, I know," Noah sighed. "But can't Mrs Henry want the best education for me *and* not give me a year's worth of homework in one day?"

Chuckling, Simmy guided Noah to her office. "Come and have your morning break with me here today, Noah."

"Oh, erm. Okay," Noah replied, glancing over to where Ash, Josh, Mia and Max were eagerly waiting for him. He had promised Ash he would make an effort to catch up with them today, and shot them an apologetic shrug as Simmy closed her staff room door behind him. Noah could see their disappointed faces as he glanced at them through the window and felt a pang of guilt. He really had neglected them these past few months.

"How are you going with your work for the Realm, Noah?" Simmy interrupted his train of thought.

"What?" Noah replied, not registering Simmy's question.

"Your work?" Simmy asked again. "For the Realm. You've still got a lot of skills to learn."

Noah stared blankly at Simmy for a few seconds. "I thought Layla was the new Guardian."

"She is," replied Simmy.

"So why do I need to focus on *my* training? Shouldn't we be focusing on training her up?"

"Layla is extremely skilled at manifesting her desires. She is a hard worker, and she knows how to manipulate her own destiny," Simmy said. "Whether she knows it or not," she added as an afterthought.

"Right," Noah agreed, not sure as to what he was agreeing with.

"She needs practice in helping guide others to manifest their

140

desires," Simmy said simply.

"Oh."

"She needs to practice with you, Noah," Simmy said, her voice firmer than it had been a few seconds ago.

"Right. Well, I was actually going to catch up with some old friends of mine today. You know, reconnect with reality," Noah said, feeling stupid that he had to explain this to Simmy. He began to ask if there was more going on, but before he could, he saw movement outside indicating that his morning break had already finished, and Noah threw his backpack over his shoulder. The low rumbling in his stomach reminded him that he'd forgotten to eat while he was chatting to Simmy.

"Here," Simmy said, handing Noah a ham and salad sandwich. "I'll walk you to your next class. Eat this on the way."

"Thanks," Noah said gratefully, ripping open the cling wrap and downing the first half of the sandwich in two bites.

"English Studies?" Simmy asked as she grabbed her purse and flattened her floral printed skirt.

"Yeth," Noah replied through the large amount of bread in his mouth, following Simmy outside.

Swallowing hard, Noah briefly caught sight of his friends, who had been loitering around the staff room trying to catch Noah before he got to his next class, scattering as soon as they saw that Simmy was chaperoning him.

"I apologise for stealing you away from your friends, Noah," Simmy said as Noah shoved the last half of his sandwich into his mouth.

Watching his friends running off in all different directions, that pang of guilt returned, and Noah resolved to make an effort to chat to them all before the day was up. "It's alright," Noah replied to Simmy. "I know I've got to focus on the

Realm. I just feel like it's time for me to reconnect with them, y'know?"

Simmy stopped walking and smiled at Noah. "I know. They will be a big help to you in the future."

Noah didn't know what Simmy meant by that, but before he could ask, they'd arrived at the English hall and Miss White was ushering everyone inside. Her light brown hair, which was pulled back in a loose bun, bobbed as she counted her students.

"Remember we have lessons this afternoon, Noah," Simmy called to him.

Noah nodded in Simmy's direction, acknowledging that he had heard her, and rushed inside, uttering a greeting to Miss White.

Layla wasn't here yet for some reason, but—oh. Noah had forgotten that Max was in this class.

Noah awkwardly sidled up to a spare seat next to Max and coughed lightly. "Erm... Would it... Would it be alright if I sat here?" Noah asked timidly, thinking of how stupid he was being. He'd been friends with Max for years.

Max grinned that lopsided grin that he was so well known for and rubbed his dreads with his hand. "Don't be stupid, idiot. I saved this seat for ya. Why d'ya think it was empty? I noticed ya girlfriend wasn't around today, so I figured I'd take my chances."

Noah spluttered when Max mentioned his 'girlfriend', but before he could deny the claims Max laughed loudly and smacked Noah on the back. "I'm kidding. Sit down already. I'd almost forgotten how easy ya were to tease!"

Noah, whose back was stinging from the blow, chuckled to himself. If anyone knew how to pick things up where they'd left off, it was Max.

Miss White silenced the class from the front of the room and pulled out the reading material for the semester. Noah groaned silently to himself and opened his notebook.

"How keen are ya to pay attention to this class?" Max whispered to him from the corner of his mouth while he too pulled out his notebook.

"Less than I want your dad's lasagna," Noah replied.

Max chuckled to himself. Max's dad was notorious for being a terrible cook. The first time Noah had stayed over at Max's house, his dad had made a lasagna for dinner, but instead of using beef mince, he'd accidentally used the scrap meat that he was saving for the dog's dinner. Noah had never let him live it down, often bringing packaged lasagna's to Max's house when he stayed over after the incident.

"How about we catch up on old times and I'll grab Cindy's notes at the end of class," Max said, nodding his head towards a scowling brunette sitting a few seats back from where he and Noah were sitting.

"You're not..." Noah half laughed, half sighed, turning his head to see Cindy staring at them, disgruntled. She'd apparently thought Max had been saving the seat for her.

"Yeah," Max replied. "Been goin' with her for about a month now. Looks like she's not fond of you though," he chuckled.

"I really don't need to be making enemies today, Max," Noah tried to say sternly, but failed as a grin escaped him. "Oh!" Noah exclaimed, making sure to keep his voice low so that Miss White wouldn't get suspicious. "Speaking of enemies, does Mia know?"

The grin slid off Max's face, and he rubbed the palms of his hands over his cheeks so hard he could have lit a fire from the friction. "She hasn't said anything. But she knows… they always bloody know."

Mia and Max had known each other since second grade. They were the ones that got married on the playground with gummy rings, but a year ago they called it quits. None of the group knew why, and the couple didn't elaborate, so Nora had gone and comforted Mia, and he, Noah, had been there for Max. It had been an awkward new dynamic for the group, but everyone had been so determined to make it work that Mia and Max just had to suck it up.

"Y'know, we only started talking to each other again after Nora disappeared," Max said quietly, glancing at Noah from the corner of his eye to see if he was walking on forbidden territory.

"Oh really?" Noah replied, unsure how to answer the statement.

"They were such good friends. We all were. Are," Max corrected himself.

Grateful for the correction, Noah smiled, but decided that this wasn't the time or place for him to be chatting to Max about Nora and changed the subject. "You'd better tell Mia yourself, mate. Or Cindy might find herself *accidentally* a victim of an angry blonde. I know I wouldn't want to be on the receiving end of Mia's wrath."

"I know," Max whined, his face in his hands. "Although that might not be so bad. I don't really gel with Cindy. I only got with her to make Mia jealous because I saw her with some tall, sporty guy a few weeks ago."

Noah sighed. He'd forgotten how dramatic Max and Mia's love life was. "You're going to get yourself injured one of these days."

"I know, mate. I know."

Chuckling, Noah opened the reading material in front of him and turned towards the front of the classroom, pretending to listen to Miss White. It was nice to have some semblance of reality back. *Although,* Noah thought to himself, *I wonder where Layla is.*

The dull scratching of pens against paper was almost symphonic to Noah's ears. He hadn't been sleeping well lately, with the dreams of Garvan and the remaining eleven Guardians becoming more and more frequent. His eyes were feeling heavy, and he let his cheek rest on his hand as he absently tapped his pen on his desk.

"You will tell me where she is," Garvan's sinister voice hissed.

"Never," Nora hissed back. *"You'll have to kill me first."*

"That can be arranged," Garvan raised his staff into the air. *"Die,"* he spat.

"...And that is how you will pass the assessment this semester." Miss White's dulcet tones broke through Noah's daze. "If you have any questions, my door is always open. Class dismissed."

"Alright mate?" Max asked quietly, hiding behind the scraping of chairs and clatter of books in the background. "You look like you've seen a ghost."

Noah rubbed his face with his hands and felt a shiver go through his spine.

He *had* seen a ghost.

So that *is* how Nora disappeared. She *was* taken by Garvan. Noah's mind was racing.

"I have to go," Noah said, standing up so fast his chair toppled backwards and landed with a loud bang.

Max, looking alarmed by the change in Noah, picked his

chair up off the ground and placed it back next to the desk. "Are you sure? Maybe you should go to the infirmary and lie down for a while?" Max said, trying to give Noah as much space as he could while trying to appear like nothing was wrong, as a few classmates had turned to find the source of the bang.

"No, I have to go. I have to see Ms Johannson," Noah replied.

"You have Life Science next period anyway, mate," Max explained.

"What?" Noah replied, his mind still racing from the dream.

"Ashlee's in the same class as you. She told me on break before that she was going to try and catch up with you in class," Max said.

"Oh, right…" Noah replied. He sank down into the chair that Max had replaced for him.

"What's goin' on?" Max asked, placing a firm hand on Noah's shoulder.

"It's hard to explain," Noah replied, rubbing his tired eyes.

"Could you try to simplify it?".

Noah gave a short laugh. Simple wasn't something he would call the Realm.

"Is everything alright here, boys?" Miss White asked as she walked over to the two of them.

"Noah was feeling a bit dizzy, so I told him to sit down for a bit, ma'am," Max lied unflinchingly.

"Do you want me to take you to the infirmary, Mr Parker?" Miss White asked. "Taylor, you'd best run off to your next class."

Max nodded and started to pack his bag.

Noah stood up again. "I'd like to go to class, Miss White."

"Are you sure? You're very pale."

"I'm sure," Noah said, packing his own books into his bag.

"Well, alright then. Here, at least eat something on the way to class. This will help to pick your blood sugars up again," she said as she handed Noah a small chocolate bar.

"Oh, thank you," Noah said, grateful for her concern.

"Have a decent drink of water as well, Noah. You need to take care of yourself, otherwise you're just going to become exhausted," Miss White said kindly. "I'll write a little note for your next teacher explaining what's happened."

Ripping the note out of her pad, Miss White handed it to Noah. "No dawdling now," she said as they stuffed them into their pockets and swung their bags over their shoulders.

"Thanks Ma'am," Max said.

Miss White waved them off and walked back to her desk.

"Well, I've got maths now," Max said to Noah as they exited the classroom and hastily walked towards the courtyard.

"Life Science," Noah replied, even though Max had been the one to tell him that, shoving the last piece of chocolate into his mouth.

"Are you sure you'll be alright?" Max asked. "You gave me a scare back there, mate."

Noah sheepishly looked at Max. "Sorry, I guess I haven't been sleeping well lately. It's getting the best of me, I suppose."

Max gave Noah a sharp look and placed his hand out to stop him from walking any further. "Look mate, I know that's a lie. We all do. You're doing something, and it's taking a toll on you."

Noah opened his mouth to refute the claims, but before he could say a word, Max cut him off.

"I'm not gonna force it out of ya, but just know that we're all going to be checking up on you more from now on. There's no more hiding from us. Tell your girly mate too. You two are doin' somethin', and we're onto you," Max said sternly.

Noah hung his head slightly. Of course his friends knew he was up to something. They'd known each other since they were kids. "I won't deny it then," Noah said, "but I can't tell you what it is. Not yet anyway. There are still some questions I need answers to."

"That's fine, mate. I won't tell the others we had this chat, and I'll tell them to give you some space until you're ready," Max replied, the sternness leaving his voice.

"I'll make more of an effort to spend time with you all too," Noah insisted. He really meant it too. He hadn't realised how much he'd missed his old friends until today.

Max grinned, clapping Noah on the back. "We'd appreciate that. Now get goin', we've almost missed half the class."

Noah grinned back and pulled his rucksack higher over his shoulder. "I'll chat to you later on," he called to Max's retreating back.

Max just waved in reply.

Noah turned and sprinted towards the science building, knowing that Simmy would be wondering where he was. He knocked on the closed classroom door and waited anxiously until Simmy called, "Enter."

Trying to be as inconspicuous as he could, which was impossible as he had clearly interrupted Simmy explaining something to the class, Noah walked up to Simmy and handed her the note from Miss White.

"Alright," Simmy said after she'd read it. "Take a seat, please. There is a free one next to Miss Singh."

Noah nodded and weaved his way through his classmates. Ashlee mouthed *'Where were you?'* to Noah as he unpacked his notebook and pen, but Noah pretended he didn't see. He gazed intently at Simmy, who had waited until he'd taken his seat before continuing with her explanation.

"As I was saying before," she said, "the power of writing down your goals works in many different ways. For example, if you were to purchase a journal purely for the sake of writing down your goals over and over again, every day, you are not only writing those intentions down, but you are thinking about your goals and how you are going to achieve them. It's a very powerful process. So, today I have provided you all with a journal to write down three goals, and I want you to write down those goals ten times each. Once you have done that, I want you all to close your eyes and visualise yourself achieving them."

The class started murmuring, chatting amongst themselves about what they were going to write down.

"This is a silent task," Simmy interrupted. "There is no right or wrong answer. I will be taking these journals from you at the end of the class, and I will give them back to you at the end of each lesson we have between now and the end of the year. That way, you will be able to look back on these goals and see how much you have grown."

The class nodded at Simmy. Many people seemed itching to begin the task, while others were gazing blankly at the journals in front of them, as if having no idea where to start.

"If you're stuck, try something simple such as, 'I am happy and grateful that I remember to make my bed every morning', or 'I am happy and grateful that I passed my Life Science exam this semester.'"

The class chuckled.

"Begin your task," Simmy said to the class. "Mr Parker,

come and grab a journal from me."

Not wanting to disrupt the class again, Noah quickly crawled under his desk, rather than weaving between his classmates, and reached Simmy at the front of the room.

"You're late," Simmy said softly to him as he reached her.

"Yeah, sorry. I got stuck in English Studies," Noah replied, grabbing a blank journal from Simmy's desk.

"Miss White wrote that you were unwell," Simmy said in the same soft voice.

"Just a bit dizzy," Noah replied, keeping his voice low as well.

"I want to see you after class, Noah," Simmy replied, not giving him a chance to object.

Noah nodded and crawled back to his desk, which was much harder this time around as one of his long legs got stuck between his chair.

Out of the corner of his eye Noah could see that Ash was trying to grab his attention, but he pretended that he was focusing intently on the task in front of him.

What goals do I have? Noah thought to himself, his blank page staring back at him.

Defeat Garvan. That's definitely a goal. He wrote that down ten times.

Master my mandala. That is also another priority. Noah thought, and he wrote that out ten times as well. *Defeat Garvan. Master my mandala. And... save Nora. I want more than anything to rescue Nora.* Noah thought, writing that down ten times.

Before he could close his eyes and visualise how he was going to achieve these goals, Simmy was calling for everyone to hand back their journals as it was the end of the class.

"Do you want to walk with me to lunch?" Ash asked Noah as they packed up their books.

"Ms Johannson wants me to stay back after class. Probably to explain why I was late," Noah replied apologetically.

Ash sighed and gave him a look from the corner of her eye, but didn't push the topic any further.

"Well then, see ya," she said, walking out of the classroom.

Noah waved guiltily. He waited until the rest of the class had finished chatting about their journals with Simmy before he went to see her.

As always, Abigail was chatting avidly with Simmy about her goals, and Simmy patiently answered all of her questions, making Noah wait what felt like hours until they finished talking.

Finally, Abigail left the classroom, and Simmy and Noah were left to chat.

"Sit," Simmy said.

Noah sat.

"What did you see?"

Chapter 21 - Nora

The meeting with Garvan, the man who called himself Master, had gone well.

After Scratch had taken her to the bathing room and given her a change of clothes, Nora had begun to feel semi-normal, which allowed her to really focus on clearing the fog from her mind.

While Scratch hadn't shown his other form again, Nora could only hope that he *was* here to help her. But she couldn't rely on that. If she'd learnt anything since she'd been trapped here, it was that she had to depend on herself more than anyone else. As a twin, she'd had someone else to rely on her whole life, so this scared Nora more than anything she'd faced so far, but she had to do it.

She needed to find a way to get out of here and get back to Noah, Layla and Simmy. First, she had to get closer to Garvan. She needed to gain his trust, get access to her powers again, and maybe even find out what he had planned so that she could let the others know.

It was a long shot, but really, what did she have to lose?

To be honest, most of what Garvan said to her hadn't interested her. He'd mentioned her good behaviour, strong willpower, and a bunch of other things that Nora figured were backhanded compliments, while also trying to rile her up about her current predicament. She'd kept a blank face and answered him when it was required, but when he'd mentioned doing some jobs for him, Nora had jumped at the chance. She'd tried not to sound too eager, so he wouldn't get suspicious, but she'd shown enough interest for him to smile cruelly at her.

A feeling in the pit of her stomach told Nora that there was more to these 'jobs' than Garvan was letting on, but she pushed it aside. This was the break she'd been hoping for.

She'd ignored Scratch's clawed hand tightening on her shoulder when she'd accepted. She wasn't sure if he was reacting out of excitement for what she would be doing, or worried that she was getting in over her head, so she didn't dwell on it. If he wanted her to act a certain way, then he was going to need to tell her himself.

"Come here, girl," Garvan called when she'd accepted his offer. Even though Nora had bristled at his smug tone, she shrugged her shoulder out of Scratch's grip, flipped a scowling Tick the bird and strode up to where Garvan was sitting on a black throne draped with red and gold velvet.

As soon as Nora reached him, Garvan's arm shot out, gripped her face roughly in his long fingers and pushed her forehead to his. "Show me your friends from Earth," he breathed.

Before Nora could even think, Garvan had infiltrated her mind, probing to the very core of her being. Her eyes swam at the invasion, and she tried to fight him off, but it was no use.

He found what he wanted.

"You need a new Guardian," Noah said firmly.

153

"Yes," Simmy said, looking at Noah.

"You should train Layla," Noah replied, even more firmly.

"Wha—?" Layla exclaimed. "Me? But you're Nora's twin. Surely you'd be the next candidate to be the Guardian."

"No," Noah replied, just as firmly. "I'm not ready. I don't have nearly as much experience as Nora had, or you have for that matter. And you knew Nora just as well as I did before she disappeared. You're the right candidate."

"YOU ASSHOLE!"

Ticks' scream snapped Garvan's concentration and he pulled away, staring furiously at Tick, who was sprawled on the floor at the opposite side of the room.

Nora quickly ripped her face out of Garvan's grasp and took a shaky step back, hitting Scratch's chest as he walked up the steps, shrugging. "Tick was trying to get a closer look, so I kept her out of your personal space, Master" he said nonchalantly as Garvan whipped his gaze to him.

"Get her out of my sight," Garvan replied through gritted teeth, pointing at Nora. "She has given me enough for today."

Scratch nodded and pulled out the blindfold , but before he could put it on, Garvan reached for Nora's wrist, gripping it tightly.

"I will be in touch, sweetheart. You're going to be a great asset to me," he crooned, his slimeball mouth sliding up into a malicious grin.

Nora fought the urge to shudder, instead just nodding at him and allowing Scratch to place the blindfold over her eyes once more before shooting off back to her room.

Tossing her on the bed, Scratch turned to leave, but hesitated and turned back. "If I'm correct, and I usually am"—Nora rolled her eyes— "you should have some more freedom now. Garvan accidentally released a mental block he had placed on you when he invaded your mind just now."

Nora opened her mouth to ask what he meant by that, but he just walked away, rebuilding the barrier around her door before disappearing into thin air.

Now Nora was lying on her bed, gritting her teeth and hoping beyond hope that *she* wasn't going to be the reason that Garvan found Noah, Layla and Simmy, while also wondering what the *hell* Scratch had meant by her having more freedom. What mental blocks? She hadn't felt any different... except... she really hadn't been able to *feel* her energy since she'd been here.

Still, the barrier at her doorway felt stronger than ever, and she hadn't been able to bathe again since seeing Garvan, so she definitely didn't feel any freer.

Pushing herself up in frustration, Nora threw her arms up, willing anyone or anything to give her a sign as to what Scratch meant.

Immediately, a warm sensation prickled through Nora's fingertips, and she slowly dropped her hand to her face so she could see it. Her fingers were glowing with her amber energy, the feel of it was stronger than it had ever been before.

Jumping up and down on her bed stifling a laugh, Nora wiggled her fingers before creating a small energy ball, rolling it over the top of her fingers, practising her control.

A tear rolled down her cheek as she let out an exhausted breath. *Freedom,* she thought to herself. This is what Scratch had meant. How he'd known that Garvan had accidentally released her mental chains was beyond her, but she wasn't going to question it.

There was no way in hell that she was going to let him

invade her mind like that again. She added practising mental barriers to her list of things she'd need to perfect, but it was a start.

It was a step forward.

Taking a deep breath, Nora could have sworn she saw the shadowy figure of Scratch standing outside her barrier, but she ignored it. It didn't matter if he saw her, and she wasn't waiting another second.

Chapter 22 - Noah

"What?" Noah asked.

"What did you see?" Simmy repeated.

"How did you..." he started to ask, but the panicked look on Simmy's face made him trail off, and he relayed to her what he'd seen in his dream.

"Layla," Simmy called over her shoulder after Noah had finished his story, "come out here, please."

A door at the back of the classroom opened, and an exhausted Layla appeared.

Before he could think, Noah rushed over to her and caught her as she stumbled over her feet.

"Thanks," Layla mumbled as she allowed him to lead her to the chair he'd just vacated.

"What happened to you? Where have you been all day?" Noah demanded, looking from Simmy to Layla.

Simmy walked up to Layla, knelt in front of her and put a hand on her knee. "Are you alright?" she asked softly.

"Tired. But I've managed to ward him off for now."

"What are the two of you talking about?" Noah asked loudly, frustrated at how uninformed he was.

"Garvan is somehow aware that I am training another Guardian," Simmy said to Noah as she pulled up another

157

chair for him to sit on.

"What?" Noah replied, dumbfounded.

"Yeah," Layla croaked, her voice sounding as tired as she looked. "But he's been coming for you," she said, looking at Noah.

"Me?" Noah replied. "Why me?"

Layla looked up at Noah and took his hand in hers. "We don't know, but Garvan plans to attack your mind. We think he wants to weaken you from the inside out. His plan was to strike today during your classes, when your mind was preoccupied."

Noah just stared at her. He didn't have any words.

"That vision you saw today, Noah," Simmy chimed in, "was an attempt from Garvan to get to you. Layla has been blocking his attempts all day."

"So," Noah croaked, "the vision I saw wasn't real?"

"I can't confirm nor deny that," Simmy replied, forcing Noah to look her in the eyes. "I don't know if Garvan was just trying to find your weakest point, or if he was so frustrated with himself for not getting to you sooner that he just bombarded you with his last evil act."

"Right," Noah replied, letting out a cough to clear his throat. "Well, I guess I'll have to find out for myself whether or not that vision was real."

"I'll help," Layla said, her eyes determined.

"I'll, of course, be with you too," Simmy agreed as she grasped both of their hands. "He is my responsibility, and I cannot lose anyone else.

"So," Noah said after a moment, "where do we begin?"

"Layla?" Simmy asked. "You're the next Guardian of the Realm. What do you suggest we do?"

Layla looked taken aback at the question. "Oh, um… well, you may not like it," she said, glancing at Simmy, "but I think we should utilise the fact that Garvan is trying to get to Noah."

Simmy raised her eyebrows but nodded for Layla to continue.

"Well," Layla said hesitantly, "while I was blocking Garvan today, I managed to catch a glimpse of what his plan for the Realm was. He has this notion that he can dispel the twelve Guardians and become something that he called 'the Master of the Realm.'"

Noah saw Simmy react to this out of the corner of his eye, but she didn't stop Layla's explanation, so he pretended that he hadn't seen anything.

"I'm not entirely sure what he meant by that," Layla continued, "but it's the only advantage we have over him at the moment."

"I'm up for it," Noah said straight away. "I'm not going to sit back and do nothing while Garvan wants to become some 'Master'."

Simmy looked hesitant, then sighed. "You're right, Layla."

Noah and Layla both looked at each other, shocked.

"Really?" Layla asked, her eyes lighting up.

"Yes," Simmy replied. "But it's going to be dangerous."

Noah narrowed his eyes and looked from Simmy to Layla and back again. "What's going on?" he asked the both of them. "This is too easy. What are you hiding?"

Neither Simmy nor Layla said anything for a few moments, until finally Simmy said, "I've decided that I need to go back to the Realm to try and stop Garvan from the inside"

"What!?" Noah exclaimed. "Why would you do something like that? You know he's been looking for you! He'll turn you

159

to stone like he has your siblings!"

"I'm aware of the danger, thank you Noah," Simmy replied firmly, "and I wouldn't be taking this risk if it wasn't something I thought was necessary."

"Why is it necessary?" Noah demanded, throwing his hands in the air.

"Please don't use that tone with me, Noah," Simmy said, her voice still firm. "I will explain to you why this has to happen."

Noah, not at all appeased by the promise of an explanation, paced the room and looked at Simmy expectantly.

"Take a seat please, Noah," Simmy instructed.

Noah took his time walking over to the beanbag that Layla had relocated to, and was patting for Noah to join her, and squashed in next to her.

Layla jumped in her seat a little at the addition of Noah's weight, and they both shuffled around until they found a comfortable position.

"Thank you," Simmy said after the two of them had settled. "First things first, I have been planning this trip back to the Realm for well over a year now."

Noah opened his mouth to give his two cents, but Simmy held up her hand to stop him.

"You may give your opinion at the end," she told him.

Noah closed his mouth.

"When I started training Nora to become the new Guardian of the Realm, I knew that I would have to return to face Garvan," Simmy started, "but I never expected the events that unfolded to occur."

Noah felt a pang in his chest. He was starting to believe more and more that the vision he'd seen today was more than just an attack on his mind, and that what he'd been shown had actually happened.

"Had everything gone according to plan, Nora would be a new Guardian of the Realm right now, and my siblings and I would have started the process of restoring the Realm back to its former glory. During that process, we would have trained Layla up to improve her skills and help Nora with her Guardian duties, and Noah, we would have asked you to join us, but the plan was for the Realm to be much healthier when you did, not the dark wasteland you have seen.

"My siblings can no longer hide my energy signature from Garvan. They are growing weaker by the day. The only reason I have been able to live here on Earth undetected for so long is because my siblings have been actively keeping Garvan off my trail, forgoing the opportunity to use their own powers to keep me safe. But even they are unaware of where exactly I am. The energy block they created around me is weakening, and they've lost too much life force in their petrified state. The evil in the Realm is growing at such an alarming rate that it's causing their hearts and minds to weaken, and so their energies are weakening as well."

"You're going to find Garvan before he finds you," Noah murmured.

"Yes," Simmy answered. "It is the only way to keep you both safe and to give you a real chance at taking back the Realm."

"Aunt Simmy?" Layla asked.

"Yes?"

"What do you think really happened to Nora? Do you think Garvan really did attack her like he showed Noah?"

Simmy's face turned grave, and Noah knew that this was something that she'd hoped she wouldn't be asked. "I have a hunch."

Noah and Layla both looked at her expectantly.

"I have done a lot of research into Garvan over the past few months, and I believe that this was a trick to try and lure me out of hiding. But Garvan forgets that he is not the most powerful being in the Realm yet, and I'm unable to give myself away to him that easily. I physically can't do it, the Primary Guardianship doesn't allow me to."

A loud CRASH forced Noah and Layla to their feet as suddenly the ceiling exploded, and a blinding white light engulfed the entire classroom.

Noah rubbed his eyes as he tried to protect his burnt corneas from the offending light. It took several minutes until he could open them, although what greeted him made him close them again, as there was no way what he was seeing was real.

After opening his eyes a second time, Noah turned to the right to make sure that he could see Layla, who was also rubbing her eyes with the palm of her hands.

Standing behind Simmy was an enormous figure, whose huge hand was on Simmy's shoulder. Noah didn't know how Simmy wasn't doubled over by the weight the hand must have been putting on her.

"Hello, young ones."

A deep voice caused every nerve in Noah's body to come alive. He'd never felt so uncomfortable. The buzzing energy coming off the figure sent shockwaves through him, but at the same time he felt completely at ease. It was almost like it had been a part of Noah his whole life.

Layla shuddered beside him, and he knew that she was experiencing the same shockwave he was.

The enormous figure gave a deep laugh, which made Noah smile for reasons he couldn't explain.

There was something about this... being... that made Noah feel like he was exactly where he was meant to be. That everything that had happened in his life was to lead him to this exact moment.

Noah's eyes finally adjusted to the light that had engulfed the classroom, and he could see Simmy looking from him to Layla, giving them a quick once over, checking to see if their bodies were able to take in this new energy.

"Noah, Layla," Simmy said, "what you're experiencing right now is the raw energy of the Realm.

"But... how?" Layla said, her voice cracking slightly. "I've been around you for basically my whole life, and I haven't experienced anything remotely close to this before."

"I made sure that you were only dealing with energies that I knew you could cope with," Simmy replied.

"So how are we exposed to these energies now?" Noah asked, unsurprised to find that his voice was cracking as well.

"I'm sure you can both see the man behind me," Simmy said.

Noah could, although 'man' seemed too... mediocre... to describe the figure behind Simmy. Noah would have been more inclined to call him an 'All-Powerful Being'. That was the vibe he was getting.

"This man is my father," Simmy continued. "He is the creator of myself and all my siblings, Garvan included."

"Why is he here?" Layla asked, unable to take her eyes off him.

"I am here because Simmy asked me to come," Simmy's father's voice boomed, "and you can call me Zion."

Suddenly, the bright light engulfing the classroom dimmed, and Zion transformed from an enormous figure standing beside Simmy to a tall, chiselled man with tanned skin, long golden hair pulled back into a low ponytail, and piercing blue eyes. A white toga covered Zion's torso and knees, and the gold chains that held it in place glistened under the classroom lights.

Noah noticed a neatly trimmed beard covering Zion's face and immediately decided that he was going to grow one himself.

Even though Zion had assumed a human figure, the power emanating from him was still enormous, and Noah couldn't help but feel like he was staring at the face of a god.

"You created Simmy *and* the other Guardians?" Layla asked Zion incredulously.

"I did. And I am here to guide you as much as I can on your journey while Simone returns to the Realm. Hand over your mandalas." Zion held out his large hand.

Noah had almost forgotten he even had a mandala. It had been so long since he'd taken it out of his bag.

The mandala was squashed at the bottom of his backpack, and Noah picked it up by the packaging, silently apologising to the relic.

Handing it over to Zion, both himself and Layla stood back and watched as Zion ran his hands over the edges, apparently making sure that they were still in good condition.

"I see," Zion said to himself. "These two mandalas were created with the intention of being joined." Zion chuckled. "He is a crafty man, my brother."

Noah and Layla looked at each other nervously.

Zion passed the mandalas to Simmy. "Could you hold these for me, please?"

Simmy took them from him and held them out on the palms of her hands.

164

Raising his hands, palms facing towards the mandalas, Zion closed his eyes, and a magnificent golden energy ebbed from his fingertips.

Suddenly, a flash of bright white light pierced the mandalas, and Noah hid his eyes in the crook of his arm. As soon as the light dimmed, Noah dropped his arm and looked towards Simmy and Zion.

"What happened?" Layla cried out next to him.

Confused, Noah tried to see what Layla was looking at.

Zion took something large and round from Simmy, and turned to face Noah and Layla.

Noah gasped. They had become one. In place of the two smaller mandalas was a large mandala with sunstones that shone brighter than any gemstone Noah had seen before. The power it was producing made the hair on his arms stand on end.

"I have bound your two mandalas together," Zion said. "I have also transferred some of my own energy to the mandala."

"Does that mean that Layla will be fighting this battle by herself?" Noah asked, even though he knew, should Zion say yes, he was still going to fight to find out the truth about Nora.

"No," Zion replied, handing the mandala back to Simmy. "You are now on this journey together. Both of you, as Guardians."

Chapter 23 - Noah

"What?" Noah asked blankly.

"You will both be Guardians," Simmy said slowly. "Together."

"But... I thought you were only looking for one Guardian," Layla replied.

"Garvan is too powerful right now for you to succeed on your own, Layla," Simmy said. "Originally I was going to be fighting with you, but now I need to go back to the Realm earlier than planned and get ready to face Garvan by myself. The two of you will follow me once you're ready. Garvan will be able to sense my return to the Realm, so it's not safe for you two to travel with me."

Noah and Layla turned to each other.

"The two of you will have to train extremely hard to make this work," Zion's deep voice rang as he held up the mandala he had just fused and watched the sunstones shine under his gaze. "This is an extremely powerful relic."

Noah hesitated for just a second. "Layla's a lot stronger than I am. She's had years of training to get to the level she's at. We don't have enough time to train me as well."

"Layla's power will amplify your own," Simmy replied to him. "Also, you have a natural ability to work with the energies within the Realm."

"Why?" Noah asked. "Where did this natural ability come from?"

A pained expression crossed Simmy's face as she tried to answer Noah's question, but nothing came out. Zion placed a reassuring hand on her shoulder, smiling at Noah. "She's unable to tell you that yet. But you'll find out—"

"When the time is right," Noah finished for him, sighing.

"You will need some training in control, but because Layla will be guiding you, your training will take significantly less time, especially with the two of you wielding the mandala," Simmy continued, as if the interruption never happened.

"You're going to be fine," Layla said confidently, nodding in Noah's direction.

A fire burned in the pit of Noah's stomach. Becoming a Guardian meant that he would be on the front lines when it came to getting Nora back. He nodded back at Layla.

"It's going to take a lot of hard work," Simmy said, looking at the two of them, "and I won't be here to train you the whole time."

"We know," replied Noah, "but we've been working with you for months now. And if our powers are linked because of the mandala now—"

"We *will* make this work," Layla interjected.

Zion chuckled behind Simmy. "I don't think we need to worry about these two."

"No," Simmy agreed, a sad smile on her face.

"As I said before, I have transferred some of my life energy into your mandala," Zion went on, "but it will only work if you are truly ready. Knowing that you have the power but not believing in yourself isn't going to work. You need to know you have the power, while also believing in not only yourself, but in the people who are on this journey with you. It is a major mental battle. The hardest thing the two of you will encounter on this journey will be making sure that you keep each other accountable for both your mindsets and actions. The two of you are physically ready for this, but mentally, you have a lot of work to do."

Noah's mind briefly flickered to his parents, who had already lost one child and could now potentially be losing another in the rescue attempt. "What about my parents?"

"I think your parents will understand what you're doing without you needing to explain everything to them in detail," Simmy said, the same pained expression on her face as before.

"Alright," Zion's deep voice boomed, "I think that is enough for today. The two of you will need to work closely with Simmy before she leaves in order to get your Guardianship training underway."

"When are you leaving?" Noah asked Simmy.

"In three days," Simmy replied.

"Three days!?" Noah exclaimed.

"Simmy has been here too long. She needs to return to the Realm as soon as possible. Even another month here could do irreparable damage to her body," Zion said to them, placing his large hand on Simmy's head.

Layla nodded. Her face had gone pale at the thought of the journey to come, but she gritted her teeth. "We will make this work," she repeated determinedly.

"We will start your training tomorrow during our lessons after school," Simmy said.

"Not today?" Noah mumbled, staring at the mandala that Zion was still holding.

"Not today," Simmy confirmed.

"I will keep this for now," Zion replied. "You are not yet ready to manage its powers."

Noah picked up his backpack from the floor. "I'll be able to handle it. I'll make sure of it."

"I never doubted for a second," Zion replied.

Noah nodded to him and walked with Layla out into the courtyard, waving to Simmy and Zion as they closed the door, continuing their conversation in private.

"We're on a dangerous mission," Layla said to Noah as they walked.

"I know," Noah replied, "but it's something we need to do."

"To find out what happened to Nora," Layla agreed.

"And to make sure it doesn't happen to anyone else."

Layla gave Noah's arm a light punch. "We've got this."

Chapter 24 - Layla

Layla's head spun as she stared at her ceiling. She had a bunch of unread messages from James, but she didn't care. She didn't have the energy to see him right now. There was so much going on.

Usually, whenever she found herself frustrated or lost, James would be the first person she reached out to. Physical activity always got her brain seeing things from different perspectives, but this time she wanted to be with Noah.

Not because she wanted him to replace James—no, definitely not—but because he was literally the only person who could understand what she was going through. There was so much to process.

The fact his messy blond hair always fell into his eyes and made her want to reach up and brush it out of the way had nothing to do with it.

Groaning, Layla rolled over to her side and pulled her pillow over her face.

She didn't even have her mandala with her anymore to escape to the Realm. Even though she knew it was dangerous, and that Simmy would be furious with her if she found out she was still going to the Realm for a couple of minutes every now and again, she couldn't help herself. She'd grown up with the Realm's energies thanks to Simmy. It felt like part of her was missing whenever she stayed away for too long.

Layla's message tone snapped her back to reality. She fished around her blankets for the offending item without lifting her head, finally finding it half-hidden under her second pillow.

She glanced at the message and groaned when she saw that it was James again, throwing her phone back onto the bed. She really needed to reply to him and let him know that she wasn't going to meet up with him today, but she really couldn't be bothered.

Her mind drifted back to the conversations that she'd had with Simmy and Noah over the past few days. How hadn't she known that Simmy wasn't just not telling her what was going on, but that she was physically unable to?

It made her feel better knowing that Simmy had wanted to tell her as much as possible, but it also left a feeling of dread in the pit of Layla's stomach as she wondered what else Simmy knew but wasn't able to share.

And Zion... Zion was a whole different story. What even *was* he? He had to be a Celestial, for sure. One of those all powerful, eternal beings, but how was he created? And *he* was the one who created Simmy and the other Guardians? How much power must he have? He'd mentioned something about a brother too. Did that mean that there was another one of him roaming around the Realm somewhere?

Throwing the pillow off her face, Layla sat up abruptly and stretched her arms above her head. What she wouldn't give to be able to chat with Simmy openly. She had so many questions.

The most prominent question being whether they would really be able to rescue Nora and stop Garvan without killing themselves, or getting themselves killed in the process.

It seemed pretty far-fetched, but she had to believe that it was possible, otherwise Simmy wouldn't be sending them on this journey… right?

Right. If Simmy had needed to keep everything in the dark until now, it must mean that this was the right time for them to make their move. That right now, the Realm was ready for them to take over the Guardianship.

There was so much that she needed to do. Still so much that she needed to learn. Would she be able to do it in time? While also helping to train Noah?

Noah was great, but he was still so green when it came to the Realm.

To be fair, Nora had been green too, but she'd had that natural ability. Although Simmy said Noah had it as well.

Layla rubbed her forehead, wondering what the natural ability was. From what she'd learnt over the years it was unusual for humans to have much sway over their own abilities, often needing guidance from the Realm to turn their desires into reality.

Frowning, Layla leant back, grabbed her phone and shot a quick reply to James saying that she wouldn't be able to meet up, then grabbed her pyjamas. She was going to have a long bath, relax and sink into a meditation to clear her head.

There was no point in her stressing over these things when there was literally nothing she could do about them right now.

She just had to surrender and trust that Simmy and the Realm were guiding her in the right direction.

* * *

Layla splashed around in the water restlessly. She was still exhausted from blocking Garvan's mental attacks on Noah all day, and she hadn't been able to settle properly. She kept feeling like someone was trying to reach her.

Well, actually, the name she kept hearing was *Noah*, but maybe now that their mandalas were connected, they somehow had a mental bond as well.

Layla wasn't sure.

But every time she tried to tap into the voice, it disappeared.

She didn't get her hopes up that it could be Nora. Layla still didn't know exactly how she was going to rescue her, just that she was determined to do it.

With Noah, just as determined, by her side, there was no way they were going to fail.

She hoped.

Was determination enough for this mission?

There was still so much for them to learn as well. When were they going to start learning how to wield their energies to their will like Simmy and the other Guardians could?

When Layla was still a little girl, Simmy showed her an amazing trick where she brought her red energy to the surface of her hand and turned it into a beautiful flower, which shimmered when Layla poked it with her finger.

It was a warm and happy energy. Simmy had always been such a nurturer and her energy in the Realm mimicked that.

Layla had always been called fiery. Fiery hair, fiery temper, fiery personality.

She wondered if this meant she'd be breathing fire with her energies in the Realm.

Letting out a light laugh, Layla pulled the plug out of the bath, grabbed her towel and dried herself.

Soft footsteps let her know that Simmy was home, and, from the fact she didn't knock on the door, not quite ready to talk. Honouring that she needed space, Layla took her time drying her hair before quickly shuffling to her bedroom.

A static call of *Noah* caught her attention again, and Layla flopped down on the bed, trying to concentrate on the sound.

But instead, sleep found her.

Chapter 25 - Nora

"What the f—" Nora started to mumble to herself as she dropped to the floor, looking at the hole she'd just blasted in the wall.

Quickly crawling over to her doorway, she checked to make sure no one had heard the commotion of her reducing a section of the wall to smithereens, before jumping back to her feet and quickly sweeping the broken pieces into her hands. Hoping to the Realm that this would work, Nora placed the pieces against the wall and willed her energy to the palm of her hand to stick them back together.

To be honest, she wasn't convinced that this would make any difference, but she wasn't ready for Garvan to find out that he'd given her access to her powers yet, so she was damn well going to try.

First shifting her fingers a little to see if any of the debris would fall away, Nora tentatively pulled her hand back and did a silent cheer as the wall remained in place.

It looked like shit up close, like a toddler had come and stuffed playdough on the wall, but it was better than nothing. It was definitely less obvious than the gaping hole that had been there previously.

It wasn't completely unrecognisable though, and she hoped

that no one would notice it when they came to throw in her meals during the day. No one ever actually came into her room when they came by, so there was no reason why they *would* see it. But still, there was a first time for everything.

Nora sighed, walking backwards towards her bed. With her current run of luck right now, she wouldn't be surprised if Tick was feeling extra nosey the next time she came around to check on her. Scratch hadn't been to see her since Garvan had summoned her that first time, and Nora had spent more time than she wanted to admit wondering where he'd gone.

Sometimes she wondered if she'd imagined the dark-haired man she'd seen squatting by the thrones that day. She didn't think she had, but Scratch seemed to be a permanent fixture here, judging from Tick's scathing reports of him messing things up for her. Tick would complain to anyone who'd listen about Scratch taking the good jobs while she had to come and babysit.

Nora gave the wall one last look before shrugging and walking the few steps to her bed, sitting cross-legged on top of it. Alongside practising her control and various energy blasts, Nora had also been trying to get in touch with Noah again. It was proving to be a lot more difficult this time around. Even though she'd been able to connect with him enough to bring him to her location while he was sleeping, she hadn't yet been able to gain enough traction to chat with him directly. Something must have been going on with him though, because the dreams that she'd been trying to send him lately hadn't been catching.

"Oi."

Nora scowled at the doorway.

"Oi!"

"I heard you the first time," Nora replied, glaring at Tick, who was obstructing her pitiful view of the Throne Room outside and running a long, clawed finger down the barrier keeping her trapped.

"Garvan wants to see you," Tick said, taking her time opening the barrier with her claw, every so often letting it drift off course so it sounded like nails scraping down a chalkboard, sending shivers down Nora's spine.

"Where's the bath stuff?" Nora asked, once Tick had finally opened the barrier. Tick laughed.

"Not this time." Tick's hand stretched out at the speed of light, and she gripped Nora's arm tightly. Not hard enough to break her bone, but tight enough that it would bruise later. Nora gritted her teeth as Tick forced her to her feet into her waiting arms. "Close your eyes. You're not going to enjoy this."

"Enjoy wh—" Nora started to ask, but before she could get it out Tick sped off into the temple so fast that everything became a blur. Without having the chance to close her eyes, her eyelids were flapping in the wind. Once Tick had stopped moving, she pushed Nora away so quickly that she stumbled forwards onto her knees, retching. She hadn't had enough to eat lately to actually bring anything up, but it took a good few minutes for her stomach to settle. When it finally did, she still couldn't stand up without feeling nauseous.

"I thought you were made of tougher stuff," a low voice mocked. Nora raised her head to find a pair of polished black boots walking towards her.

Not really caring to show her respect, Nora dry retched one more time as her stomach churned, and then gasped loudly as Garvan gripped her by her hair, pulling her to stand on her tiptoes and leaning in to whisper in her ear.

"You've been working against me," he breathed menacingly, sending more unpleasant shivers down Nora's spine. She cringed at the close proximity of the two of them, wanting nothing more than to rip the strands of his beard that were ticking her cheek out of his old, sunken cheeks.

"How so?" Nora replied coolly, forcing herself to be aloof.

"I have been working to get into your brother's head, the boy I saw in your mind, but I am unable to do so," Garvan replied, his voice still low and dangerous in her ear. "You have something to do with that, I presume?"

Nora laughed genuinely. "Not me, *Master*," she replied, and Garvan's eyes narrowed at her tone. "I haven't been able to do shit with you keeping me locked up in my room all this time. How am I supposed to be keeping you out of my brother's head?"

Garvan licked his lips, and Nora fought down a shudder as the tip of his tongue—she hoped accidentally—brushed the outer shell of her ear. "Show me," he said before roughly turning her to face him and slamming his forehead into hers, holding her head in place with the hand that was still gripping her hair.

Nora grit her teeth. This is what she'd been preparing for, so she kept her breaths even and allowed Garvan into her mind only enough to show that she didn't know anything, not giving him the opportunity to dig any further.

Finally, after minutes of trying to invade every corner of her mind, Garvan pulled away and threw her to the floor. "Nothing," he spat. "I can't see a thing! What is protecting him?"

Nora shrugged, her tailbone aching from where Garvan had

thrown her to the floor. She subtly flipped Tick the bird when she heard her cackling from her position near the doorway.

Frustrated, Garvan threw a wave of energy throughout the room, flinging Nora back. Pain shot through her as she hit the wall roughly, and she gasped as she felt a bone in her leg snap.

Quicker than lighting, Scratch was there, gently lifting her up and making sure there was no pressure on her leg.

"Leave her," Garvan snapped to him. "She's of no use to me. Come, tell me what you've learnt."

"You're not using her properly," Scratch replied, not letting go of his hold on Nora, who was searching his eyes for any sign of the man she'd seen when he arrived.

Garvan turned slowly, menacingly, towards Scratch. "What did you say?"

Unfazed, Scratch shrugged the shoulder that wasn't supporting Nora. "I said you're not using her properly. Man, your body really *is* old, isn't it?"

Garvan's jaw twitched, and if his interest hadn't been piqued, Nora was sure that Scratch would be a pile of ash right now. "And how exactly do *you* suppose I *use* her?" Garvan asked slowly.

"She has direct access to the new Guardian and her trainer. It would be stupid of us not to use that to our advantage," Scratch replied, refusing to look Nora in the eye, even when she whispered a horrified *"No."*

Garvan looked between them for a moment, before turning back around and stalking to his throne, lazing on it comfortably. "Make it your mission to get anything and everything out of her. In any way you need to," he added, sneering at Nora.

Scratch nodded at him, before lifting Nora off her feet completely and carrying her back to her room, fast enough that it took no longer than five minutes but slow enough that nothing jolted painfully during the trip.

Nora glared at him the whole time, tears threatening to fall. Everything she'd been working for—everyone she'd been trying to keep from Garvan—would be exposed. And for what?

Scratch gingerly rested Nora on her bed, his eyes lingering on the horrible patchwork she'd created on the wall for a few seconds before turning back to her. He sent a blue healing light coursing over her body.

"If I heal you too much, Garvan will just hurt you even more next time," Scratch murmured. He healed her enough that she wasn't in agony anymore, but not enough that her leg was able to take her full weight.

"Why do you even care?" Nora spat, wiping the tears from her eyes furiously.

Scratch shrugged, before standing and turning on his heel, leaving her in the room by herself. She glared at the energetic barrier that kept her locked inside.

* * *

"C'mon," Nora whispered. "C'mon!"

Nothing she did would connect her to Noah.

She didn't know why. The only thing she could think of was that he, Layla and Simmy had added some stronger mental shields around him. They must have noticed that Garvan had been trying to get into Noah's head.

While she was glad that he was safe from Garvan, she had

to stop herself from gritting her teeth into dust in frustration that she couldn't connect with him anymore.

Wincing as she tried to roll over, Nora used her arms to change positions in the bed. She was sure she was getting bed sores from lying on her side all the time.

Letting out a breath, Nora blew a rogue strand of oily hair out of her face as she brought her amber energy to her fingertips, playing with it as it rolled over the tops of her fingers.

What's Garvan going to make me do? she thought to herself. *Bloody Scratch, why did he have to go and suggest that to Garvan? Noah can't be forced into this any more than he already is.*

Chapter 26 - Noah

Noah waved goodbye to Layla, who was heading to her maths class for the day, and gasped when he came face to face with his old friend Mia, who was sporting an accusing look on her face.

"We missed you at lunch the other day, Noah," she said, narrowing her eyes.

Noah gave a guilty laugh. Mia was never one to beat around the bush. "Yeah, I had to talk to Ms Johannson about a project I'm working on," he replied, inwardly sighing.

Mia kept her eyes narrowed and fell into step with him as he started walking towards his next class.

"Where are you going?" Noah asked her. She looked like she was heading towards the Woodwork classroom as well.

"Woodwork class," Mia replied.

"Oh," Noah said, trying to remember when Mia joined his class.

"I was originally in another class, but I changed my major so I had to shift a few lessons around," Mia said, answering Noah's silent question.

"Oh," Noah said again.

"You spend an awful lot of time with Layla Forrest," Mia went on, her eyes still narrow and burning a hole in Noah's head.

"Do I?" Noah's voice rose a couple of octaves as he nervously ran his hand through his hair, messing it up even more than its usual untidiness.

"You do," Mia confirmed. "I hadn't realised you two were such good friends."

"She was close with Nora," Noah said, hoping that the mention of Nora would get Mia to drop the subject.

"I know," Mia replied. "But I didn't think you knew that."

"I didn't. But I do now, so we're friends."

"She's very protective of you," Mia stated.

Noah tripped over the path. "What?" he spluttered. "No she's not."

Mia rolled her eyes, the hazel in them overly apparent from the action. "Whatever you say," she said, and hurried into the classroom before Mr Garcia closed the door.

Noah stared blankly at the back of Mia's head for a second before hurrying after her, but before Noah could enter the classroom, Mr Garcia stopped him by placing a hand on his arm. "A word please, Noah."

Mr Garcia was from Spain, and Noah really enjoyed working with him. While his accent had disappeared a little, his curly dark hair, tanned skin and sharp brown eyes pierced Noah as he looked at him.

"Uh, sure," Noah replied, shuffling back and waiting for Mr Garcia to give instructions for the class to continue working on their projects.

A few minutes later, Mr Garcia stepped back outside and faced Noah.

"I understand that you're going through a tough time at the moment, Noah," he said. "And I know you're working towards getting back to your regular classes, but I would like it if you would work with Mia Weir on her project for the next couple of weeks, as she is still finding her feet in this class. You will both be graded on what you accomplish between now and the end of the semester. We're halfway through now, and I don't want to pressure you into completing your own project in that short timeframe."

Mia, who had already been informed of the situation, was looking at Noah from behind Mr Garcia's back. "Yeah, of course, that's fine," Noah replied as he hitched his backpack a little higher.

Mr Garcia patted Noah on the shoulder and led him into the classroom.

"Everything alright?" Mia asked as Noah made his way over to her workstation.

"Turns out we're workshop buddies until the end of term," Noah crooned. It was his turn to narrow his eyes at her.

"Oh really?" Mia said flippantly. "I suppose that's a good thing in the long run. You now have someone to keep you accountable."

"Mmmhmm," Noah murmured in response. "It's also a good excuse to have a chat…"

Mia didn't respond.

"You organised this, didn't you?" Noah whispered accusingly.

Mia looked at Noah for a few seconds and then started to brush the sawdust off her apron. "You've been through a great trauma," she said simply. "It was an easy way to make sure you were okay."

"It was for purely selfless reasons then?" Noah replied sceptically.

"Fine. It's also a way to find out what's been going on with you," Mia replied brashly. "You've been acting weird, Noah Parker, and I'm going to find out why."

"This isn't just an excuse to take your mind off Max?" Noah drawled, a cheeky grin forming on his lips.

Mia forcefully thrust the hammer she was passing Noah into his stomach, knocking the wind out of him. "Max can suck an egg," she replied hotly, and said nothing more.

Noah chuckled, rubbing his aching belly.

Chapter 27 - Noah

"The two of you are going to need to really concentrate," Simmy said to Noah and Layla. They had finished their classes for the day and had met Simmy out the front of her classroom as usual. "There is going to be danger at every turn. Not only physical danger, but mental danger as well. You're going to need to keep your senses alert and your minds sharp."

Noah, who'd been trying to concentrate on his breathing for the past five minutes, found his thoughts constantly wandering. It was as if someone was trying to break into his mind every few breaths, which meant he had to reinforce his mental shields over and over to keep them out.

Ever since Layla had taken the brunt of Garvan's attacks on him, he had demanded that Simmy show him how to block his own mind. It was simple enough; just imagine a wall surrounding your mind where nothing is welcome inside unless you allow it. The execution of it was easy, but the maintenance was hard work, especially because it felt like someone was trying to break into his head all day, every day.

"If you're struggling to keep your mind clear, focus on the point between your eyebrows and imagine a white light flowing through you," Simmy instructed, forcing Noah back to reality.

It may not be physical, but mental work was exhausting! Blowing his sweaty fringe out of his face, Noah crossed his legs where he sat on the floor and tried to focus his mind on what needed to be done.

Find Nora, he thought, running through his mental list, *take the Realm back from Garvan, return the other eleven Guardians to their unpetrified forms, make sure Simmy comes out of all of this alive, and while I'm at it, make sure Layla and I come out alive too.*

Noah groaned. The tasks didn't even sound doable while he was sitting safely in a classroom, not to mention that each one of those tasks had hundreds of mini-tasks that needed to be completed in order for them to succeed.

Opening his eyelid the tiniest crack, Noah peered over to where Layla was sitting, and saw she had face in her hands and Simmy whispering in her ear.

"Is everything alright?" he called out.

"There's too much," Layla replied. Noah could hear that her voice was thick with tears. "There's too much to learn, too much at stake, too much to do alone."

"You're not alone," Noah replied, walking over to her and leaning down so that his face was near hers. "I'm here, Simmy's still here, and we have Zion protecting us now. We have more power now than we did before."

"But we don't know how to *use* it!" Layla replied, frustrated. "We're here, trying to learn how to control a power that will help us by *sitting down and breathing.* For all the inner work we're doing, we have absolutely nothing to show for it. We're no closer to learning how to control Zion's power than we are learning to fly!"

"We don't have a choice, Layla," Noah said softly. "We're going to overcome the odds, because the only alternative is to lose Nora forever and let Garvan control the Realm permanently. There's too much to lose if we don't do this."

"But what are we going to do if we can't beat Garvan? What are we going to do if we never find Nora? What if we can't work together and we wind up hating each other, and then the Realm gets completely overrun by Garvan and his Shadow Beings?" Layla demanded, tears streaming down her cheeks.

Noah gave a small smile and placed both his hands on Layla's shoulders.

"We could never hate each other. Could you imagine what Nora would say if her brother and best friend hated each other? We'd be locked in a room for days until we sorted ourselves out," Noah chuckled, wiping a tear from Layla's chin.

Layla let out a laugh and nodded. "That's true. But what about all the other issues? What about Garvan?"

"I can't promise that we'll beat Garvan," Noah said, standing up and looking at Simmy, who had been watching their exchange. "But we're the best chance anyone has right now. We're the ones that have been chosen to become Guardians and protect the Realm. Plus, we have Simmy, Zion and the other Guardians rooting for us too, so we won't be fighting alone."

Simmy walked over to the two of them and pulled them into a hug. "We are all going to be with you every step of the way, even if we aren't able to be there physically."

Noah, who was bent quite awkwardly to accommodate Simmy's short stature, wrapped his arms around her and patted her on the back. "I know," he replied.

Layla nodded at the two of them and wiped the tears from her face.

"You two will be amazing," Simmy said, releasing Noah. "You both know what you need to do. You just need to learn to control your energy when you get to the Realm."

Layla walked over to where Simmy had laid the new and improved mandala she'd received back from Zion and reached forward to touch it.

"Don't touch that, Layla," Simmy, who had followed her, said quietly.

"What will happen?" Layla asked.

"You'll be forced into a situation you aren't yet ready to handle," Simmy replied.

"What does that mean?" Noah asked, curious as to why they couldn't touch something that was meant to help them.

"I mean that you haven't formed a strong enough bond between yourselves, the mandala, and the Realm," Simmy explained. "You will be transported to a part of the Realm that is overrun by Garvan and his minions.

"Why would that happen?" Noah questioned. "It sounds a little extreme."

"Not when the future of the whole Realm of Intention is at stake," Simmy said. "We need to make sure that the person who is trying to master the power genuinely wants to help the Realm, instead of trying to use the power purely to help themselves."

Noah paused. He *did* want to help the Realm, but the only reason he'd agreed to help was so he had a chance at finding Nora. Was that selfish? Would he be able to use the power Zion had shared with them? Or was all the work he was doing going to be for nothing?

Chapter 28 - Simmy

Layla and Noah seemed to be progressing well, even though they were struggling with their limitations here on Earth. Unless they were able to tap into the Realm while they were here, it was going to be near impossible to teach them how to hone their powers properly. Not that Simmy would be able to tell them that. The moment she did, they'd run straight to the Realm, and all hell would break loose. So Simmy had to watch them from the sidelines, guiding them as best she could while knowing they weren't able to reach their full potential yet.

And she hated it.

There was a reason she'd become a teacher here on Earth. She loved seeing her students grow, learn and become more confident in themselves.

Nora had grasped the concept of the Realm and her energy pretty quickly while she was training, but Simmy had been allowed to guide her in more depth and had allowed her to travel to the Realm in order to hone her skills. Layla had gone along with them for a few trips, but even though she had been exposed to the Realm's energies through Simmy almost her entire life, it hadn't been the right time for Layla to learn how to harness her energy to its full potential.

Simmy hadn't known why until right now. Looking at her niece and Noah working together, she noticed that their bodies were in total sync, even though they didn't realise it.

It had frustrated Simmy at the time, knowing that Layla was capable of so much more and being unable to guide her properly. Everything she did needed to be in the best interest of the Realm.

Even Zion had tried to break the Realm's hold on her as its Primary Guardian while still allowing her to keep the position, but as soon as he foresaw what would happen, he backed down. Garvan would have felt the shift immediately, and everything they had been working towards would have been for nothing.

Simmy held back a groan as she shifted positions in her chair. She had been in this body here on Earth for so long that it was starting to take a physical toll on her. That was why she needed to go back to the Realm soon. Zion had told her that if she put it off much longer, she'd risk her body completely giving out, and since she wasn't in the Realm, there was no way for her to regenerate into her new life. She'd simply cease to exist.

She kept her eyes on Layla and Noah, who were building their mental shields and strengthening their mindsets. There was so much more she wanted to show them, so much more they needed to learn. Sure, they needed to know how to build strong mental defences, but that wasn't going to keep them safe in the thick of things. They needed to know how to protect themselves on the offence too. Unfortunately, there was no way for them to learn that here. Not with her. Not while she was in this state.

Clapping her hands, Simmy waved Noah and Layla to the

front of the classroom. "You have both done so well today. I'm so proud of you," she said, smiling even though a pang of guilt shot through her at the thought of how underprepared they were.

She just had to trust that the Realm and Zion would be able to keep them safe until she could make her way back to them, even though Zion was restricted with what he could do to help as well. The Realm wouldn't allow him to assist in the destruction of one of the children he'd created, forcing him to watch the Realm he loved so dearly crumble before him.

Inwardly sighing, Simmy ran her hands over her long pleated skirt out of habit, catching Layla's eye as she looked at her with a frown on her face.

"You two should head home now," Simmy said to them. "You must be exhausted, and there is still more to learn tomorrow."

"I'll stay here and help you pack up," Layla said to her, smiling and waving at Noah, who hadn't hesitated to escape.

As soon as Noah shut the door behind him, Layla whirled around to her aunt, her hands on her hips. "What's going on?" she asked. "Why are you nervous?"

Simmy refused to look in her eyes, instead smoothing her skirt down again.

"This, see!" Layla continued. "You only play with your skirt like that when something's wrong."

Simmy pulled her bottom lip into her mouth and chewed, forgetting that she was supposed to be a forty-something-year-old woman, and looked up at Layla from where she was sitting. "There's so much I can't tell you. There's even more I can't help you with," she said softly, feeling the back of her eyes prickle.

Layla quickly pulled her aunt into a hug and buried her

nose in Simmy's hair. "You're not letting us down," she gently scolded her. "We know you can't do more than you already are, and while, yes, it's frustrating sitting down and working internally all the time, we know that if you were able to show us more, you would. You and Zion both."

Simmy sniffed, pulling out of Layla's arms and looking at her. "I don't want anything to happen to you."

"Nothing will," Layla replied, determined. "The time is finally right for me"—she smirked as Simmy cringed, thinking back to all the times she had told Layla she would know when the time was right—"and nothing will keep me from making the most of my chance. Noah's the same. He's desperate to find Nora and help her."

"What did I do to deserve you?" Simmy asked, pulling Layla back into a hug.

"Realm only knows," Layla laughed, and she tightened her arms, squeezing Simmy in her hug.

Chapter 29 - Noah

Noah took his time walking home that afternoon. He was mentally exhausted and drained of all his energy, even though he hadn't physically done much.

"Noah?" a voice called to him.

Noah sluggishly pulled himself from his thoughts and turned. "Mum?" he asked. "What are you doing here?"

Jen Parker was patiently waiting for him two blocks away from their house, and she smiled when she saw him walk towards her. "Hey darling, you're later than usual, so I thought I'd see if I could meet up with you. I just had a feeling you might like some company today."

Noah looked at his mum for a few seconds, smiled, and gave her a hug. "Can we get a milkshake, like we did when Nora and I were kids?"

Jen wrapped her arms around her not-so-little boy and returned the hug. "Of course we can, sweetheart. Same place?"

"Yes please," Noah said, feeling like he was six years old again.

Jen gave Noah's hand a squeeze and took his backpack from him like she used to do when he was little, and in silence, the two of them walked towards the corner takeaway shop. Noah looked at it and reminisced about all the pocket money he'd spent there as a kid.

The sugar clouds had always been his favourite treat. He and Nora always split their lollies in half to share. Then they would climb up to the tallest branch of their favourite tree and chat endlessly about their favourite cartoons and what they were going to buy the next week with their allowance.

Then, when the sun started to go down, they'd try and sneak back into the house without being noticed. They weren't allowed to stay out when it got dark, and the wrath of Jen Parker was something they tried to avoid as often as possible.

Noah smiled to himself and refocused on his surroundings, just in time to see his mum place a vanilla milkshake with chocolate chips and a bag of sugar clouds in front of him.

Grabbing a spoon to scoop the frothy top layer off his milkshake, Noah felt an intense shiver run up his spine.

He looked up at his mum, seeing that she had experienced the same sensation and was returning his gaze with a sincere sadness. "You need to find Nora," she said, placing her hand on top of Noah's.

"What?" Noah replied, not sure he'd heard his mum right.

"The Realm. I have a feeling that Nora's in the Realm."

"You know about the Realm?" Noah exclaimed. Had everyone known about the Realm before him?

"I took Nora here just before she left us as well," Jen reminisced, and Noah saw her blink away a thin sheen of tears.

"Left us? Don't you mean before she disappeared?" Noah asked.

"No," Jen answered. "I was so distraught when she first

went missing that it took me a while to figure it out, but I don't believe she was taken against her will. She would have given herself up to protect others. I have a suspicion that she's trapped in the Realm somewhere, trying to bide her time before you can meet her."

"You do?" Noah said quietly.

"Yes."

"And you think I should go to the Realm to meet her?"

"I think the Realm needs you. And I think that you have an important role to play in something bigger."

Noah didn't say anything for a while. His mind was racing, trying to process everything his mum was telling him. "How do you know about the Realm?" he finally asked.

Jen smiled and brought her cup of tea to her lips, taking a deep sip. "I met Simone... Simmy, when I was just a little girl."

"You did?" Noah exclaimed. "How?"

"I lived on the farm with my parents growing up, as you know," Jen replied, "and one day I noticed that all the animals started gathering near the edge of the forest. I went over to take a look at what was going on, and I found Simmy sleeping in a tree, looking a bit worse for wear."

"You found Simmy?" Noah asked slowly. "You found her when she arrived on Earth?"

"No," Jen answered. "She had already been here for a few years when I found her. Simmy had already begun searching for a new Guardian before we met, and her journey brought her to our farm."

"Was she searching for you?" Noah asked. It would make sense if his mum was originally meant to be the replacement Guardian of the Realm but had passed the role over to himself and Nora.

"No, she was looking for you two!" Jen laughed. "Although she was a few years too early. You can imagine my surprise when she woke up, saw me, and asked where my twins were."

Noah stared at his mum in disbelief. "She knew you were going to have twins? How old were you when you met her?"

"I was only fifteen!" Jen exclaimed. "Far too young to be raising twins!"

Noah laughed, imagining a young Jen Parker spluttering in disbelief at the request of a stranger in one of her trees.

"But she stayed close to me and the farm as I grew up," Jen said, continuing her story. "We became quite good friends, to be honest. I spent a lot of time learning about the Realm and the skills to connect to our guides up there." Jen paused, smiling at the memories with her friend. "Simmy was actually the one who introduced me to your father. She'd met him one night while he was wandering the streets looking for a place to eat. She was meeting me for dinner and invited him along to join us. Gosh, that was a fun night," Jen laughed to herself.

Noah smiled at his mum. He'd never heard how his parents had met before, and the fact that Simmy and his mum had been friends for years blew his mind. Why had they never met her before they started university? Did that mean that his parents had known Layla's parents as well?

"Layla's a lovely girl," Jen said, almost as if she had read Noah's mind.

Noah made a non-committal sound at the back of his throat, but his mum was too lost in her memories to interrogate Noah about his romantic endeavours.

"I went to school with Layla's dad," Jen mentioned quietly. "He was a few years ahead of me and was very handsome."

Noah looked at his mum, not daring to say a word in case he missed anything.

"Layla got her red hair from him, but I only met her mum once. Simmy introduced us just after I had started dating Paul. They were living together for a few years."

"Mum?" Noah asked tentatively.

"Hmm?" Jen hummed in response.

"Why didn't Nora and I grow up knowing Simmy if you'd known her for such a long time?"

"Simmy wanted Paul and me to raise the two of you on our own. She didn't want to have any input into how you grew up. I still wasn't sure why she'd been looking for the two of you when we first met, but I knew that I could trust her, so we parted ways after I gave birth," Jen explained. "I believe that she'd had the same intentions with Layla's parents, but unfortunate circumstances caused Simmy to adopt Layla," Jen said softly.

"Is that a bad thing?" Noah asked his mum. Layla was the one who brought Nora into all of this and started this chain of events, and he wasn't sure if, maybe, that was all part of a bigger plan.

"It's not a bad thing," Jen answered. "I'm not sure what it means for Layla, but from what I've seen of her through her friendship with both you and Nora, she's got a very promising future ahead of her."

That's good, Noah thought to himself. The last thing he wanted was for Layla to lose her path, especially with Garvan becoming more powerful every day.

Taking a sip of his milkshake, Noah stirred the straw around with his teeth, thinking about the information his mum had just shared with him.

Nora was calling him to the Realm for reasons he wasn't yet sure of, but the more he was exposed to all of this new information, the more desperate he became to find her and save her. And now he'd just found out his mum and Simmy had been friends for years, that Simmy had known that his mum was going to have twins, *and* she had introduced his parents to each other. There was too much of a connection for these events to be a mere coincidence. It made Noah think that his whole life had been leading him to this point.

Layla's parents dying hadn't been part of Simmy's plan. But Simmy adopted Layla, so Layla must have meant a lot to her, or Layla was on a similar journey to himself and Nora. Well… Nora was originally meant to be the Guardian, which is why she and Layla had met. He, Noah, was only on this journey because Nora had been taken, right?

Jen watched Noah while he was processing all the new information. Her tea, which had been forgotten, was now cold.

"I have to go soon, don't I?" Noah asked after a long pause.

"That's your choice to make," Jen replied.

"I've only just started reconnecting with my friends," Noah said, a light pang piercing the pit of his stomach.

"They'll understand. They love Nora too," Jen answered.

"I'll have to leave you and Dad," Noah said, his voice thick.

Jen smiled, stood up, and pulled her son into her arms in a warm embrace. "You aren't leaving us," she said into his hair as she hugged him. "You're going on a brave journey to make all of our lives better. And we will always be with you."

Noah took a deep breath which filled his lungs right up, releasing it slowly as his mum hugged him. As soon as he released the long breath his mind cleared, and he was transported to the same green plain that he had seen the first time he'd touched his mandala.

A rustling sound caught Noah's attention, and he turned toward it.

"Nora?" Noah cried. Walking up behind him on the hill was his sister, looking exactly as he remembered her.

Nora nodded and took Noah's hand in her own. "I've missed you," she said to him, her voice distorted, the hand holding Noah's flickering as she spoke.

"This isn't really you, is it?" Noah asked quietly. "Where are you?"

The Realm Nora smiled at him. "I am here physically within the Realm, but not here with you right now. I'm sure you know where I really am by now."

"With Garvan," Noah murmured, squeezing his sisters fingers tightly.

Nora took her hand from Noah's and clicked her fingers. Instantly the greenery surrounding them disappeared, and he was once again looking upon the gallery with the eleven petrified Guardian siblings.

Turning to Nora, Noah's eyes wide and mouth agape, he tried to express his horror.

She pressed her finger to her lips, silently telling Noah to keep quiet, and pointed him in the direction of a dark room behind the thrones.

Noah looked blankly at the room and followed Nora, who was beckoning to him.

A churning sensation filled Noah's stomach. He wasn't sure he was ready to see what Nora wanted to show him, but he followed her nonetheless.

The walk to the room took an uncomfortably short amount

of time, and as soon as Noah's eyes adjusted to the dim lighting, he had to stifle a gasp.

Inside, the real Nora was sitting on her bed, extremely bruised and battered, while Garvan paced in front of her.

"It's almost time," Garvan muttered. "It is an unfortunate necessity in this current form, one that I am looking forward to shedding once I complete the transition into Master of the Realm, but a necessity nonetheless."

"What is he talking about?" Noah whispered as quietly as he could. He turned to where Nora had been standing next to him, only to find that she'd disappeared.

"You!" Garvan shouted curtly, causing Noah to jump a foot in the air.

Regaining his composure, and looking wildly around the room to make sure no one had seen him, Noah ducked even further into the darkness, keeping watch on the events that were unfolding before him.

"Yes, *Master*?" The wounded Nora stepped forward into the light, looking at him, expressionless.

"You've been here a long time now," Garvan said to her, waving his hand in the direction of the room.

Noah hoped that Garvan was indicating the entire temple and not just this dark room, but Nora just nodded at Garvan, not making any sound.

"You have proven you are worthwhile keeping alive, for now," Garvan continued.

Noah wondered what Nora had been exposed to in order to prove her worth, but he threw the thought from his mind. He couldn't bear to know.

"You are needed for the next phase of our plan."

"How can I assist you?" Nora asked, lifting her face just

enough so that Garvan could see her eyes.

Noah groaned inwardly at Nora's bloodied lip and black eye, but he knew that he couldn't move from where he was. Nora had brought him here for a reason.

"I need you to keep watch over the eleven siblings. Make sure that they don't attempt to make any contact with their sister while I am gone," Garvan said, eyeing Nora.

"I understand," Nora replied.

"Ask him where he's going," Noah hissed quietly, but deep down he knew that she couldn't, not without great risk anyway. He would have to ask Simmy if she knew where Garvan needed to go so urgently.

"Good," Garvan replied. "Don't let me down."

Nora nodded and shuffled back against the wall as Garvan removed himself from the room.

Noah noticed that she wasn't putting much weight on her left leg, and rubbed his face in his hands as he realised that it was probably broken.

When Noah opened his eyes again, he'd been transported back to the takeaway shop with his mother. The time he'd spent in the Realm had passed as a mere second on Earth. He was still being embraced.

"There," Jen said, smiling, unaware of the journey that Noah had just been on.

"I need to go to the Realm," Noah said softly.

"I know," Jen replied. Noah waited for her to say more, but whatever she was thinking died on her lips and, instead, she gave him a small, sad smile, her blue eyes swimming with tears once more.

Nodding, Noah slurped up the rest of his milkshake and stood up too. "I have to chat to Simmy and Layla."

Jen smiled at her son and took him by the crook of his arm. "You'll be back," she said to him. "I know that it feels like you're going to have to stay in the Realm forever, but you'll find your way back when you're ready."

Silence followed that statement, and Jen and Noah walked back to their home.

When they arrived at the house, Paul Parker was waiting with a freshly cooked meal. "Did you sort through everything?" he asked the two of them.

Noah nodded, eyeing up the roast which was crackling away on the dining table.

"It's all been sorted, dear," Jen said warmly to her husband, kissing him on the cheek before she sat down for dinner.

"You'll be leaving us then?" Paul asked Noah, sharpening his carving knife in the kitchen before walking over to cut the meat into serving sizes.

"I need to," Noah said to his dad as he watched him work. He didn't bother to ask how he knew what was going on. Nothing would surprise him anymore.

"That Simone has always known more than us, hasn't she, dear?" Paul said to Jen.

"She's always known the twins were made for more than just an average life, that's for sure," Jen said. The tone of her voice was tight, making Noah realise just how much his parents wished that Nora and himself *were* made for just an average life.

"I'll come back," Noah said to his parents. "I promise I'll find a way back."

Both his parents smiled at him, and Paul sat down, having finished dishing up the plates.

"A 'see you soon' meal then," he said. "One that we can have

203

again when you and your sister return home."

"It's a promise," Noah replied, lifting his cup of water in the air in a toast for his parents.

The rest of the meal was eaten in silence.

The sound of clinking cutlery filled the house as the family each pondered about the days ahead, not knowing what was to come or whether they would see each other again.

"Thank you for the meal," Noah said to his dad as he scraped the final piece of meat onto his fork and savoured the last bite.

After taking a sip of his water, Noah stood and started collecting the empty dishes for his parents.

"Don't worry about that, Noah," Paul said to him, taking the plates out of his hands. "You need to be somewhere, don't you?"

Allowing the plates to be taken from his hands, Noah nodded. "I need to see Simmy and Layla. I have some information that will be able to help us in the Realm."

"Go," Jen said to him, still sitting in her chair. "That is more important right now. Go."

"I'll be back," Noah said to them as he rushed, heart racing, brain spinning with urgency to grab his backpack. His breath came in short, sharp gasps, until the weight of his backpack dragged his shoulders down, and he realised he had stopped thinking clearly as he reached the front door. He paused, hand on the knob, taking a steadying breath, then turned and paced back inside to his parents. Kissing both of them on the cheek and giving them a quick hug, Noah ran out of the house.

Noah had just enough time to look back for a second to see Jen had followed him outside and was holding her hand over the cheek he had kissed, while the other one covered her eyes as tears streamed down her face.

A pang shot through Noah's chest, and he knew that he might be leaving them for longer than he wanted to, maybe forever, but he couldn't think of that at the moment. Garvan was going somewhere, and he needed to tell Simmy and Layla about it.

Chapter 30 - Nora

Exhaustion hit Nora like a freight train.

Every time she tried to move, her muscles ached and resisted painfully. Even her earlobes were aching. How that was possible, she didn't know, but she didn't have enough energy left to even try and heal herself.

She'd *finally* been able to connect with Noah, and even though everything he'd seen hadn't happened the way she'd shown him—it had happened, just in Garvan's Throne Room—she hadn't had the energy to show him more than she had, even though there was still so much he needed to know. Garvan had never come to her room, though. He hadn't been here since the day she'd almost broken free of the barrier, often opting to send Tick to collect her or pass on his messages.

She hadn't seen Scratch for a while either. Now would be a great time for him to come and visit, though she'd give anything to have someone come and heal her properly, even if it was just to take the edge off. She was so exhausted her own poor attempts hadn't amounted to anything.

"You look like crap."

Nora scowled, not bothering to lift her head at the voice. "Is that the only greeting you know? Most people say 'hello'."

Maybe she'd wished too soon. She didn't want to see Scratch after all.

Hearing his low chuckle as he disabled the barrier, Nora tried to pretend she was simply uninterested in his visit rather than literally and completely unable to move.

It wasn't until she felt his warm healing energy, saw the blue light and experienced immediate relief that she even realised he'd made his way over to her.

"You don't need to do that," she said, making an effort to sound nonchalant.

"Alright," Scratch replied, the energy immediately subsiding. Nora let out a whine of protest before she could help herself.

Her cheeks flushed bright red at the noise and Scratch's smug grin. Quickly scowling, she turned away from him, even though the small movement made her head swim.

Scratch clicked his tongue before placing his shadowy hands over her once again, letting his blue healing light engulf her, replenishing her energy levels and healing her broken body.

"Why do you always pretend you're fine when you're not?" Scratch asked softly as he worked.

"Why are you parading around as a Shadow Being when you're not?" Nora shot back, more harshly than she'd intended. She internally winced as Scratch halted his healing. His eyes widened for a brief moment before he let out another low chuckle, letting the illusion he was wearing melt away.

Nora couldn't help but be drawn to his sapphire blue eyes as he gazed into her amber ones, looking as if he could see the depths of her soul.

"Better?" he asked, resuming his healing.

"Better," Nora confirmed, her voice nothing more than a croak.

Clearing her throat, Nora watched him work for a few minutes, allowing him to check her body for any further bruises or marks, but there were none.

"Garvan's not going to remember how bruised you were the last time he saw you," Scratch murmured, offering up an explanation of why he was healing her fully this time around. Happy with his work, Scratch lifted his hands from her before holding one out for her to help her sit up.

Grasping it tentatively, Nora's eyes roamed over him, taking him all in. "I wasn't sure if I imagined it," she breathed, still holding his hand even though she was completely upright.

"I wasn't sure if you'd seen it either, but it was a chance I had to take."

"What's your name?"

"Aaron," he replied, gently letting go of Nora's hand and placing it on her thigh.

Nora's face flushed bright red again as she snatched her hand away, holding it to her chest, the lingering heat of Aaron's hand burning her.

"Are you here to help me?" Nora hated herself for asking it, but she'd been alone for so long now that she was desperate for someone to shoulder some of this burden with her.

Aaron stared at her for a minute, his eyes intense as they burned into her own, before sighing. "There are so many different routes that this can take."

"What does that mean?"

"It means that I want to be able to help you, but I am limited in what I can do, especially if things shift… unexpectedly."

Tears prickling the back of her eyes, Nora quickly pinched her earlobe to stop them from falling. "So, I'm not your priority?" she asked thickly.

"Your role is... undetermined," Aaron replied, reaching for her hand once more, but Nora pulled it away. "I will do what I can, like come in to heal you when you need it, for example."

Nora let out a small chuckle, but her heart was thudding against her ribs. Aaron hadn't come here to help her. Who was he talking to when she first saw him then? Lifting her face to look at him, Nora set her jaw. There had been some part of her—some small, hidden part of her she'd been determined to ignore—that had been hoping he would get her out of this mess. But that wasn't the case. She really was on her own. Garvan had told her in his Throne Room that she'd proven herself worthy to him, so she would just have to keep proving her worth until she was given the freedom she needed to escape.

"Nora?" Aaron asked, placing a finger under her chin to tilt her face back to his. "You *are* a priority, but the events unfolding around you aren't determined yet, so I'm unable to step in. The Realm... there are things that even the most powerful beings in the Realm are unable to do due to their ties to it."

"And are you one of those all-powerful Realm dwellers?" Nora drawled, her voice tight as she tried to look away again, but Aaron held her face in place with his thumb.

"I'm sure you know the answer to that yourself," he said, and Nora scoffed. Only someone with the title 'Most Powerful Being in the Realm' would have the audacity to give that answer.

"I'm going to have to do things my own way now," Nora said quietly to him. He was holding her chin so tightly that she couldn't look away even if she'd wanted to, and her lips tingled despite the plan she was forming.

"I don't doubt that," Aaron replied, leaning in so his breath tickled her ear as he spoke into it. "Don't get yourself killed."

Nora let out a slow laugh and pulled away from him. "I'm not that stupid."

Aaron chuckled once more before letting go of her face and standing up. Nora shivered as his heat left her.

Running his hands over himself, Scratch stood before Nora once more. He gave her a mocking salute before stalking back out of her room, making sure the barrier locking her in was as impenetrable as ever, and striding away without a backwards glance.

Nora flopped back onto her bed, her body aching again, but for a completely different reason.

Chapter 31 - Aaron

It had taken every ounce of willpower he'd had to pull away from Nora and walk out that door. Aaron mentally berated himself for getting attached to her. There was so much going on. It was stupid of him to be so taken by her.

He wasn't able to help her yet. Even though there had been plenty of chances for him to sneak her out and get her to safety, he couldn't.

Physically couldn't.

And it drove him mad.

What was the point of having all this power if he couldn't save a single human from the horrors that Garvan was putting her through?

She hadn't done anything to deserve this, and Aaron struggled against the Realm's bond every day to see if he was able to help her.

He couldn't.

He'd even tried to ask the Realm what her role was and why she needed to be trapped like this in order to fulfil it.

Do you think he got an answer? No, of course he didn't.

When Zion had told him that there would be a human girl in the temple while he'd be playing his role as Scratch, he hadn't thought anything of it. He was here to see the damage

211

that had been done to the eleven Guardians and determine whether it could be reversed. To see whether the siblings had any chance of being able to guide the Realm like they had before.

No part, not a single part of the plan, had involved him becoming invested in the wellbeing of the human girl.

But there was something about Nora.

There was something dwelling within her that he wasn't able to put his finger on. But it was powerful.

He wondered if Garvan had realised the same thing and if that was why he had kept her alive all this time.

Aaron had heard the story of the day that Garvan had come to Earth and taken Nora. It was a happy accident that he had stumbled across her while trying to find Simmy. He'd sensed some Realm energy coming from her and grabbed her. The blast that Nora had created while she was submerged had been powerful enough to actually scald Garvan. The fact that Garvan hadn't anticipated it made Nora a powerful adversary, and potentially, an even more powerful ally.

That had to be the angle that Garvan was playing.

While Nora hadn't shown that level of power since she'd been here, she had still been surprising her captors with what she *had* accomplished, especially since Garvan had placed a lock on the amount of her energy she could access in the beginning.

He had to keep playing this part, though. If there was any chance of him getting as many people as possible out of this alive, his role was here, as Garvan's loyal lackey.

A shiver ran through him as he remembered the vision, which Zion had sent him the night before, of the blond boy and the red-haired girl arriving in the Realm earlier than planned. While it would be incredible to leave this post earlier and guide them while they were in the Realm, Aaron secretly hoped that wouldn't happen.

He'd have to leave Nora here by herself, and that wasn't something he was mentally or emotionally prepared to do yet.

Running his hands over his shadowy face and cursing that he needed to wear this bloody disguise, Aaron took a breath and calmed his mind. He threw on the *'couldn't give a shit'* smirk that Scratch wore so well and stalked into Garvan's chambers. "You rang, majesty?"

Garvan snarled as his tone but merely waved him forwards. "I have need of you," he said absently.

"Whatever you desire," Aaron crooned, fighting the urge to gouge the gaunt eyeballs out of Garvan's head as he gave him an arrogant grin.

Chapter 32 - Noah

Noah sprinted to Layla and Simmy's house as fast as his long legs would take him. Everything was about to change. There was no doubt in his mind as to what he had to do, but he needed more first. The most pressing matter being to figure out where Garvan needed to go so badly that he'd put Nora in charge of watching over the eleven Guardian siblings.

Puffing heavily and holding a stitch in his side, Noah reached Layla and Simmy's front door and banged on it loudly with his fist.

"Noah?" Layla asked as she opened the door. "What are you doing here? You're still in your uni clothes. Is everything alright?"

"Come inside, Noah," Simmy said to him, her auburn hair swaying as she peered around Layla.

Noah walked into the house and gratefully accepted the cold glass of water Simmy offered after she'd ushered him into the living room.

"What has happened?" Simmy asked after he had caught his breath.

"Nora's definitely with Garvan." Noah puffed out a breath,

willing his heart rate to slow down.

"What? How do you know?" Layla exclaimed.

"She came to me when I was out with my mum just now. She brought me to the Realm with her through a vision."

Simmy didn't reply, a grave expression shadowing her face.

"So... this means that we can bring Nora back with us when we defeat Garvan, though. Doesn't it?" Layla interjected. "I mean, I know we have to win first, but this is fantastic!"

Noah looked at Layla. The thought had crossed his mind as well, but there was a feeling deep in his gut that told him bringing Nora back to Earth wouldn't be that simple.

"We can't think about it until we've removed Garvan from the Realm for good," Noah said. "Look, there's something else I need to tell you two."

For the next hour, Noah relayed everything that had happened to him that afternoon.

"...and then I ran here," Noah said, finishing his story.

Layla and Simmy processed the information. While Layla looked like she was ready to jump into the Realm that very second and storm Garvan's lair, Simmy had a more thoughtful expression on her face.

"Garvan is still a regular Guardian," Simmy murmured to herself. "When was the last time...?"

She stood up and briskly walked to one of the bedrooms at the end of the corridor.

Noah and Layla looked at each other in silence while they waited for her to come back, neither one wanting to be the reason that Simmy lost her train of thought.

Looking flustered, Simmy quickly paced back to the living room with an old, dusty book, and Layla shifted uncomfortably in her seat.

Noah couldn't see what was on the cover as she gingerly placed it on the coffee table.

Simmy gently pried it open and sifted through the pages as carefully as one would handle a newborn child as it looked like it would fall apart at any second.

Inside were rows and rows of names and dates.

"This is the complete record of our lives as Guardians," Simmy said to the two of them as she leafed through the pages. "It has the date on which we were born or reborn, the names that we choose for ourselves, the gender that we chose and the date in which we then underwent the rebirthing process. Although, you might have already guessed that for yourself," she said to Layla as she shot her niece a look from the corner of her eye.

"I didn't… quite… figure all that out," Layla mumbled, her cheeks flushing.

Noah looked between the two of them, confused.

"I took this book to Nora before she was taken," Layla said softly to him, her cheeks still stained pink. "We thought it might give us some answers as to what was going on in the Realm."

Noah just nodded before bringing his eyes back to Simmy.

Simmy eventually paused at a page and murmured something to Layla, who nodded, ran to the kitchen and came back with a notepad and pen. They both paused before Simmy started to point at different entries written within various pages of the book. Layla hastily wrote down the information Simmy pointed at, and for a while, the only sound filling the room was the scratching of a pen on paper, and the light rustling of pages being gently turned.

Finally, Simmy reached the last entry of the book. Carefully closing the cover, Simmy took the notes Layla had written and studied them.

Anxious to find out what the two of them were doing, Noah coughed lightly to remind them he was still there.

Layla glanced at him briefly before returning her eyes to her notes, while it seemed Simmy hadn't heard anything, and she continued to pore over the information in front of her.

Settling back down in his chair, willing patience from every fibre of his being, Noah started the process of clearing his mind to pass the time.

He closed his eyes, took a long deep breath in through his nose, and a long deep breath out through his mouth before repeating the process; a long deep breath in through his nose, and a long deep breath out through his mouth.

Every so often, a flyaway thought would drift through his mind, but instead of spending any time on it, he just let it continue on its way and focused on his breathing.

In and out. In and out. In and out.

"Noah?" a woman's voice called to him. "Noah?"

Unwilling to open his eyes and remove himself from his pleasant trance, Noah wiggled his fingers and his toes to get the blood moving through his body again.

After a few seconds, Noah released a long, deep breath and opened his eyes.

Both Simmy and Layla were standing over him, the notes clasped firmly in Simmy's hands.

Remembering what had been happening beforehand, Noah jumped out of his chair, almost landing on top of Layla.

"Oof! Sorry Layla," Noah said as he raised awkwardly to his feet. "What did you learn?"

"Well," Simmy began, "I think I know where Garvan needs

to go so desperately."

Noah nodded for her to continue, not daring to get his hopes up.

"Sit down. I'm too short to show you while you're standing," Simmy said to him, motioning to the leather couch Noah had just jumped out of.

Noah sat and looked expectantly at Simmy.

"Do you remember when I was telling you about how we Guardians have a lifespan, but then we are reborn?" Simmy asked Noah.

"Yes," Noah replied.

"Well, Guardians don't have a specific timeline that decides how long we live for. We are reborn with certain lessons that we need to learn throughout our lifetime, and once we have learnt those lessons, it is time for us to move on to a new life."

Noah looked blankly at Simmy. "What do you mean by lessons?"

"We are much like humans, who are born on the Earth with lessons that need to be learnt to become the people they are destined to be, lessons such as patience, respect for others, spirituality and many many more. Guardians also have lessons that we need to learn," Simmy replied.

"But unlike humans, who have an unpredictable life expectancy, us Guardians cannot move onto our next life until we have fully completed our lessons. Humans, whose lives can range from dying in the womb to reaching over one hundred years of age, carry their lessons from one life to the next if they haven't learnt what they've needed to."

"How do humans know what lessons they need to learn in a lifetime?" Noah asked. "Is there a set path for us?"

"No," Simmy answered, "there isn't a set path as such. Before you are born, your spirit chooses the life they want to live as their new self on Earth. Often these lives are based around the lessons that need to be learnt."

Noah still didn't quite understand, so Simmy explained further.

"For example, someone who needs to learn patience might consistently be put in situations where they have to wait. Someone who needs to learn to love themselves might be put in situations where they need to trust their own abilities. Someone who needs to break a poverty mindset in their family might be put in a position to earn great wealth and show their own children how to do the same.

"Much like the lessons we bring from previous lives, we also tend to meet the same people over and over again. We are always attracted back to the people we love. Now, these people will always play different roles in our lives. We may not marry the same person every lifetime, and our parents from one life may become our children in the next while our lovers in one life may become our good friends in the next. There is no set path."

"What's this got to do with Garvan's plans?" Noah asked.

"Isn't it obvious?" Layla said, pointing at the notes she had written. "Garvan has learnt his lessons for this lifetime, and it's time for him to be reborn."

"I believe that Garvan has put off learning his last lesson for as long as he could in order to stay in his current body, but the body is getting older and is now starting to deteriorate," Simmy said to both Noah and Layla. "While we are powerful beings, we are not immortal, and we must adhere to the nature of the Realm and fulfil our life cycles."

"Why wouldn't Garvan want a new body? Wouldn't this

older body be a hindrance to him?" Noah asked.

"Garvan has created a life that he is proud of in this current lifetime," Simmy replied. "There is no guarantee how many lessons he needs to learn in his next lifetime, or even if he will remember everything that he had accomplished during his time in this body."

"He won't remember his time during this life?" Layla asked. "I thought you all remembered everything you learnt from your previous lives."

"We retain our lessons," Simmy answered, "but whether or not we remember what we accomplished during our previous lives is all dependent on what we need to accomplish during our next life. If we are determined to remember, the process takes much longer. Which brings me to this list." Simmy lifted the piece of paper in her hand up and held it out to Noah.

"These are all of Garvan's previous lives?" he asked.

"Yes," Simmy replied. "I want you to take a good look at it."

There aren't many lives recorded, Noah thought to himself. Not nearly as many as he was expecting.

"Are the dates in the Realm equivalent to the dates on Earth?"

"They are close," Simmy answered.

"So Garvan has been in this body for over two hundred years!?" Noah exclaimed.

"Closer to three hundred," replied Simmy. "This is why it is necessary for him to move on. I also doubt Garvan will risk losing everything he has built in this lifetime, which gives us an extra edge because he will have to stay in his rebirthing chamber for longer in order for him to retain his memories. Also, because he has waited so long to undergo the rebirth process, it will take longer still, which means that we have that extra time to work with as well. Garvan is too arrogant to risk losing any of his powers."

"We can make our move when he undergoes the rebirthing process," Layla said, clasping her hands in front of her. "There's no reason why we can't."

"Exactly," replied Simmy. "We just have to wait and train until the time comes. It will be soon. I only have another two days left on Earth, so we are going to have to work exceptionally hard."

"Right," Layla and Noah exclaimed together.

"We will have one night of rest tonight, and then early tomorrow morning, we will start," Simmy said. "Now off to bed, the two of you. Noah, you can sleep in the spare room, third door on the right down the hall."

It was only now that he knew he could rest that Noah realised just how tired he was, even though his mind was racing a mile a minute. He thanked Simmy as he found his way to the bedroom. There were a long couple of days ahead of him.

Chapter 33 - Simmy

A familiar white light filled the living room after Layla and Noah had gone to bed, and Simmy waited patiently for Zion to sit down before looking over'. "There are too many different scenarios of how this is going to work out. A lot of them have the kids facing more danger than we want them to," she said, wringing her hands.

"You have to trust that they will be able to handle it," Zion replied, although he looked grim.

"Is there nothing we can do to help them? No way we can train them more, or keep them here longer?"

"You know that there is only so much they can do here. They need the Realm's energy to unleash their true potential. Keeping them here would only hinder them further."

Simmy began to object, but Zion held up his hand to stop her. "I have prepared for all worst-case scenarios. While they may face harsher trials than we wish them to, they will be supported. You need to focus on your own mission now, Simone. You play an important role in this too."

"I am aware of my role," Simmy snapped, then sighed, sinking into her chair, her hands covering her face. "If anything happened to them, I'd never be able to forgive myself."

"You have done everything you can with the resources you have available to you," Zion replied gently. "There is nothing more you can do other than let them know that they have your full support. Remind them of how capable they are and make sure they know that they are not alone."

Nodding, Simmy didn't lift her head from her hands.

"Have you still got their mandala?" Zion asked her, standing up.

"Yes, I have it with me here."

"They are going to need it soon."

"Are they ready?"

"No, but they are going to need it anyway."

A bright glow shone through Simmy's fingers, and when she finally pulled her hands away from her face, Zion was gone.

Chapter 34 - Noah

His body was crying out for a good night's sleep, but there were so many different scenarios running through Noah's head that he tossed and turned restlessly.

Just as he was going out of his mind trying to clear it, there was a light knock on his bedroom door.

"Noah?" a voice called softly.

Quietly rolling out of bed, Noah tiptoed across the room and leant his forehead against the door. "Layla?"

"Can I come in?"

Noah turned the handle as softly as he could so Simmy wouldn't hear him. As soon as the door opened, Layla slipped inside and, just as quietly, shut the door behind her and leant against it.

"Couldn't sleep either?" Noah whispered as they walked over to the bed and flopped down on it together.

"No," Layla whispered back. "There's too much to think about."

"I know," Noah replied. "There's so much we need to do, but none of our efforts will be worth it if we can't control the mandala."

Layla made a noise in the back of her throat that confirmed

to Noah that she'd been thinking the same thing.

"Sunstones are extremely powerful," Layla said after a while, "which is great for battle, but we're going to have to be really in sync."

Noah nodded, before realising Layla couldn't see him properly in the dark room, so he hummed his agreement instead.

Layla shifted slightly on the bed, and Noah's heart jumped as he became acutely aware of how close they were. All thoughts of the Realm flew from his mind as he tried to convince himself the right side of his body wasn't about to burst into flames, thanks to their close proximity.

"Is it hot in here?" Noah asked, fingering the collar of his t-shirt.

"No," whispered Layla, shuffling around on the bed again, causing Noah's heart to skip another beat.

"Oh, okay," he squeaked, forcing himself to lay still.

Unfortunately for him, Layla saw through his act immediately.

"What's wrong?" she asked, leaning up on her elbow.

"Nothing!" Noah insisted enthusiastically. Too enthusiastically.

"Really?" replied Layla, sounding thoroughly unconvinced.

Noah laughed nervously, trying to appear as though lying in bed with a girl was a normal situation for him. *Does she need to be so damn attractive?* The flyaway thought crossed his mind.

Noah jumped up, as if to throw the thought from his body, but Layla had leaned in closer to see what was going on with him, and as he jumped, the two of them collided.

A resounding crash echoed around the room as they both

landed on the floor next to the bed.

There was a sharp pain in Noah's lip, and he wondered if he'd bitten it on the way down.

But in the couple of seconds it took for him to find his bearings, he realised that *he* hadn't bitten his lip… Layla had.

And she hadn't yet come to her senses.

So Noah was lying on the ground in an extremely uncomfortable, twisted position, with Layla lying on top of him in a painful, toothy kiss.

Unsure what to do, Noah stayed as still as possible, one arm stuck underneath him, the other hanging awkwardly in the air, praying Layla would come to her senses soon.

Time seemed to run in slow motion as Noah watched Layla pull herself up, rub her head and turn to face him.

"You're a terrible kisser," she said as she brushed a few rogue strands of red hair out of her face.

"What? That wasn't a kiss! *You're* the terrible kisser!" Noah spluttered, pointing an accusing finger at her.

"Calm down. I was joking," Layla laughed, pushing his finger away with her own.

Muttering under his breath, Noah willed his heart to stop pounding as he rearranged his body into a sitting position.

"You *have* kissed a girl before though, right?" Layla asked slyly.

"Of course I have!" replied Noah hotly. "I had my first kiss when I was ten!"

"Ten? Wow," Layla replied with a laugh. "Have you kissed anyone since then?"

Noah huffed and didn't reply.

"You haven't, have you?" Layla answered for him.

"I haven't wanted to," Noah justified.

"It's not a bad thing," replied Layla, holding her hands up in surrender, "but if we're going to be working closely together you need to be comfortable around me, and if you can't even lay on a bed with me without getting all hot and bothered then how are we going to spend all that time together in the Realm?"

Heat rose to Noah's face at Layla's blunt statement. He should have realised she'd have noticed how he acted around her. She noticed everything.

"Kiss me," stated Layla abruptly.

Noah's heart almost leapt through his chest. "What!?" he exclaimed. "No!"

"Okay," Layla shrugged, and brushed a piece of lint off her pyjama top.

Noah spluttered for a few moments, before deciding that he *was* curious about what it would be like to kiss her…

"I'm not very experienced," Noah said quietly.

"I'm not going to score you," Layla replied drily.

"You think that this will help us be able to work together better?" Noah asked, shifting himself around so that he was facing Layla directly.

"There's only one way to find out," Layla replied, rising so she was sitting on her knees.

Nodding, Noah fidgeted, trying to think of a reason not to do it, but the truth was he *wanted* to do it. And if the end result was that he would be able to stay focused on defeating Garvan, then all the better.

It was just a kiss.

Just a simple kiss, and then he could focus on becoming a Guardian and finding Nora.

"Okay," Noah said. "What do we have to lose?"

227

"Exactly," she replied, and Noah was pleased to hear she sounded a little nervous herself.

"Do we count down, or…?"

"I am *not* counting down to a kiss!" Layla exclaimed. "Just sit still and I'll do it."

Nodding, Noah took a deep breath, and as he did, the moon came out from behind the clouds, illuminating the bedroom.

Surely it wasn't Noah's imagination that Layla's green eyes seemed to look brighter than usual, and he could have sworn her face was a little flushed. But before he could dwell on either of those thoughts, Layla had placed her hands on Noah's cheeks and gently closed the distance between them.

Soft, was the thought that crossed Noah's mind.

It was as if his body was moving of its own accord because, before he knew it, Noah was tangling one of his hands in Layla's wild red hair while the other hand drifted to her waist, pulling her closer to him.

There was no resistance from Layla, who, in return, dropped her hands from his face and wrapped her arms around Noah's neck.

Noah had never felt anything like it before. His whole body was alive. Like every one of his nerves was on fire while electricity ran through his veins.

Layla appeared to be supercharged as well because the next thing Noah knew her hands had moved from resting around his neck. One gripped his messy blond hair, while the other dug into his back as her lips moved against his.

Nervously, Noah opened his mouth a little more and held back a sigh as Layla's tongue slipped inside.

All coherent thoughts flew from his mind as he leant deeper into the kiss, pulling Layla onto his lap, his hands gripping her waist like she would disappear as soon as he let go.

It was as if the two of them were fighting to get as close to each other as possible, trying to meld their bodies into one.

Noah didn't know how long the kiss lasted, or how long Layla's legs had been wrapped around him, but he knew the blood pumping through him would become noticeable soon, so with every ounce of willpower he possessed, Noah gently pulled away, both of them gasping for air as he did.

Now, even though he didn't have much experience with kissing, Noah was sure this reaction wasn't normal. Max and Mia had plenty of kissing experience, and neither one of them ever mentioned their bodies near exploding when *they* did it.

"Noah, look," a breathless Layla insisted, holding her hand up to Noah's face.

There was an emerald green energy surrounding it, the same colour as her eyes. Noah lifted his own hand to his face and saw that it was also surrounded by energy. Amber, just like his eyes.

Noah reached out his hand towards Layla's.

The second their hands touched, there was a blinding flash of light, and Noah had to shield his eyes with his other hand because the one that was connected with Layla's wouldn't budge.

As quickly as it had come, the light dimmed, and in its place was the sunstone mandala. Both himself and Layla were gripping a side of it, their energy running through the relic like electricity.

"We can touch the mandala," Noah breathed.

"Amazing," Layla replied, her voice breathless as well.

The two of them stayed silent for a while, just watching the beauty of the sunstones mixing with their own unique energy source, until they felt their bodies start to relax, and they both leant back on the side of the bed for support.

Soon the sunstones in the mandala dimmed, and Layla took it from Noah and placed it on the floor next to her.

"I wasn't expecting that," she said to Noah, her cheeks flushed pink as she lightly touched her lips with her finger.

"Neither was I," Noah replied, forcing himself not to pull her fingers away and replace them with his lips once more.

"I don't think we'll have an issue controlling the mandala now," Layla said. "I think enough of our energy flows through it now for it to be safe to use."

"That's good," Noah replied, looking at his hands. "At least that will knock some time off our training tomorrow."

"Yup," agreed Layla.

There was a small silence, then Noah groaned inwardly. "Look, Layla—" he started, but before he could say anything else, there was a sharp knock on the bedroom door.

"Layla! Noah!" came the stern voice of Simmy. "I don't know what you two are still doing awake, but get to sleep now. Both of you!"

Layla jumped up off the floor with the mandala and turned guiltily to Noah, "Well, I guess I'd better go now."

Noah stood up as well, nodding at her, trying to keep his legs from wobbling.

Smiling, Layla looked up at Noah before lifting up on her tiptoes and kissing him on the cheek. The unfamiliar sensation of electricity flew through Noah like a shockwave once more. "Goodnight, Noah. We have a busy day ahead of us. Make sure to get some sleep," she said to him.

"You too. Goodnight," he replied as he watched as Layla went up the hall and back into her bedroom, closing her door behind her.

Closing his own door, Noah flung himself onto the bed, rubbing his cheek that was still popping with electricity.

"What a crazy night," he said to his pillow.

Taking a few deep breaths to calm his mind, Noah closed his eyes in an attempt to fall asleep, but his traitorous mind kept drifting back to the kiss and the last thoughts he had before Noah drifted off was of fiery red hair and of the sharp tingles that refused to leave his body.

Chapter 35 - Layla

Layla practically sprinted back to her room, her hand covering her mouth as she launched herself onto the bed, the door she had flung behind her closing with a loud *click*.

Panting, Layla pulled her pillow over her head as her mind raced.

She hadn't meant to ask Noah to kiss her, it had just slipped out, and there was no way she was going to back down from it after the look he'd given her. The shock and desire that flashed through his eyes were enough to get her toes curling, and she didn't know what she would have done if he'd turned her down. Her lips had been tingling at just the thought of kissing him.

Groaning, Layla rolled onto her back, hugging her pillow to her face.

What had happened with their energy though? It was so unusual for their life energy to show its form on Earth. Usually they would have to be in the Realm to be able to see it like that.

She slid her hand over the bed until she felt the comforting warmth of the mandala that had appeared before them. A smile tugged at Layla's lips as the familiar energy zinged over her fingers.

Absently running her index finger over the sunstones, Layla took a deep breath in through her nose and out through her mouth, embracing the energy which was flowing through her.

There was so much they still needed to learn, but at least they had the power to control the mandala now. They'd had so many conversations, while they were supposed to be focusing on their breathwork, wondering how they were meant to become Guardians if they couldn't even manage to work the mandala. Even if they didn't know *why*, exactly, they needed it. But Simmy had one, and Layla was sure that Zion would have a relic as well, so it must be a vital part of being a Guardian.

Stilling her hand, Layla's thoughts drifted to Nora. *Sorry for kissing your brother,* she sent out, as a telepathic message to her friend, and she grinned as she was imagined the image of Nora doubled over laughing.

There was no way Layla could tell her about this. There wasn't a chance Nora would let her live it down.

But if it became a regular occurrence... Layla's face flamed at the thought, and she immediately pushed it from her mind.

Once she knew being a Guardian would take up most of her time and energy, she'd called things off with James, much to the boy's dismay. While it had been lots of fun, she didn't want him getting in the way of her mission. Maybe that's why she'd told Noah to kiss her tonight. She was used to a certain amount of attention that she wasn't receiving anymore.

Sure, let's go with that, Layla thought, forcing all other thoughts away as she tried to relax.

It's a good thing Simmy came along when she did. Otherwise, it may have gotten way out of hand.

Simmy... oh shoot. Simmy must have felt the energy shifting too. That must be how she knew the two of them were together. Layla was *sure* that Simmy had gone to bed by the time she'd knocked on Noah's door.

"Oh crap," Layla whispered to herself, pulling the pillow off her face.

She was going to have to explain this to Simmy in the morning.

Chapter 36 - Noah

Morning came far too quickly for Noah's liking. After a night of tossing and turning, his eyes felt dry and heavy.

"Noah, time to get out of bed," Simmy called through the door, knocking as she walked past.

Groaning, Noah stretched his body and pulled the doona over his face.

Closing his eyes again, Noah slowly took a deep breath in through his nose, held it for five seconds, and then slowly released it out through his mouth.

Climbing out of bed, Noah stood and stretched one more time before changing into a pair of jeans and a t-shirt that Layla had given to him yesterday. *I took them from your place that morning I was over, in case you ever needed a change of clothes here,"* she'd said.

By the time he reached the kitchen, Simmy and Layla were talking quietly.

"Morning," Noah called out to both of them, stifling a yawn.

"Good morning, Noah," Simmy replied cheerily.

"Morning," Layla replied, with a quick glance in his direction, her cheeks flushing as she looked at him before turning back to Simmy.

"I've got a toiletry bag all set up for you in the bathroom, Noah. Go and have a shower and freshen yourself up for the day. You're going to need to be ready for your training." Simmy said, pointing Noah towards the bathroom.

With a feeling that she was trying to usher him out of the kitchen, Noah slowly walked to the bathroom, pulling his shirt off along the way. He wasn't going to complain about being asked to have a nice hot shower, though. He'd find out what the two of them were whispering about when he came back.

Noah's muscles were uncomfortably tight, and he almost moaned as the warmth and pressure of the shower relaxed him. Sighing gratefully, he let the water run over his face, clearing his mind of any thoughts that were trying to ruin his bliss.

There was plenty of time to worry in the coming twenty-four hours. He was going to enjoy these ten minutes to himself.

When he couldn't put it off any longer, Noah sauntered back to the kitchen, feeling relaxed after his hot shower, drying his hair with the towel that Simmy had put out for him. He paused as soon as he walked through the kitchen door, when Simmy and Layla turned to him, solemn expressions on their faces.

"Noah," Simmy said gravely, "I need you to show me what you did last night to infuse your energy with the mandala."

Thud.

The towel hit the ground, landing in a pile on the floor in front of him, and Noah's heart just about leapt out of his chest.

Gaping wordlessly at the two women in front of him, Noah tried to come up with any excuse as to why the mandala was flickering with amber and emerald energy, when suddenly Layla burst into a fit of laughter. Even Simmy cracked a smile.

"Sorry, Noah. That was a joke. You don't need to show me what happened," Simmy said to him, trying to keep the smile off her face. "I am well aware of how your energy became infused with the mandala."

"Oh great, well that makes me feel heaps better," Noah muttered, picking the towel up off the floor and drying his fringe to hide his burning face.

"She was going to find out sooner or later," Layla said, in an attempt to comfort him after she'd stopped laughing.

"I'd have rathered later than sooner," Noah mumbled to her, walking over and knocking her elbow lightly with his fist.

Noah looked up to see Simmy watching the exchange between them, and immediately he turned away from Layla and walked to the fridge for some breakfast.

"Well, the good news is that the two of you have significantly reduced the training time needed to master the mandala, so whatever happened doesn't need to happen again," Simmy stated.

Noah's heart gave an uncomfortable lurch at her words so he grabbed an apple before walking back over to the two of them.

"Unless, of course, you want it to," Simmy continued, with an innocent look.

"Okay, okay, enough," Noah said loudly, desperate to change the subject. He knew his face was bright red, and he took a loud bite out of his apple to distract himself. He was surprised, though, to see that Layla's face was also sporting a red tinge.

Chuckling to herself, Simmy passed the mandala to Noah. "You now need to learn how to use the power within the mandala."

The mandala felt heavy in Noah's hands, and he ran a finger over one of the sunstones. Even though it had been inside the cool house all night, the stones were warm.

"Can you feel its power?" Simmy asked, as she watched him.

"It's warm," replied Noah. "It wasn't this warm before."

"That's because you have infused your own energy within it now," Simmy explained. "It acknowledges you as a master."

"Does it know that I'm going to become a Guardian?" Noah asked, placing it in the palm of his hand.

"It knows you are powerful, and it's responding to that. You as well, Layla," Simmy said, gesturing to her.

Noah looked up as Layla walked towards them and held the mandala out for her. The heat he felt now had nothing to do with the mandala.

"It feels... happy," Layla murmured, when she took the mandala from him.

"It knows that the two of you are going to use it to restore the Realm," said Simmy. "Noah, you take hold of the other half."

Grasping a side of the mandala with a warm hand, Noah felt shockwaves run through him.

"Take a deep breath, and close your eyes."

Simmy's voice sounded distant.

Closing his eyes, Noah tried to concentrate on his breath and ignore the tingling sensation running through his body.

"In order to utilise the mandala, you first need to control the power running through yourselves and harness it by visualising what you want. If you need to attack, visualise your target. If you need to open a portal, visualise the place you wish to be transported to. If you need to heal, visualise yourself fully healed. It's all about bending the mandala's energy to your will. The two of you will need to be on the same page throughout each process. Two bodies, one mind. Now concentrate," Simmy coached them.

Noah tried to concentrate on his breathing, but it sounded off-beat to him, which didn't make any sense. How could his own breathing be off-beat?

Whenever he breathed in, he felt like he should be breathing out.

Layla, Noah realised. He needed to be in tune with Layla's breathing.

Two bodies, one mind. They needed to be completely in sync if they were going to fully harness the power of the mandala.

Concentrating on the feel of Layla's breath, Noah paused his own to learn her rhythm.

Breathe in, two, three, four... breathe out, two, three, four, five.

This was different to Noah's breathing pattern, which was in for four and out for three, but he could adapt.

After three attempts at trying to match Layla's breathing, Noah finally got the hang of expanding his lungs and breathing out for longer.

In two, three, four. Out two, three, four, five. In two, three, four. Out two, three, four, five.

The energy from the mandala started to fuse with his own again, and Noah felt electric. As long as he could utilise this power, nothing, not even Garvan, would be able to stand in his way. He would be able to save Nora.

Nora was firmly implanted in Noah's mind as the mandala's power surged through him, and with one last exhalation,

Noah felt he and Layla would be ready to move on to more rigorous training.

"No! Wait! Stop! Clear your mind!" Simmy called desperately, breaking Noah's concentration. He opened his eyes.

The last thing Noah saw was the kitchen, and Simmy, disappearing, before he was transported to a very familiar room.

Chapter 37 - Nora

something was about to shift. Nora didn't know what it was, or why it was happening, but the air around her was crackling with tension.

Even Aaron hadn't been back to see her since he'd shown her his true form, which annoyingly sent shivers of anticipation down Nora's spine.

She still didn't know how long she'd been here, but she was spending her time much more wisely than she had been before. Instead of purely training to wield her energy—which was still being blocked to some extent—she was also training her body; pushups, situps, agility training, well, as much as she could train her agility in her small room, and even her fighting skills.

Without anyone here to train her, she really didn't know what she was doing, but she practised anyway, trying to remember anything and everything she could from the action movies her and Noah had watched as a kid.

The only time anyone came to see her was when Tick strolled by and opened a small crack in the barrier surrounding her door, just big enough to toss her in some food and water three times a day, before disappearing again.

It was the lack of her snarking that had initially tipped Nora off that something was happening. Well, that and the fact Tick and Scratch were now permanently situated as guards in the Throne Room.

Nora hadn't been given any more instructions on what her role in watching over the Guardians would be once Garvan went, wherever it was that he had to go, and Nora hadn't pushed the subject. The thought of what she might have to do sent more shivers down her spine, and not the nice ones. She knew there was more to this task than Garvan was letting on, and if he'd forgotten about it, then all the better. She would spend her time training her mind, body and energy while she figured out a plan to escape.

She began practising her punches as her heart gave a twinge as she thought about Aaron and how he hadn't come back. Whatever role it was that she had to play, it was clearly something she had to do by herself, so much so that Aaron hadn't even attempted to help her, even though she was sure he was strong enough to withstand anything that might be thrown his way.

Whatever. If he couldn't help her, then she couldn't be held responsible for what she had to do to ensure her own plan didn't fail.

"You've been keeping yourself busy."

Nora had been so consumed with her thoughts that she hadn't heard anyone approaching. She held back a scream, mid-punch, turning quickly to find Garvan standing in her doorway, leaning on his golden staff.

Nora let out a growl of impatience, silently thanking the Realm she hadn't been practising with her energy when he'd walked in. As far as she knew, he wasn't aware that she'd gained back any control of it.

"What can I do for you, Master?" she crooned. Garvan narrowed his eyes at her tone, watching as she took a sip from the pitiful cup of water she'd been given with her most recent meal of stale bread and cheese.

"I hope you haven't forgotten that I've requested your assistance with the Guardians," Garvan said, keeping his eyes on Nora as she wiped the sweat from her brow.

"I haven't," Nora answered, in the same purr, "but I was hoping you had. My time is precious. After all, I'm very busy here." She waved a hand around her bare room to emphasise her sarcasm.

"So it would seem."

Nora could have sworn that she saw Garvan's mouth twitch in a mocking smile, but she ignored it, peering into his wrinkly blue eyes instead.

"Scratch, come here," Garvan called over his shoulder. Scratch appeared next to him in an instant, having teleported from where he'd been standing guard in the Throne Room. "What were you telling me Nora should be doing this morning?"

"She has the ability to see what her brother and his friends are doing. The friends that you think are the ones you've been looking for all this time. You should use her to get to them." Scratch's voice was dull as he explained, but Nora could barely tell the difference over the ringing in her ears.

"What?" she hissed, not daring to look at Aaron as betrayal tightened her skin. "What did you say?"

It was Garvan's turn to purr. "You're to get in touch with your brother, in any way you see fit, and lead him to me. This is your new mission."

With that, he turned on his heel and stalked out of the room, leaving the barrier down so Scratch could leave once he was done.

"I didn't have a choice—" he tried to explain, but Nora shot him a furious look, fighting back the tears that were burning in the back of her eyes.

"I don't care if he threatened to skin you alive," she hissed. "I don't care if your sad, miserable life was on the line. Because it is now. Everything I do now will be to spite you."

Aaron's eyes flashed. "Don't get in the way of my mission."

"I'm going to do whatever the hell I want," Nora spat. "Now get out."

"Nora—"

"Get. Out."

Gritting his shadowy teeth, Aaron stalked out of the room, returning to his post in the Throne Room. He cast Nora looks every now and again, looks that Nora pointedly ignored as she seethed.

How could Aaron throw her under the bus like that? He *knew* Noah was important to her. They'd never openly spoken about it, but he knew. She knew he knew.

In that moment of rage, that moment of pure, undiluted rage where all of Nora's thoughts were honed in on Noah, she felt a tug. Someone familiar reached out to her and, without thinking, she pulled them towards her.

Chapter 38 - Noah

Knees hitting the floor painfully, all Noah could see were the petrified Guardians and the fear that was etched onto Layla's face, which mirrored his own.

"GET OUT OF HERE! NOW!" a booming voice echoed in Noah's mind, and he was shown an image of an old, deserted-looking hut on top of a hill.

Noah grabbed Layla by the wrist and, sprinting, flung the two of them behind the pillar he'd hidden behind in his dreams, trying to keep them from view.

No sooner had he done that, two horrifying, shadowy masses skulked over to the Guardians, looking directly at where they had been a split second before. "I'm sure I saw something here a second ago," a feminine voice, akin to the sound of nails on a chalkboard, exclaimed. "It looked like two humans."

"You're as blind as you are useless, Tick," the other replied, in a deep, scratchy, male voice. "Very," the male explained, at Tick's confused expression.

Tick hissed furiously, a black energy ball expanding in her hand. "What was that, Scratch?"

Noah could have sworn that the hollow sockets, where Scratch's eyes should have been, rolled in exasperation. "Only an idiot would put *you* in charge," he heard him mutter.

"What did you say?" Tick asked again, the ball of energy in her hand crackling dangerously.

"I said we'd better get back to our post," Scratch exuded more loudly, not even trying to hide the fact this was clearly not what he'd said.

"Of all the people I'm stuck with," Tick muttered furiously, the energy ball in her hand dissolving into thin air.

Noah watched as the two of them skulked back to their posts and breathed a sigh of relief.

"They're gone," Layla hissed in his ear. "Concentrate on that hut."

Nodding, Noah closed his eyes and tried to focus on his breathing, instead of the pounding of his heart, but after five unsuccessful attempts to energetically connect with the mandala, Noah let out a low, frustrated, groan. "It's not working," he muttered to Layla. "We need to get out of here."

"I know that!" Layla hissed. "How are we supposed to concentrate when we're in some random place with Shadow Beings everywhere?"

"You don't know where we are?" Noah asked, surprised.

"Of course I don't!" Layla replied in a loud whisper. "We must be in the Realm, judging by those Shadow Beings, but we could be anywhere! This place must be run by Garvan though, if he's asked his minions to keep watch."

Noah contemplated not telling Layla where they were, so she wouldn't freak out any more than she already was, but then remembered that the two of them needed to be completely in sync to be able to use the mandala.

"Dammit," Noah muttered to himself, then explained to Layla, "We're not just in any part of Garvan's territory we're right in the centre of it all. This is the Guardians' Temple."

"What?" Layla replied, her face paling. "So… those statues in the middle of the room…"

"They're Simmy's siblings. The eleven Guardians."

Layla's face went from a look of fear to one of absolute terror. She grabbed hold of Noah's shoulders with a vice-like grip and looked him dead in the eyes. "We. Need. To. Get. Out. Of. Here."

Noah pulled Layla to his chest. "We will," he said, more confidently than he felt. "We managed to harness enough power to get *to* the Realm, we can do it again to get *out* of the Realm. I think this is my fault anyway. My mind wasn't clear when we were at Simmy's. I was thinking about Nora, which must be why we were transported to this spot."

"You're an idiot," Layla whispered, her voice wavering as she pulled herself out of Noah's arms. "Do you think we can get back to Simmy's?"

"I doubt it. If we could, I think whoever told us to get out before would have told us to go there, instead of to that hut," replied Noah.

"Hmm," Layla hummed in reply. "Okay, but first we need to get out of this room. Seeing those Guardians is giving me the creeps, and I need to focus. Those two minions of Garvan's didn't seem the smartest. Do you think we could get past them?"

"We don't have any other choice. I don't know my way around the temple," Noah breathed, risking a look around the pillar to check their surroundings. Keeping the mandala tightly squeezed in their hands, Noah and Layla quietly moved along the outer walls of the room. Breathing and moving as silently as possible was hard, and Noah had to force his teeth not to chatter. Judging from how hard Layla was gripping Noah's elbow, she was fighting to keep her own fear at bay as well.

Scratch was standing near a large window, his shoulders slightly slumped, like he would rather be anywhere else but here, and Tick was sitting on a long lounge with a high back, flicking through a magazine, clearly bored out of her brain.

"It doesn't look like we'll be able to get out with Scratch standing there. He could see us at any second," Layla whispered from behind Noah's left shoulder.

"We'll have to try and create a distraction—" Noah stopped talking abruptly, his heart lurching with more fear than he'd ever felt in his life.

Tick was looking directly at them.

Layla's nails dug into Noah's arm painfully, but he could barely feel it for the adrenaline coursing through his veins.

In the blink of an eye, Tick went from lounging on the couch to menacingly standing in front of them.

Noah couldn't move. His mind was screaming at him to do something—anything!—but his body was frozen stiff.

Tick's eyes went from Noah's face to the mandala that was tightly clasped in his hands.

Sneering, Tick took a step back to fully take in her victims. "I'll be taking that from you now," she hissed viciously. Swift as a cat, Tick lurched forwards and grabbed the mandala in her shadowy claws. But as soon as she touched it, the mandala rejected her, and a burning hot surge of white energy exploded from the sunstones, causing her hand to completely melt away. Tick screamed in agony, holding her melted stump in front of her face.

Scratch, distracted, hadn't noticed anything until this point and turned sharply to see where the commotion was coming from. In an instant, like Tick had done, he'd transported himself from his post to right in front of Noah and Layla.

Tick's screams woke Noah's frozen body up, and pure adrenaline took over. "Run!" he screamed at Layla, holding the still-burning mandala out in front of them, forcing her to move her legs as he pushed forwards.

"KILL THEM!" Tick screamed at Scratch, throwing a ball of black energy at Noah and Layla's retreating backs, missing Noah's right ear by millimetres.

Sprinting desperately towards a red, shimmering doorway in the corner of the room, Noah could see that Layla was still in shock.

"Snap out of it, Layla!" Noah screamed desperately. "I need your help!"

His screams seemed to have worked. Layla finally gripped the mandala tightly in her hand and swung it—and Noah—around to face the two Shadow Beings. "Burn them!" she shouted, pouring her life energy into the mandala.

Feeling the same burning sensation as before, Noah concentrated his own life energy into the attack, visualising the two Shadow Beings becoming wisps of smoke in front of them.

BOOM!

A giant ball of emerald energy was fired from the centre of the mandala, hitting the Shadow Beings dead on.

"We got them," Layla choked, pausing to see the damage.

As the smoke cleared, Noah's heart dropped as he saw the two Shadow Beings standing, unscathed, before them.

"Did you really think a weak attack like that could hurt me?" Tick screeched, her eyes shining a furious red.

She raised her uninjured arm above her head, forming a

black energy ball, electricity crackling around the outside of it.

Noah knew that they were in trouble. Their attack had done nothing, and no matter how fast they ran, Tick and Scratch could teleport to them in an instant.

In the same moment that thought crossed Noah's mind, Scratch had teleported from beside Tick to standing directly in front of them.

"Move Scratch, or I'll kill you too!" Tick screeched.

Noah was frozen again. It was the end. Everything leading to this point had been for nothing. Garvan would control the Realm, and he would never see Nora again.

He felt Scratch's clawed hand dig painfully into his right shoulder. Closing his eyes, Noah waited for death, but instead felt a lurching sensation.

Tick screamed furiously in the distance.

Chapter 39 - Nora

What the *shit* was going on outside?

One moment Nora was tugging on that bond, and the next she was trying to peer her way through the red barrier surrounding her door to find out what the commotion outside her room was.

Five minutes was all it took for dread to settle in her stomach as she managed to glimpse Noah sprinting towards her room, tugging Layla behind him, followed by a raging Tick aiming an enormous, crackling, black energy ball at them.

"Noah! Layla!" Nora screamed, pounding on the barrier, even going so far as to cover her hand in her own energy and punching it multiple times to see if it would break. It didn't, and judging from the agony in her hand, she'd broken a few fingers instead.

Desperately trying to peer through the barrier again, she saw the blurred figure of Aaron as Scratch appear right next to Noah and Layla, his claws digging into their shoulders. Nora's heart lurched as she saw him shoot her a look she couldn't decipher before disappearing into thin air.

They were gone.

All three of them had left her.

A sob wracked Nora's body as she slid to the floor, clutching her broken hand.

She was alone.

Again.

Chapter 40 - Noah

Noah's knees buckled as he hit the ground, and his stomach lurched uncomfortably as he tried to keep his breakfast down.

He couldn't hear Tick anymore.

Forcing his eyes open, the first thing he saw was the hut he'd been shown when they first arrived in the Realm from the bottom of the hill where he had landed.

What are we doing here?

"Stay away from me!" Layla screamed. "Noah! Help me!"

Snapping his head up, Noah turned, wildly searching for Layla. He found her next to the hut, with the large shadowy form of Scratch standing over her.

"Layla!" he screamed, snatching up the mandala that was lying next to him.

Noah focused all his energy into an attack, but the mandala flickered uselessly in his hands.

"The mandala isn't going to attack me, Noah," Scratch said, slowly looking at him from his perch on the hill.

"Why did you bring us here?" Noah demanded, ignoring Scratch's last statement, trying to focus his energy once more, but again, the mandala refused to work.

"Dammit," Noah muttered angrily, shaking it. "Work!"

"I've already told you, the mandala won't attack me." Scratch flicked his finger towards himself in a come hither motion, and the mandala came flying out of Noah's hands, floating willingly towards him.

Before Noah could open his mouth in protest, Scratch grabbed hold of the mandala with a clawed hand and, instantly, it lit up like a miniature sun. Noah felt a soft warmth fill him from the tips of his toes to the top of his crown.

Why was the mandala working for Scratch but not himself?

The light continued to shine so brightly that Noah had to shield his eyes with his hands. He could vaguely see Layla leaning against the wall of the hut as she struggled to stay upright, but he couldn't sense that she was in any danger. After a few moments, the mandala's light began to dim.

Once the white spots in his vision cleared and Noah's eyes had adjusted again, his mouth dropped open. Standing where Scratch had been was a tall, extremely good looking man with cropped black hair, tanned skin and vivid blue eyes.

A cheeky grin stretched across his face at the look of shock on Noah's.

"Um." Noah drew the word out, hesitating, "You're not a Shadow Being?"

"Nope," Scratch replied.

Noah continued to gape at the stranger, until he noticed Layla struggling to stand up.

Turning to look at her, Scratch gave Layla a guilty smile. "Ahh, sorry about that. We had a bit of a rough landing."

Noah took a hesitant step towards Layla and saw that her leg was twisted in a very painful-looking angle. His stomach gave another uncomfortable lurch. He'd never been good with broken bones.

Before he had a chance to turn away, Noah saw Scratch mumble something under his breath, which made Layla's cheeks turn pink, and the mandala turned a warm blue colour.

Even with her pink cheeks, Layla looked hesitant as Scratch moved the mandala over her injured leg, but she didn't try to stop him, nor did she complain.

Noah guessed that she was curious about Scratch too as the mandala needed a strong connection with someone for it to work.

After five minutes of treating Layla's leg, Scratch stood up and wiped the sweat from his brow with his forearm. "Phew. It's been a while since I've healed with a relic. I'm a bit out of practice. Luckily it was a simple break. You should be able to stand now," he said to Layla.

Layla hesitatingly tried bending her knee.

Noah's mouth dropped open again as the leg that had been badly broken a few minutes earlier was healed to the point that Layla could hop on it.

"Who are you?" Noah turned to Scratch and asked. "The mandala doesn't listen to just anyone. Why does it work for you?"

"Because I created it," Scratch answered simply. "And my name is Aaron."

Layla had stopped hopping as soon as those words left Aaron's mouth. "*You* created the mandala?" she asked incredulously. "How old are you?"

"I'm Zion's younger brother. So fairly old," Aaron chuckled.

Both Noah and Layla were lost for words. A Shadow Being they'd thought was going to kill them less than half an hour ago had turned out to be Zion's younger brother *and* the craftsman of their mandala.

The day had taken an unexpected turn.

Aaron allowed the two of them to gather their thoughts as he pulled a chequered handkerchief from his pocket and started to clean the mandala.

Noah could have sworn he saw the mandala shiver under Aaron's touch.

Noticing that Noah was watching him, Aaron held the handkerchief out. "Would you like to try?" he asked. "It's important to take care of your relics."

Noah nodded wordlessly and made his way to the top of the hill and sat down on the grass next to Aaron, who handed him the handkerchief and the mandala. "This mandala's name is Vajrayana," he explained. "It means *'the mind is a power source representing various divine magic at work in the universe.'* Since a mandala is a symbol for an enlightened mind, I thought it would be the perfect name for this relic, don't you think so?" Aaron questioned as he watched Noah carefully cleaning Vajrayana.

Vajrayana gave a shudder, and a hiss of steam puffed from its largest sunstone.

Noah gasped and tossed the mandala in the air.

Chuckling, Aaron caught it and handed it back to him. "She likes to be called Ray though."

Noah nodded wordlessly, taking back Ray. He was concentrating so hard on polishing the sunstones that he forgot to reply, but it didn't seem to bother Aaron, who sat there twiddling his thumbs, watching Noah from the corner of his vivid blue eyes.

After a while, Layla, who'd been testing out her healed leg, sauntered over to where the two of them were sitting and joined them on the grass.

The three of them sat in silence, Noah concentrating on Ray while Aaron appeared to be very interested in his fingernails as Layla stared unwaveringly at him.

"Why were you pretending to be a Shadow Being?" Layla fired at Aaron bluntly.

"Zion asked me to," Aaron replied, equally as blunt, without lifting his eyes.

"Did you know that we were going to arrive at the temple? Were you there to guide us?" Layla shot again.

"No," Aaron answered, this time lifting his eyes to look at Layla. "The two of you showing up was not part of our immediate plan. In fact, it's thrown quite a spanner in the works."

"Oh," replied Layla. Noah knew she was unsure how to respond to that.

Noah took a moment to look up from Ray and scrutinise Aaron. He couldn't sense any hostile energy coming from him. In fact, it felt to Noah that Aaron was happy to be out of the temple. "You're overjoyed to lose the restrictions of being a Shadow Being, aren't you?" Noah asked him slyly.

A grin stretched over Aaron's face. "It's nice to be free. I'm able to be my own person again. That Tick is a nasty piece of work, but she's smart. I had to work hard to not give away that I wasn't actually a Shadow Being."

Noah chuckled. Aaron didn't seem like such a bad guy.

Layla, on the other hand, didn't look convinced. Narrowing her eyes at Aaron, she waited a few moments before firing more questions at him.

"Why are you so excited that a task Zion entrusted you with is over before it was meant to be finished?" she demanded.

"Because it was an awful, tedious task," Aaron groaned,

flopping onto his back and dramatically covering his face with the back of his hand.

"It was in order to stop Garvan though, wasn't it?" Layla fired again.

"Yes…" Aaron drew his answer out. "But I don't think I'm needed there anymore. You two arrived earlier than expected, so it was really quite lucky that you ran into me as quickly as you did."

Layla responded to Aaron with an untrusting grunt, keeping her green eyes glued to him as if trying to x-ray him.

This didn't go unnoticed by Aaron, who threw his hands in the air in jest. "Calm down, Layla! I'm not a bad guy. Just ask Noah. He can sense energies, can't you?" Aaron turned to him and continued, "Do you sense any evil intent in my energy?"

Noah, who had no idea what Aaron was talking about, gave an awkward "Err…" in response.

"You're just trying to confuse him," accused Layla.

"No, I'm not," Aaron replied calmly. "Focus, Noah. You've sensed energies before. Now you just need to concentrate on being more specific. Keep your eyes open. You can't go and close your eyes every time you need to feel something. That's a very easy way to get killed."

Noah, who'd closed his eyes as soon as Aaron had said 'concentrate', opened them with a guilty expression on his face.

"No need for distress." Aaron waved a dismissive hand at Noah, a smile on his face. "These are new tricks you're learning, you're not going to master them straight away. But concentrate now. Don't look at me, look through me. Look deeper than the outer shell that is my body and connect with the energy that courses through me."

Ray, who Noah had forgotten he was still holding, shuddered between his fingers. *Look through him, not at him,* Noah thought to himself.

"You don't need to do this," Layla said to Noah, but he could tell by the tone of her voice that she was curious as to whether or not he would actually be able to.

Taking a deep breath and clenching his fingers tighter around Ray, Noah focused on connecting with his own energy first.

An amber light filled Noah's senses. It was his energy, the same light that had entered Ray back on Earth.

Using the energy within himself, Noah focused on feeling the same sensation around Aaron.

It only took him a couple of tries to connect his own energy to Aaron's life energy, and, like Aaron had said, Noah couldn't feel a single negative vibe. It was actually the opposite. Noah felt like laughing.

A grin slowly began to spread across his face, and no matter how hard he tried to stop it, his smile could soon rival the Cheshire cat's.

"What are you grinning about?" Layla asked suspiciously. "What are you doing to him?" she demanded of Aaron.

Aaron, whose grin matched Noah's, laughed. "I'm not doing anything," he insisted. "Noah's just sensing my energy and it's making him happy. Isn't that right, Noah?"

Noah shook his head and cleared Aaron's energies from his own. "Yeah, he's right," Noah said to Layla as soon as he felt back to his normal self. "I couldn't sense anything negative from him."

Layla sighed. "I thought you'd say that. But don't you think it's too convenient that we've landed in the Realm and met up with Zion's brother straight away?"

"There was always a chance of this happening," Aaron replied to her. "There are infinite futures available to us. Every choice we make has the ability to impact which one we experience, and this was one scenario that Zion warned me about. Although, to be honest with you, there was a very slim chance of it happening."

"So you knew we were coming?" Noah asked.

"I didn't know you would land right in the middle of the Throne Room," Aaron said, grimacing, "but I knew that there was a chance that you would be leaving Simmy's guidance earlier than expected, in which case, I would then need to take over."

"You were the one who showed us the image of the hut and told us to get out when we first arrived, weren't you?" Layla asked.

"I was," Aaron replied. Noah noticed a flicker of something cross Aaron's face. Fear? Regret? What would he have to be afraid or regretful of?

Sighing again, Layla stood up and stretched her legs. "Is there any way we can get in touch with Simmy to let her know we're safe for the time being?" she asked.

"I'm sure she's already been informed," Aaron said. "Zion wouldn't let her undergo her mission with her mind focused on the two of you." His tone implied there was to be no further questions regarding Simmy or her mission. Noah cast his eyes down, and even Layla stopped firing questions.

"We don't have much time before you two need to make your move," Aaron said seriously. "I can train you, but I'm not going to go easy on you. If the two of you really are the

Realm's last hope for peace, then you need to learn a lot of skills in a very short amount of time. Are you up for it?"

Noah and Layla looked at each other and then at Aaron. "We made the decision back on Earth that we would become the new Guardians," Noah said. "We knew the risks, and that it wouldn't be easy."

"Good," Aaron straightened, all traces of humour leaving his face. "A lot of people are relying on you."

Layla took Ray in her left hand while Noah continued holding the mandala in his right. "Anything you can teach us would be appreciated."

"First things first," Aaron said, as he took them both in, "Show me what you know, and we'll work from there."

Chapter 41 - Noah

Aaron's training was rigorous. The easy-going demeanour he'd projected when they'd first met was gone, and in its place was a tough, knowledgeable man who pushed Noah and Layla to their limits.

Noah and Layla would practice a new skill for hours until Aaron felt they'd truly mastered it. If there was even the smallest error in their output, Aaron ordered the two of them to work on their technique until they were able to complete it successfully over and over again, then he would make sure they'd be able to use it while under fire as well.

And Aaron fired at them without hesitation.

"Again!" Aaron shouted from his perch at the top of the hill. "If you're not able to block your enemies' advances, you're not going to have an opening to stop them."

BOOM!

A blue energy ball flew past Noah's right ear as he grabbed Layla, throwing the two of them on the ground to dodge it.

"We've been going at this for hours!" Layla screamed at Aaron, wiping dirt off her face with even dirtier hands.

BOOM!

Another energy ball hit the ground directly in front of Noah's feet, barely missing him as he scrambled back.

"You're not going to get a break when you're fighting Garvan and his cronies," Aaron called, a hard edge to his voice.

"It's almost dark now. We've spent all our energy today. It would be pointless to keep going," Layla said, her voice cracking from exhaustion.

"I need a break too, Aaron. We can start again in the morning," Noah said, standing and pulling a shaky Layla up off the ground.

Aaron hesitated for a second, then his latest ball of energy dissolved back into the palm of his hand. "If that's what you two really want. But you're not going to get stronger by stopping the second you hit the walls of your comfort zone. You're going to need to dig deeper."

Noah walked Layla back to the hut, gently nudged her inside and closed the door behind her as she flicked on the lights, remaining outside to finish his conversation with Aaron.

"We know," he said, "but we've been at this since we arrived here, and nothing's pushing us past that point right now, regardless of how hard the training's been today." Noah slumped onto the steps near the front door, pushing a piece of sweaty blond hair out of his eyes before dropping his face in his hands, not bothering to wipe away the sweat running down his nose. Another droplet would just take its place anyway.

Aaron counted on his fingers as he spoke. "You've mastered sensing other energies around you, how to hide your own energy so no one can sense you, a camouflage cloak, a simple attack blast, and you've almost mastered blocking," he said, "but there is still much for the two of you to learn. You've barely scratched the surface of what you're capable of."

263

"How much time do we have?" Noah asked, knowing this would be the major factor in their skill level when they finally came face to face with Garvan.

"Maximum amount of time, one and a half days. Minimum amount of time, we're discovered right now and have to fight," Aaron replied. "Tick would have told Garvan that I helped the two of you escape almost as soon as it happened, so he will be on the lookout, along with his new advisor. I'm sure you know who Garvan's advisor is by now." Aaron gave Noah a pointed look.

Noah could have sworn that he saw a flicker of guilt flash through Aaron's eyes, but he blinked and it was gone. Noah answered quietly, "Nora."

"I know she's your sister, Noah, but she's been exposed to Garvan's darkness for a long time now. It would be in your best interest to not trust everything she tells you," Aaron said softly.

Noah didn't reply. He knew what Aaron was saying made sense, but he trusted Nora. She wouldn't lead him astray.

"Has Garvan started his rebirth?" Noah asked, after a pause.

"He hadn't when you two arrived, but he's putting off the inevitable. There is a chance he may have decided to postpone it after he found out about me," replied Aaron.

"Is there any way we can find out?" asked Noah. "Wouldn't it be best to attack while Garvan is preoccupied?"

"It would be best for you two to gain as much exposure to the Realm as possible and improve your skills before barging into a warzone," Aaron answered drily. "With the state the two of you are in now, you'd be killed within seconds."

"Oh, right," Noah reluctantly agreed, "That makes sense."

Pulling blades of grass out of the ground, Noah tried to

focus on everything he'd learnt today, but his thoughts kept on drifting to his parents and Nora. He was sure none of them knew where he was right now. And what about Simmy? She'd planned to train him and Layla until they were ready to travel to the Realm safely. He'd really messed up.

But Aaron said himself that Simmy and Zion had planned ahead for this. Well, it would have been nice if they had told him and Layla about their plans. They weren't the ones who had to go up against Garvan!

Ray let out an angry hiss of steam, burning Noah's hand and bringing him back to reality as he gritted his teeth and dropped her. His hand was now red and throbbing painfully.

Once the pain subsided, Noah sighed and picked her up again, stroking Ray's largest sunstone to calm her down.

Ever since coming to the Realm and meeting Aaron, Ray had come alive.

The more skills Noah and Layla learnt, the more connected the three became.

It was nice in a way, but it also meant that Ray could sense when negative thoughts were entering their minds, and there was no time for that. All their energy needed to be spent on perfecting their skills.

Aaron gave a little chuckle. "I did make Ray quite sassy. She'll keep the two of you in check."

Noah placed an arm behind his head, laid back on the stairs and held Ray up in front of his face. "Is there any way to train faster? We still need to learn more attacks, don't we?"

"Yes," replied Aaron, lying down next to Noah, "but I had to take measures to ensure that if we were separated tonight, the two of you would at least be able to hide yourselves effectively. No attack will be useful if you're dead."

Aaron had a habit of speaking blunt truths. He didn't beat around the bush when it came to acknowledging the danger they were in now that Noah and Layla had made it to the Realm, which was something that Noah felt Simmy had tried to shield them from.

"In regards to learning the skills faster," Aaron continued, "why do you think I've been blasting you with energy balls all afternoon? For enjoyment?"

"Yes," Noah replied drily.

Aaron gave a guilty laugh. "I'll admit I enjoyed it a little, but I needed to put you two under a certain amount of pressure to release your potential. You can't keep tapping into your energy source with your eyes closed, taking deep breaths. Yes, that is the most accurate way of tapping into your full potential as a newbie on Earth, but if you're doing that in the middle of a battle here in the Realm you're going to get yourself killed. Unless, of course, you create a powerful enough shield around you that can block out all enemy advances, but you'd need to do that under pressure as well. You'll learn these skills a lot faster by doing them whilst having to focus on something else. This way, you two will know you're able to manifest anything you need while still being able to focus on the task at hand."

Noah didn't say anything, instead nodding absently. While focusing on his breath and visualising everything he needed was powerful, he knew that they couldn't rely on that in the midst of a battle.

"Go and get some rest," Aaron said to Noah after a pause. "You need to keep your energy levels up. There's food inside the hut."

"Okay," replied Noah, sitting up with a groan.

"Give Ray to me," said Aaron, leaning up on his elbow and holding out his hand. "She's been out of work for a while and needs some fine-tuning. You'll find she'll be easier to use in the morning."

"Ah, thanks," Noah said, handing Ray over and standing up, stretching his arms to the sky. He enjoyed the pull in his muscles for a couple of seconds before making his way inside the hut. "Thanks for today. We appreciate your help."

Aaron grinned at Noah as he began tuning Ray with his own energies. "No problem. You're the saviours of the Realm, after all. We need to get you in tip-top shape."

Noah laughed. "Sure, sure. You were just having fun with us this afternoon."

Aaron didn't reply, but he grinned as each of his fingers shot out a different coloured energy beam into Ray's sunstones.

Noah watched as the sunstones changed colour to match Aaron's energy and then shot the light back into Aaron's fingertips.

After a moment, Aaron and Ray began to exchange energies in a pattern, almost as if they were playing a song.

Entranced, Noah watched the two of them for a few more minutes before deciding to head inside. He was filthy and needed a long, hot shower.

Opening the door to the hut, Noah saw Layla sitting on a long squishy couch, watching Aaron from the window.

"He's incredible," she breathed, not taking her eyes away from Aaron.

Noah felt a small twinge in his gut but quickly pushed it down. This wasn't the time for jealousy.

"I mean, look at the way he can control his energy. Ray is pretty much singing in his hands," Layla continued. "To think, we'll be able to do that soon."

"I think Aaron's had a lot more practice than us," Noah replied to her, his voice harsher than he'd intended it to be, but it fell on deaf ears. Layla either hadn't heard Noah, or she was blatantly ignoring him.

"Well, I'm going for a shower," Noah muttered, but again, Layla gave no indication that she'd heard him, opting to continue staring at Aaron from the window.

Pulling off his shirt, Noah grabbed a towel from the cupboard and sauntered to the bathroom.

Inside there was a spare toothbrush and even a razor for Noah to use. Zion had indeed planned for all possible futures, having provided enough supplies for both Noah and Layla to live in the hut for a short amount of time.

Looking in the mirror, Noah noticed the stubble on his cheeks and the bottom of his chin, which seemed to grow back straight away these days, and started to shave them off. Doing it without shaving cream was awkward, but Noah hated the stubble. It made him itch. *Aaron could pull off a five o'clock shadow,* he thought to himself, then yelped as he nicked himself with the razor.

"Dammit!" he muttered, frustrated at himself for letting something as stupid as Aaron's facial hair get under his skin.

He needed to sort things out with Layla if they were ever going to have a chance of fully becoming united as one mind. They were very obviously two bodies and two minds right now, and they needed to clear all baggage before they could hope to move forwards.

Irritated, Noah chucked his razor in the sink and turned the shower to its highest pressure, trying to drown out the world for a few minutes. He waited until steam filled the bathroom, then stepped into the pouring water, letting the heat wash the day away.

After a few minutes, Noah's muscles finally relaxed, and he slipped into a silent meditation, taking deep breaths and thanking the Realm for everything it had provided for them. It was only a small amount of time, but Noah's mind became much clearer. The frustrations he'd been feeling beforehand slipped down the drain with the water.

Opening his eyes, Noah came to a new resolve. He grabbed the soap off the shelf and gave himself a quick wash to remove the dirt that had accumulated after being blasted by Aaron so much that afternoon.

He needed to talk to Layla.

Noah's heart was skipping beats erratically as he thought through his plan, and he took his time drying off and dressing so as to pluck up the courage to actually follow through with what he needed to do.

Taking a deep breath, Noah flung open the bathroom door with more force than he'd anticipated, scrunching up his face as it slammed into the hallway wall.

Aaron and Layla, who had been chatting, stopped and turned to Noah.

"Sorry," Noah whispered to the two of them, tiptoeing into the bedroom, his damp hair falling into his eyes.

Softly closing the bedroom door behind him, Noah ran to his bed and hid his head under the pillow, mentally berating himself for hiding away and not going straight to Layla like he'd planned.

The soft creak of the door went unnoticed by Noah, but the pressure on the mattress from someone sitting next to him on the bed didn't.

Stiffening, Noah didn't dare move as he felt a soft hand gently rest on his back.

"Noah," Layla called to him lightly. "Get out from under the pillow. You look ridiculous."

The words were harsh, but the tone of voice Layla used was so gentle that Noah felt he had no choice but to pull the pillow off his head. Rolling over, he saw there was nowhere to escape in the small bedroom. He moved to sit up, but Layla placed her hand on his chest.

Abs burning and heart pounding, Noah stopped moving as he took in Layla's flushed face, noticing a hint of determination in her eyes.

Not one to beat around the bush—something Noah realised she'd picked up from living with Simmy for so long, as it appeared to be a trait of Realm inhabitants—Layla spoke. "We need to become two bodies and one mind, right?" she asked. Noah nodded. "And we're not going to do that with the confusion from our kiss last night."

Noah nodded again. This was what he'd wanted to speak with her about, but he had to admit he was grateful she was the one bringing it up instead of him. He knew his voice would've been shaking.

"Ray has become more powerful. She knows that there is unresolved tension between the two of us," said Layla, her face flushing even more.

Noah didn't say anything. He was preoccupied with Layla's flushed cheeks.

His heart skipped another beat.

"I'm not very good at chatting about... feelings," said Layla quietly.

Noah swallowed the lump in his throat. "Me either," he

croaked.

Layla's face moved closer.

There was a freckle under Layla's right eye that Noah hadn't noticed before.

"They say that actions speak louder than words..." Layla whispered.

"That's true," Noah's voice was barely audible.

Layla closed her eyes at the same time Noah did.

A soft pressure sent tingles down Noah's spine as Layla gently brushed her lips against his.

Electricity exploded through his veins, and he responded by pushing himself up into a sitting position and pulling Layla against him as he tangled a hand in her red curly hair.

Their two hands that were an inch apart on the bed had green and amber energy sparking and connecting in the middle, but Noah barely noticed. His mind was completely overrun by the feeling of Layla's lips against his and the way she tilted her head, giving him more access.

He could have stayed like this forever.

BOOM!

A loud explosion forced the two of them apart.

"Sorry!" a muffled apology called from the living room.

Looking wildly at each other, the unspoken energy crackling between them gave Noah goosebumps as they caught their breath.

Not wanting to leave the bedroom but deciding to make sure everything was alright, Noah stood up. As he walked outside he forced a massive grin off his face. He didn't want to explain to Aaron what had just happened.

Chapter 42 - Aaron

T he kids weren't very subtle.

The energy that was flowing into Ray was palpable. So much so that Aaron had to put her down, tuning her now out of the question.

Rubbing the bridge of his nose with his thumb and forefinger, Aaron doubled over, a stab of pain pierced his gut.

He knew where it had come from.

Well, actually, he knew *who* it had come from.

There was no way Nora hadn't noticed what had gone on outside her room. Noah and Layla had been so close to her when he'd had to teleport them away. If he'd been in his current form, he would have had to open a portal, but Garvan had given them a small fragment of his energy that had allowed him and Tick to teleport anywhere at will.

He wondered if Garvan had taken that gift away from Tick now that Aaron had abused it.

But Tick wasn't the one who was behind this ache in his stomach. Nora was. They had become connected when he'd shown himself to her, connected in a way he hadn't been with anyone before. The only people that were important in his life were his brother Zion and his nieces and nephews. But this was different. Nora called to him on a different level, and not running straight to help her was proving damn near impossible.

No matter how hard he'd tried to go against the Realm's guidance and get her out of that miserable room, he hadn't been able to. His role as a Protector of the Realm kept him from drastically changing the events that needed to unfold.

He didn't know *why* Nora needed to be with Garvan, but whatever reason it was, changing it would create a rift in the Realm so large that the entire Realm could collapse. So, no matter how much it destroyed him, he had to keep guiding Nora in small, almost unnoticeable ways.

Not that she would ever know that.

She probably felt like he'd just up and left her. Judging from the rage she was shooting at him, it sure felt like that's what she believed.

Sighing, Aaron let his hand glow in a blue, healing light and placed it on his stomach, relieving the stabbing pains in his abdomen. While he was doing it, he tried to reach out to Nora telepathically, using the moments the two of them had shared together to connect.

But as soon as he got close, a solid amber wall of telepathic energy slammed into him, hitting him so hard that he physically shot back into the couch, his hands splayed beside him.

Eyes wide, Aaron waited for the onslaught of energy to recede before daring to move.

What was that? he thought to himself, panting as the energy slowly ebbed away.

Risking the connection once more, trying to make sure Nora was okay, Aaron sent out a tentative tendril of sapphire energy in her direction.

"LEAVE ME ALONE!"

273

The message slammed into his mind, snapping his head back painfully causing a loud BOOM as it hit the wall.

A trickle of blood leaked out of Aaron's nose, and he slowly wiped it away, panting.

Where did that power come from?

Looking at his sleeve that was now smudged with red, Aaron leant back into the couch, exhausted.

That power... Maybe she harboured more than he realised. Maybe that's why the Realm had stopped him from interfering with her, because she could tip the table of this battle in an instant.

Grinning, Aaron held back the desire to reach out to her once more, if only to see how she would react, knowing it would end up hurting him again.

Maybe I should just let this play out, he thought, making a mental note to check in on the Throne Room more often.

The creak of a door pulled his attention, and he gave a quick thumbs up to Noah, who had peeked his head out to check if everything was okay, before picking Ray back up again, absently shining her with his chequered handkerchief.

Chapter 43 - Nora

That insufferable bastard had woken her up. She'd been having such a pleasant dream about kicking the shit out of him for leaving her here.

It had taken her *hours* to get to sleep, and then he'd just come along and bothered her for no reason.

He didn't care about her. He'd done nothing to try and help her while he was here. Why the hell was he reaching out to her now?

Letting out a frustrated sigh, Nora looked at her shaking hands.

She'd let out a bit more anger than she'd intended to, and now she was exhausted.

Once she'd managed to get to her feet after the others had left, she'd spent the rest of the day training. There would be no more relying on others. There would be no more false hope that someone would get her out of this.

This was her battle now, and she would do whatever she had to in order to free herself.

Gritting her teeth, her thoughts flashed to Noah.

He'd known she was in here. She'd shown him this room in the vision. He should have tried harder to get to her.

If Noah had been one hundred percent certain that you were here, he would have come for you, her thoughts reasoned with her.

Nora sighed.

He *was* pulling Layla to her door right as Aaron grabbed them and teleported them away.

Nora let out a low growl. *"Aaron,"* she hissed. If only he'd done more to help her—if only he'd actually cared about her enough to get her out of here—maybe they could have worked to overthrow Garvan together!

A silent tear rolled down Nora's cheek as her stomach clenched. She ignored the dull ache in her heart that told her she'd begun to rely on him too much. But she genuinely thought he was starting to care about her… thought he *wanted* to help her… thought something was starting to blossom between them.

Clearly, she was wrong.

And she wouldn't be making that mistake again.

Throwing on a cool mask of nonchalance, Nora wiped away the rogue tear and schooled her face to show nothing.

She was in charge now.

"Good, you're awake," a dry voice said to her through her barrier. "I have a job for you."

Nora turned to Garvan, twisting on her bed so she was facing him. "Whatever you need," she purred.

Chapter 44 - Noah

After a surprisingly restful night's sleep, Noah woke up the next morning to a series of obstacle courses set out down the hill near the hut.

"What's all this?" Noah asked Aaron, who was balancing on top of a very tall wooden pole.

"Part training, part distraction for anyone who may decide to pop around today," Aaron replied, jumping down from his perch and lightly landing in front of Noah.

"Right…" Noah said slowly, wondering if he'd be able to do that one day.

"Here," Aaron said, handing Ray back to Noah. "She's in tip-top shape now. Seemed to enjoy a large influx of energy last night," he drawled, giving Noah a sneaky look.

Noah's face flushed, but he said nothing as he took Ray from Aaron.

"Good morning," Layla called cheerily to the two of them as she walked outside. "I'm ready for a full day of training."

"I bet you are," Aaron mumbled, throwing Noah a sly look, which Noah pointedly ignored even though his face flushed even hotter.

Passing Ray to Layla, Noah couldn't help but give her a shy smile, which was returned as a quick peck on the cheek.

Aaron's smirk turned into a full grin as his eyebrows all but disappeared into his hairline.

Noah shoved Aaron in the ribs with his elbow and quickly dodged the playful energy ball that was sent his way.

Layla, who'd been ignoring the two of them, placed Ray in both her hands and weighed her. "Aaron," she said, "Ray seems heavier than yesterday."

"That's to be expected," replied Aaron. "I tuned her yesterday, so she's picking your energies up a lot easier, and you both gave her a good feed last night, so she's full to bursting."

Layla, whose face flushed as red as Noah's, merely nodded.

"Alright, let's finish off what we started yesterday. Blocking attacks. Remember, you need to learn to work as one mind. Don't get distracted," Aaron said, floating back up to the top of the pole where he had been perched earlier and aiming his hand at them.

"Ready?" he called, but shot a ball of energy at them without waiting for a reply.

Noah ran to Layla, grabbed her hand in one of his with Ray still clutched in the other, and jumped to the side to dodge Aaron's blast.

Neither of them had to say a word to know what the other was thinking, and Ray reacted at the slightest instruction.

Aaron shot another energy ball at them, and with a single thought of *'block'*, Ray produced a mirror-like surface in front of Noah and Layla, causing Aaron's energy ball to rebound straight back at him.

Catching the ball and sucking his energy back into his body, Aaron clapped and floated back to the ground. "Well done! Looks like you two are in complete unison today. Alright, let's move on to more advanced techniques. You can block now, so you need to learn how to attack properly. Everyone's skill sets are different, depending on the type of person they are. Simple energy balls, like the ones I've been using on you and the one I taught you yesterday, can be used by anyone, but they don't do much damage."

"Speak for yourself," Layla muttered, rubbing the bruises she'd accumulated.

Grinning, Aaron chose not to reply. "For example, I connect with music on a deep level, so I incorporate that into my attacks. Watch."

Aaron clicked his fingers and a tiny blue ball of energy the size of a pinhead appeared, hovering above his index finger. Next, Aaron whistled a tune, causing the ball to shudder and begin to fly around Noah and Layla, weaving in and out between their legs and around their ears.

Aaron then clapped his hands, and the energy ball stopped so suddenly that Noah looked everywhere trying to find it.

"Yah!" Aaron yelled, pointing his index finger in the direction of the pole he had been standing on.

The energy ball flew towards it and seemed to disappear, but a loud *CRACK!* Caused Noah to jump as the pole snapped in half and then disintegrated.

Gaping, Noah and Layla were lost for words. How powerful was Aaron, really?

"So that, for example, is the type of attack I can create by utilising musical influences like clicking, clapping, whistling and different vocal sounds," Aaron said calmly.

Not giving Noah and Layla a chance to bask in his glory, Aaron held out his hand for Ray, who flew straight to him.

"You two need to figure out an attack without Ray. In an ideal Realm, the two of you would be able to stick together for the entire journey, but we know that may not happen. You need to be able to rely on your own powers, as well as Ray's. Take ten minutes to figure out what you're good at, and we'll then be able to create an attack suited to your needs," Aaron instructed them.

"I don't need ten minutes," Layla replied instantly. "I already know what I can use."

"Perfect," Aaron said, clapping his hands together enthusiastically. "Well then, Noah, you get thinking while I help Layla."

"Oh, right, yup," Noah said, as he watched Aaron and Layla walk towards the hut and sit on the steps.

Sitting cross-legged on the ground, Noah thought about what he was good at.

There was nothing that immediately came to mind, no matter how hard he tried to think of his accomplishments, and before he knew it, Aaron strolled over to him while Layla was practising her attacks on the hut's steps.

"What did you come up with?" Aaron asked, as soon as he reached Noah.

"Erm…" Noah hesitated, racking his brain for anything that might be useful to him. "I'm not really good at anything," he finished lamely.

"Nonsense. Think harder."

Noah scrunched up his face and concentrated. "I mean, I'm good in the garden. I can take care of plants well. But I don't know how that's going to help me, unless I want to swing from vines and take Garvan out with a mushroom."

Aaron laughed. "No need to become a jungle man. Good in the garden… hmm…"

Noah watched as Aaron started to move his hands in

different angles in front of his body.

"Noah," said Aaron after a couple of minutes, "I want you to pick some grass."

"Uhh… Okay," Noah replied, unsure what this had to do with his training.

Pulling a few strands of grass out of the ground, Noah held them out in the palm of his hand.

"Yah!" yelled Aaron, pushing some of his energy into the blades.

The strands began to float in front of them, one of them growing larger and larger until it became a wooden bow.

"How did you do that?" Noah asked in awe, touching the bow with his fingers. It felt warm.

"I just inserted my energy into the grass to create something physical," Aaron replied simply.

"Uh-huh," Noah said slowly, not understanding what Aaron meant.

"You can take images that you've created in your mind, nurture them, and then bring them to life with your energy," explained Aaron. "Think of something that you can attack with and create it with another one of those little blades of grass."

"Attack with…" Noah mused. "Alright then."

Staring at the little blade of grass, Noah thought about a plastic dagger he used to play with as a kid. The silver blade, bronze hilt and small ruby that glistened at the top.

Noah thrust his own energy into the blade of grass with a "Yah!" and watched as it began to grow before his eyes. It was a little flimsy, but the shape was there.

Letting out a breathless laugh, Noah took the dagger in his hand and felt its grip. It was heavy.

"Throw it," Aaron encouraged.

Grinning, Noah focused on another thin pillar that Aaron had created for the obstacle course and held the dagger by its hilt, lifted his arm and threw it.

It hit its mark perfectly, being guided by Aaron's energy, and embedded itself in the hard wood.

"Wow," Noah said in awe.

"Wow indeed," Aaron replied. "Now you need to practise. Create some arrows to go with that bow, and think of other weapons you can create with those blades of grass. Everything made from an earth structure is intertwined, so there are no limits to what you can bring to life."

Nodding, Noah plucked out some more grass and turned them into wonky arrows in the air in front of him. A stark contrast to the perfect Bow Aaron had created.

"Now, keep your hand out and focus on your weapon," Aaron coached.

Concentrating on the arrows, Noah felt a heaviness in the palm of his hand as his energy expanded.

"Expel that energy into the arrow by pushing it from your hand. You might feel the inclination to yell when you do this, which is fine, don't fight it. Yelling is a natural way of allowing your body to release that force."

Unable to reply, Noah focused all his might on the arrows. "Yah!" he yelled.

For a split second, Noah could see his amber energy forcing its way from his hand and into the arrows.

It flickered for a moment before disappearing.

Disappointed, Noah turned to Aaron, who looked like Christmas had come early. "That was amazing!" he cheered. "I wasn't expecting you to do so well on the first go. Incredible!

Now keep practising while I go and check on Layla."

Feeling better about his attempt, Noah grinned. There was no way he was going to get it on the first go, he reminded himself. He also realised he'd been comparing himself to Aaron, which was ridiculous because Aaron was probably thousands of years old and had been fine-tuning his skills that whole time.

"Okay," Noah said to himself, slapping his cheeks. "Again."

He plucked the arrows from the air in front of him and focused his energy to the palm of his hand, this time expecting the heaviness that came.

"Yah!" yelled Noah, forcing the energy from his hand into the arrows in front of him. Like the first attempt, they glowed amber for a second before the energy disappeared into thin air.

"This is harder than it looks," Noah said to himself, panting from the effort.

"No slacking over there!" Aaron called to Noah from the hut. "Keep going until you've perfected it. Unless you want to train while being bombarded by energy balls again?"

"Yeah, yeah, I'm working," Noah hurriedly replied. There was no way he'd be able to master his new technique while trying to dodge those blasts.

So he trained. For hours. It was well into the afternoon by the time Noah had successfully embedded his energy into an arrow, and another hour until the arrow hit its mark in one go like he had done with the dagger that Aaron had helped him with.

Ignoring the need for a break, Noah pushed himself further by making sure he could create more weapons so he could attack more than once. He knew that Aaron was watching, and he needed to perfect this before he could rest.

Another hour passed, and Aaron walked over to Noah, placing a hand on his shoulder. "Good work," he said warmly. The hand on Noah's shoulder glowed a warm blue, and Noah's energy levels instantly felt replenished. Aaron was using the same healing technique he'd used on Layla their first night.

"You worked hard today. Your offence will be extremely powerful with more practice. You may even be able to produce something other than an arrow," laughed Aaron.

"Har har," Noah replied sarcastically. "Soon I'll overtake you," he said, shooting Aaron a crooked grin.

"In your dreams, little boy," replied Aaron, elbowing Noah in the ribs.

Grunting, Noah took the shock and then laughed, allowing his stiff legs to rest as he laid down on the grass.

"Can I create anything from an earth-based substance then?" Noah asked Aaron.

"Yes," Aaron replied. "Anything from vines to arrows, to wheat for food, as long as you focus the right energies into them. An attack energy will burn up wheat, but a nurturing energy will turn wheat into bread. It's all about focusing on what you need at the time and utilising it properly."

"How did you go today?" Layla asked Noah as she walked over to them.

Noah looked up at her and could see that she was covered in dust and visibly tired. He sat up and patted the grass next to him. "Good, I think," he replied as she sat down. "It took all day, but at least I know I can cause some damage when I need to."

"That's awesome," Layla replied, stretching her legs out in front of her.

Noah noticed that Aaron took this chance to silently slip inside, leaving the two of them alone.

"How about you?" Noah asked, tucking a strand of curly hair behind her ear.

"I managed to perfect mine today," Layla said, her face flushed a little at Noah's tenderness.

"Amazing," said Noah quietly. "You're amazing."

Layla's eyes flickered under Noah's gaze, and Noah's heart pounded as he placed a finger under her chin and lifted her face so that he could look her in the eye.

The gap between them grew smaller.

"Here you are, you insignificant worms," a familiar voice sneered at the two of them.

Noah and Layla jumped apart and looked wildly around to find the source of the voice.

BANG!

The door of the hut flung open, and Aaron burst out onto the dimly lit hillside, the sun beginning to set after their long day.

"Get out of here," he screamed at the two of them. "Run!"

Drawing a large circle with his arm, Aaron pushed a portal towards Noah and Layla. "Jump into this! It will take you somewhere safe!"

Checking to see that Layla was holding Ray, Noah frantically pulled her to her feet and ran towards the portal.

"Not this time!" the voice screeched, and the portal shattered into smithereens with the force of the black energy ball thrown at it.

"No!" Aaron yelled. "Tick! Tick! Where are you, you cow?"

An evil laugh came from directly behind Noah and Layla. Turning on his feet in an instant, Noah pulled Layla behind him, but she had other ideas.

"Take this, you bitch!" Layla yelled, pushing the palm of her hand out in front of her.

A large orange flame was thrown above their heads, illuminating the hillside, and Tick was thrust into the spotlight.

"Argh!" Tick screamed, covering her eyes with her clawed hands.

"Run! Now!" Aaron yelled. He sprinted towards the two of them, using an energy shield to push them down the hill while creating a lasso out of another beam of blue energy, pulling Tick towards himself.

Running faster than he ever had, somehow managing to keep a hold of Layla's hand, Noah and Layla flew down the hill at a frightening speed.

Noah dug his heels into the grass to slow their descent and turned to see Aaron and Tick battling at the top of the hill. Tick had snapped the lasso in half in her rage.

The power emanating from the two of them was overwhelming. Aaron had produced a tiny energy ball and was whistling so it stabbed through Tick again and again, impaling her with every attack.

Tick, being a shadow, became increasingly irritated by the blows, but they weren't enough to keep her down, and in a second when Aaron had to catch his breath, she had created an enormous black energy ball with purple electricity crackling around the outside and thrown it directly at Aaron.

Aaron's scream, as Tick's attack hit him square in the chest, sent chills down Noah's spine. He watched Aaron hit the floor.

"Aaron!" he yelled, turning to run back up the hill.

"Noah!" Layla called to him, gripping his hand tighter to

stop him from running away. "We can't."

"Let go of me, Layla!" Noah screamed, trying to pull away from her. "We need to help Aaron!"

"Aaron's fine," Layla said to him hurriedly. "A little attack like that won't keep him down."

Noah looked back up the hill, and, sure enough, Aaron was standing again, this time controlling two energy balls, piercing Tick at lightning speed.

"Noah, look! Noah!" Layla said urgently.

Still trying to escape from her iron grip, Noah turned to Layla, frustrated, to see what she wanted him to look at, and he paused in shock.

Walking towards them was Nora.

Chapter 45 - Layla

L ayla opened her mouth to call to her friend, but paused.

There was something off about her.

Nora kept her eyes firmly on Noah as she stalked towards them, a menacing smirk on her face.

It was only when a particularly loud shout from Aaron caught Nora's attention did she turn to see Tick standing over him, one of her sharp claws scraping across his neck, trying to separate it from the rest of his body. Aaron held her at bay, his hands covering her shadowy face, a bright light forcing its way through her body.

Nora's smirk turned even more sinister. She flicked a look at Layla for a brief moment, and Layla's head snapped back as something was flung into her.

"Good, you're awake," a dry voice said to her through her barrier. "I have a job for you."

Nora turned to Garvan, twisting on her bed so she was facing him. "Whatever you need," Nora purred as he stalked into her room, looking her up and down in her filthy state.

"If you'd bothered to let me bathe regularly, I wouldn't look like this," Nora said lazily as she waited for his eyes to stop roaming over her body, fighting down the shiver of disgust as he did so.

Garvan just gave her a cruel smile, slowly raising his eyes to hers. His wrinkled face seemed to have sagged even more since the last time she saw him.

"You're aware that I have somewhere else I need to be," he said, his long finger tapping the hilt of his golden staff.

"I am," Nora drawled, inspecting her fingernails as if she couldn't be less interested in this conversation.

If Garvan was irritated by Nora's lack of interest, he didn't show it. Instead, he stamped his cane into the ground once, creating a red and gold adorned stool for him to sit on.

"Old age getting the best of you?" Nora crooned, watching him slowly take a seat, the nimble agility that she had seen from him when they'd first met on Earth gone.

Garvan ignored her, keeping hold of his cane as his eyes roamed over her once more.

Nora forced herself to not grit her teeth at the sleazy look.

Garvan spoke once he'd finished taking in his eyeful of Nora. "It seems like your brother and your friend came to pay me a visit today. It was very rude of me not to attend them, so I'm going to need you to go in my place while I am otherwise occupied."

"I'm your messenger pigeon now, am I?" Nora asked, sitting up fully on the bed, resting her back against the wall and crossing her ankles in front of her.

"If that's what you'd like to call yourself, be my guest." Garvan waved her off absently, "I thought you might like to take this with you." Garvan tapped his cane on the floor one more time, and as he lifted it, a silver staff ascended out of the ground, a large mandala with black obsidian encasing the top of it.

"And what, pray tell, am I supposed to do with that?" Nora stared at the black energy surrounding the staff as every cell in her body screamed at her not to touch it.

"You'll find out soon enough," Garvan replied dismissively. "Think of it as a promotion gift." He stood, waved the stool he was sitting on away in a puff of smoke, then turned to leave her room.

"A bigger room with a bath would have been a much better gift," Nora called out as Garvan resealed the barrier behind him, but if he'd heard her, he gave no inclination.

Looking at the staff, Nora's body shook as she became covered in goosebumps.

"There's no way in hell that I'm touching that," *she thought to herself, grimacing.*

Knowing she'd have to move fast, Nora pulled a strand of hair from her head, stepped off the bed and let it softly fall onto the obsidian mandala, visualising another version of herself standing before her.

Holding back her gasp of shock that it actually worked, Nora jumped back as another Nora appeared. But this version showed no marks of the injuries she'd sustained here. It was wearing dark fighting leathers, its wavy blonde hair was pulled back into a braid, and the eyes were pitch black.

"You'll do fine." Nora grimaced as the puppet stared at her. "Do as the staff tells you," she instructed, hoping that she wasn't leading Noah and Layla to their doom.

Before she had a chance to change her mind, the puppet version of herself had picked up the staff and disappeared in a wisp of smoke. The only thing Nora could do was to quickly pull this memory from her mind and throw the silky ribbon of it into the smoke before it disappeared, willing the ribbon to find the person closest to it so they could know what was going on.

"Shit," Layla whispered, turning wildly to Noah.

Chapter 46 - Noah

"Nora?" Noah gasped, a smile slowly spreading on his face. But before he could get too excited, he realised something was wrong.

There were no signs of the bruises he'd seen on Nora in his vision a few days ago, and her eyes were no longer amber like his own. They were a deep black.

Noah gripped Layla's hand and held Ray in the other, vaguely noticing that Layla was trying to get his attention, but he was so distracted by Nora in front of him that he didn't pay her any notice.

"Hello, dear brother," Nora said in a distorted voice.

"Nora," Noah acknowledged. "Or... who are you really?"

"I'm disappointed," Nora said, placing a hand over her heart. "Has it really been so long that you can't even recognise your twin sister?"

Noah felt Layla tense beside him as she gripped his hand even tighter, trying to pull him away. Noah gripped her back absently, Aaron's words ringing in his ears: *I know that she's your sister, Noah, but she's been exposed to Garvan's darkness for a very long time. It would be in your best interest to not trust everything she tells you.*

"What do you want?" Noah asked, gripping Ray tightly in

his hand so he could block any attacks that might come their way.

"I've come to give you a message." Nora pulled a staff out from behind her back and spun it effortlessly in the air.

Noah stared at it hesitantly. It was a bit shorter than Nora, with a long, dark, silver handle and a mandala that looked identical to Ray on top, although the mandala was embedded with black obsidian stones instead of the sunstones Ray shone with.

Layla took Ray from Noah as he handed it to her, and Noah knelt down to pluck a blade of grass, using his new energy technique to turn it into a spear. He did this with his hand behind his back, praying that when he attempted to infuse his energy with it, it would work the first time.

Suddenly, a shimmering forcefield surrounded both himself and Layla, and Noah turned to see that Layla was staring Nora down.

Lazily, Nora blasted a ball of black energy towards the two of them causing the forcefield to shudder.

Noah gritted his teeth as Nora waved her hand, flinging energy ball after energy ball at them. Layla dug her heels into the ground, holding Ray in front of her to keep the shield from shattering.

Suddenly Noah's hand felt heavy, and he gripped his spear tightly, hoping that it would be strong enough to do some damage. "Dissolve the forcefield," he shouted to Layla.

Layla nodded her understanding, and as soon as the wall dissolved, Noah gripped the spear tightly and launched himself at Nora.

The spear held solid as it hit Nora's staff when she swung it to meet Noah's attack.

"Did you really think I wouldn't be able to block that?" she demanded as they matched each other blow for blow. "The number of times we fought as kids."

Noah grunted in effort, as the spear he made turned out to be extremely heavy. "What's the message you wanted to give me?" he panted as Nora blocked yet another one of his advances.

"You don't belong here," sneered Nora as she tapped her staff on the ground, throwing Noah on his back while she created a large black energy ball on top of her mandala.

Layla held Ray in Nora's direction, but before she could create another shield, Nora had knocked her back with a smaller energy ball, striking her in the chest.

Taking this chance to attack, Noah crawled forwards and took a swing at Nora's legs with his spear, trying to knock her off balance. The heaviness of the weapon and his lack of physical training was taking its toll on Noah's body. He wanted this fight to be over as soon as possible.

Nora didn't even flinch as she lightly sidestepped him. "Go home. You're not worthy of becoming a Guardian," she said coldly. "The Realm needs someone who can take it in a new direction. Someone who can tap into its true power.

"And you think Garvan is the right person to lead this revolution?" Noah replied as he spat out some grass he'd eaten during his fall.

"Garvan is the *only* person who can create this world. He will rule the Realm as its Master, and no one will be able to stand in his way." Nora's black eyes glittered as Noah helplessly looked up at her from the ground.

"NORA!" Layla screamed, creating a blinding white light, engulfing the hill.

Nora let out a cry of frustration as she shielded her eyes.

Taking the chance Layla had given him, Noah jumped up, spear in hand, and stabbed at the space where Nora had been seconds before.

A blood-curdling scream pierced their ears as Noah's spear tip hit something solid.

Not wanting to waste any time, Noah allowed his spear to disintegrate, and he ran towards Layla, grabbing her hand in one of his and Ray in the other.

He quickly stole a look at the top of the hill where Aaron and Tick had been battling, just in time to see Tick escape into a portal and Aaron fall to the ground clutching his stomach.

"We need to help Aaron," Noah insisted, pulling Layla towards him.

"Don't you dare leave your battle with Nora!" Aaron called to them as Ray relayed their message to him.

"Aaron!" Layla shouted. "Are you hurt? We can heal you if you let us."

Aaron chuckled weakly. "I'm not so feeble to be defeated by the likes of Tick," he said slowly, opening his mouth to continue, but a golden light surrounded him, and in an instant he was gone.

"He's gone," Layla said to Noah. "We're here by ourselves." She looked terrified.

"It's okay. We know enough to be able to win against Nora," Noah tried to reassure her, even though he didn't fully believe what he was saying himself.

"Do you?" a livid Nora hissed. "I was almost blinded by that attack! And my arm! How dare you!" she screamed. "Take this!" Nora slammed her staff into the ground, and hundreds of tiny energy balls shot out from the obsidian gemstones at the top.

Noah and Layla screamed, and a familiar mirror-like forcefield formed between Nora's attacks and where Noah and Layla were keeled over, panting from the exhaustion of their previous days of training and now this fight with Nora.

If it wasn't for the adrenaline running through their bodies, Noah was sure that neither of them would have any energy left at all.

Nora's attacks were relentless, and she didn't show any signs of fatigue.

"The mandala!" Noah shouted to Layla over the sound of Nora's energy balls exploding against their shield.

"What?" Layla shouted back.

"The mandala!" Noah repeated. "We need to destroy her mandala!"

"How are we going to do that?" Layla asked desperately. "She's got us covered from all angles."

"What other attacks did you learn today?" Noah flinched as an exceptionally large black energy ball shattered against their shield. "The flash one is very helpful, but we need something that will cause damage—or at the very least a distraction!"

"I can create fire."

At Noah's questioning gaze, Layla shrugged. "Fiery hair, fiery temper. It made sense to work with fire."

"Alright," Noah said. "We won't have much time between when the shield disappears and your attack needs to start. Hand me Ray, I'll use her to knock the mandala off Nora's staff."

Gripping Ray tightly in his hands, Noah waited until Layla had positioned herself to attack.

"Okay," he whispered to himself, and when Layla nodded

at him, Noah took a deep breath.

The shield disappeared, and Layla screamed in concentration. An incredible emerald green light surrounded her, and she started shooting balls of green fire in Nora's direction.

Noah heard Nora roar in frustration as she used her staff to deflect the fireballs into the hill, creating miniature craters where they hit the grass.

Knowing this was his chance, Noah sprinted forward, not caring if Nora saw him or not, and pointed Ray at her staff.

"Take this!" he screamed as he visualised Nora's mandala shattering into a million tiny pieces.

An amber energy ball shot out of Ray's largest sunstone, aimed straight for Nora's black mandala.

Noah felt like he was watching the scene in slow motion.

The energy ball hit Nora's mandala directly in its centre, and a loud crack sounded as the primary gemstone shattered.

Nora's attempt to block Layla's onslaught of attacks stopped as soon as the mandala was damaged, and the three of them watched as it fell from the top of the staff and landed on the ground near her feet.

Layla let out a victory cheer, but Noah saw the smug look on Nora's face and knew that something was wrong.

"Stay back!" Noah called to Layla, who'd started to run towards him. She paused, confused, but quickly created another fireball in the palm of her hand when she saw Nora's face.

"Noah?" Layla called hesitantly.

"Don't move, Layla," Noah replied softly. "Something's wrong."

An evil cackle escaped Nora's lips. "Idiots. Until we meet again, Noah."

The cracked black obsidian stone was in Nora's hand, and she mouthed something that Noah couldn't hear. The next minute darkness overtook his senses, and he fell to the ground, agonising pain shooting through his body.

"Noah?" Layla's voice called to him, but it sounded far away. Very far away.

The agony wouldn't stop. Noah could hear someone screaming, and it took him a while to realise that it was him.

Then, as quickly as the pain started, it stopped, and everything went black.

Chapter 47 - Noah

A soft sensation overwhelmed Noah's senses. Confusion flooded his mind as he tried to figure out where he was and what had happened.

All he could remember was being in the Realm and fighting Nora when an unbelievable pain had knocked him to his knees. Everything after that was black.

His eyelids felt like lead, but Noah forced them to open, expecting to be at the bottom of the hill looking up at the hut. But instead, the sight of his bedroom back on Earth shook Noah to his core.

What was he doing here?

Where was Layla?

What had happened with Nora?

As soon as that last thought crossed his mind, Noah's bedroom door flung open, and Nora, dressed in her favourite ripped jeans and crop, came bounding in.

"Wake up, sleepyhead," she said to him. "You're going to be late."

Noah's face went slack. "Nora?"

"That's my name, don't wear it out," Nora laughed. "But seriously, Ash wants to meet you before school. She said she had something to ask you."

The insinuations on Nora's face caused an uncomfortable shiver to run up Noah's spine. "Ash?"

"Yes!" Nora said impatiently. "Ash. You know, your *girlfriend.*"

Noah groaned and pulled the covers over his head. This had to be a dream. What had happened in the Realm for him to come back to Earth?

"Are you alright?" Nora asked him, gently pulling the covers off his face. "Did something happen between you and Ash? Did you have a fight?"

"No," mumbled Noah in response. "I just don't feel well."

"Well, Mum won't let you take another day off, not when we're coming up to exams. So get dressed because we're leaving soon."

Noah groaned at Nora, who grinned and bounced out of his bedroom.

As soon as she closed the door behind her, Noah jumped up and started looking for clues about what had happened.

Throwing the doona off his bed, he started fumbling around the sheets, hoping to find something, anything, that would link him back to the Realm.

Nothing.

Dropping to his knees and leaning his forehead on his mattress, Noah tried to focus his energy on the hut he'd just come from. But no matter how many times he cleared his mind, controlled his breathing and visualised his destination, the image of the hut always became distorted, and the energy surrounding him disappeared.

"Argh!" Noah yelled in frustration, pounding his fist on the floor. "Why am I here?"

A knock on his bedroom door pulled Noah back to his new

reality, and he haphazardly threw his doona back on his bed in a pile.

"Are you ready, Noah?" Jen Parker sharply called to him from the other side of the door.

"Almost, Mum," Noah called back, opening his wardrobe and pulling a yellow t-shirt off the rack.

"Well, hurry up. Nora's waiting for you," his mum called again with another rap on his door.

"Yeah, okay, okay," muttered Noah, pulling off his pyjamas and throwing on some jeans he'd found on the floor and the shirt.

This routine a year ago would have been nothing out of the ordinary, but now Noah felt completely out of sorts.

Walking down the stairs into the kitchen, Noah picked an apple from the fruit bowl before grabbing his backpack from a hook near the front door. Walking to meet Nora on the driveway, he shouted a quick goodbye to his parents as he left.

Noah could tell that Nora knew something was up with him, but he also knew he couldn't confide in her like he used to. Considering she'd been gone for months now, and the last time he'd seen her the pain she'd caused him had made him wake up in some alternate reality.

Not that the Nora in this life knew she'd done that.

There *had* to be a way to get back to the Realm so he could battle Garvan like he was supposed to—he knew it—so he wouldn't let himself get too attached to this alternate life. No matter how nice it was to be walking to campus with Nora again.

Taking a bite out of his apple, Noah pondered the reality he was in right now. *What happened to bring me here?* he thought to himself.

"Ash!" Nora suddenly called out, waving her arms in the air to greet the tall brunette.

Noah stopped in his tracks as Ash walked over to meet them.

"Morning," she called back, waving her arms in the air to match Nora.

Giving Nora a hug, Ash whispered something in her ear, and Nora gave a girlish squeal.

"Well, I've just remembered I have something important to do before class starts," Nora said to an unconvinced Noah. "Better be off, bye."

Before Noah could utter a word of protest, Nora bolted into the distance so fast that if they were living in a cartoon, there would have been a cloud of dust in her wake.

Awkwardly, Noah turned to Ash, who was giving him a look that made his stomach lurch uncomfortably.

Sure, he and Ash had a little history, but never in his dreams had he thought he'd wind up dating her. He was sure she liked someone else. She was always telling him she had a crush on someone she'd known for a while, so he'd never pursued her.

Realisation hit him like a brick, and it dawned on him at that moment that, maybe, she'd been giving him hints that *he* was the one she liked, and he'd been too dense to notice.

Gulping, Noah gave a wavering smile to Ash, who looked at him through lidded eyes.

"Shall we walk?" Noah croaked.

"I was thinking we could skip our classes today," replied Ash in a low voice. "My parents left for a business trip this morning, and the house is empty…"

Noah screamed internally.

"You know, we *have* been dating for three years," Ash continued, leaning in closer to Noah.

His body acting on his own, Noah quickly turned his head as Ash closed the gap between them, and her lips bounced off his cheek.

Even with the hurt evident on her face from the rejection, Ash quickly recovered. "We can just chill and watch movies if you'd like?"

"Erm," replied Noah, his mind racing at a million miles a minute. "Well, we have exams soon, you see, so I think we'd better get to class."

Ash's eyes narrowed. "Right," she said, pulling her backpack higher over her shoulder. "Right!" she said again with more force. "Well, I'll see you there then." She turned on her heel and stomped away.

Feeling exceptionally guilty, Noah rubbed his eyes. He'd been dating Ash for three years in this life. She was right to feel humiliated by a sudden rejection like this one.

"I need to find my way back to the Realm quickly before I mess anything else up here," Noah muttered out loud to himself.

All of a sudden, Noah felt something warm and heavy drop in his jeans pocket, and he quickly fished it out.

There, in the palm of his hand, was a keychain-sized Ray, her sunstones glistening as the light hit them. Even though Ray was pocket-sized, Noah could still feel an immense power coming from her. He quickly checked to make sure no one was around and then hid behind a large tree on the side of the path.

"Ray," Noah whispered urgently to the mandala. "Show me Layla."

Ray shuddered in his hands but didn't make any other sign that she had heard his request.

Gritting his teeth, Noah tried again.

"Show me the Realm," Noah demanded.

Again, Ray shuddered, but nothing happened.

Fighting the urge to throw the mandala into a nearby bush, Noah took a deep breath, calming his mind.

Three deep breaths later, Noah knew that there must be more he needed to figure out.

"Can you point me in the right direction?" Noah asked the mandala.

Finally showing a sign of life, Ray shone a thin amber light from one of her sunstones, pointing Noah in a direction away from the campus.

"Sorry, Nora," Noah whispered to himself. "Guess I won't be meeting you in class today."

Following the path that Ray led him on, Noah ducked and weaved behind trees and under shrubs to keep himself from being seen, and after a while, Noah, who was dirty and scratched from being attacked by tree branches, arrived at a familiar house.

"Simmy!" Noah said out loud. "Simmy's house, of course."

Knocking loudly on the door, Noah called out to see if anyone was home.

"Simmy?" he yelled. "Simmy, are you there?"

The front door flung open, and a very dishevelled-looking Simmy, wrapped in an old dressing gown, was standing in front of him. Her thick auburn hair was unbrushed and her brown eyes were narrowed.

"Who are you?" she barked, a significant change from the calm and collected Simmy that Noah was used to.

Taken aback, but happy to see her, Noah pulled Simmy into a big hug.

"My name's Noah Parker," he said to her. "This may sound difficult to believe, but I'm not actually from here."

Simmy pulled herself out of Noah's arms and raised an eyebrow.

"Well, I mean, I *am* from here," Noah tried to explain, "but I'm not actually from *here,* here. If you know what I mean."

"I don't," Simmy replied bluntly. "So, if you'll kindly leave, I have a busy day ahead of me." She moved to close the door in Noah's face.

"WAIT!" Noah yelled desperately, cringing as the foot he stuck in the doorway was squashed when Simmy closed the door on it.

"Excuse me?" Simmy exclaimed. "This is private property you're barging into. Leave now, before I call the police!"

"Wait," Noah said again, all his hopes riding on Simmy and her help. "Let me just ask you one question first, and if it doesn't make any sense, then I'll leave and never come back."

Simmy's expression was hard, but she didn't deny Noah his request.

"Are you a Guardian of the Realm?"

The expression on Simmy's face changed to one of shock. "How do you know about the Guardians of the Realm?" she asked, the tone of her voice sceptical.

A laugh of relief escaped Noah's lips. "My name's Noah Parker," he repeated to her, "and I was just forced from the Realm to this place—which is,well technically it's my home—but it's completely different to how my life was before."

Simmy paused, looking Noah up and down as if deciding

if she could trust him. "Alright," she said, finally. "Come in quickly before anyone sees you."

Noah obliged gratefully, closing the front door behind him as he walked inside the familiar house, although it was much grimier than he was used to. Layers of dust were piled up on the furniture, there were dirty dishes lying around everywhere and the old, floral decorated curtains were all drawn shut, dimming the usually bright house.

"First things first," Simmy said as they reached the living room. Noah looked around, trying not to wrinkle his nose and politely declined the seat and murky cup of tea that Simmy offered him. "What happened for you to come to this timeline?"

"So this *is* an alternate timeline?" Noah mused, "I'd wondered."

"I asked the question first," Simmy said sharply.

"Oh, right," Noah said, used to Simmy being able to provide all the answers. "Well, I originally came from this town here as well, but my sister disappeared a few months ago, and since then I've been working with you and Layla in order for us to become new Guardians of the Realm. The plan was to defeat Garvan and take over from you and your siblings," Noah said, feeling that the explanation of his journey these past few months was very lacklustre.

"Layla Forrest?" Simmy asked.

"Yeah," Noah replied. "Do you know her?"

"She's dead," Simmy said, her voice thick.

Noah's core shook. "What?"

"Layla and her parents were in a car accident many years ago while Layla was still a baby. Drunk driver. They all died on impact," Simmy recalled.

Noah felt his stomach leap into his throat, and he anxiously tried to swallow it. He'd been hoping to meet with Layla in this timeline.

"In answer to your question before," Simmy continued, "yes, this is an alternate timeline to the one you're used to. While we appear to be following the same time scheme, things are very different here."

"The same time scheme?" asked Noah.

"You're the same age here as you are in your own timeline, yes?" Simmy questioned.

"Uh, yeah, I think so," replied Noah, trying to measure his body to see if he looked any different.

"If we were following a different time scheme, you would be older or younger," Simmy went on. "So we would either be in the future or in the past."

"Right," Noah answered, although he wasn't confident that he completely understood what Simmy was trying to explain. "Anyway," he said. "I need to get back to the Realm."

"That's easier said than done," Simmy said, placing her undrunk tea on the table in front of her, pacing the room. "There's a Realm in this timeline too."

"Really?" Noah asked.

"Really," Simmy confirmed. "It would be easy to get you to this Realm, but getting you to the Realm in your own timeline is an entirely different feat."

"You'll help me get there though, won't you?" Noah pleaded.

"I don't seem to have a choice," Simmy sighed, rubbing the bridge of her nose with her thumb and forefinger. "I've been banished from my own Realm because I failed my mission to train the new Guardians. The least I can do is ensure that you defeat Garvan in your own timeline."

"So Garvan's taken over here already?" Noah asked glumly.

"For many years now," Simmy replied. "He threatened Zion with the lives of my siblings and told him that unless he gave up his power, there would be no one left for him to protect. So Zion was sealed away, and Garvan took over the Realm. Slowly but surely, everyone on Earth has become affected by it, and soon they will all be destined to an eternity of roaming the Realm as Shadow Beings."

Horrified, Noah gripped the pocket-sized Ray in his hand. "There must be something we can do."

"*We*," Simmy gestured between the two of them, "are not doing anything. Don't forget that you have another path to follow. You can't go risking the lives of your friends and family because you feel you have to save everyone."

"I can't just let the people here suffer. These are my friends and family too!" Noah argued angrily.

"No, they're not. These people are the friends and family of the Noah whose body you're borrowing. And besides, I'm not sitting here twiddling my thumbs. I *will* defeat Garvan, but right now, you need to prevent your Realm from being taken over."

Gritting his teeth, Noah reluctantly nodded in agreement.

"No one's destined to save everyone by themselves," Simmy said gently, patting Noah's hand. "You need to stay focused on your own journey and not get distracted by every issue that comes your way.

Noah nodded slowly. "Alright," he said, letting Ray fall back into his pocket.

"Good," replied Simmy. "Now, follow me."

Noah followed Simmy into a dark room at the end of the hallway, unsure where she was taking him.

"Get inside here," she said to him, pointing into a wardrobe that had all different sorts of crystals around the rim.

Nervous, but not about to argue with this Simmy, Noah stepped inside. As soon as he did, he felt an intense surge of energy passing through him, lighting his nerves on fire. Gasping from the shock, Noah used all his might to keep his eyes open and to absorb as much of the energy as he could, feeling his powers grow as he did so.

"You're going to need a lot more power if you're going to defeat the Garvan in your Realm," Simmy said to him from outside the wardrobe.

Noah tried to respond but couldn't force the words out of his mouth, resigning to a nod to show that he'd heard.

Simmy appeared to be very calm as she electrocuted Noah with the energy.

After what felt like hours, Noah felt the shocks begin to subside.

"Take that mandala out of your pocket," Simmy said,

Noah gripped Ray in his hand, and as he brought her out into the field of energy he was in, she began to grow back to her normal size.

"Ask her to show you your travel companion," Simmy said, her voice beginning to sound distant to Noah.

"Show me Layla," Noah instructed Ray.

A portal began to open in front of Noah.

"I can't be sure that this is your timeline," Simmy said to him, "but I've given my remaining power to ensure that you have the best chance of returning to where you need to be."

Noah opened his mouth in protest.

"Don't worry, my powers were always going to leave me," replied Simmy. "At least I was able to choose when and how they left," she chuckled. "Take that, Garvan!"

"What are you going to do now?" Noah asked, the portal growing bigger and bigger beside him.

"I'm not sure yet, but I'll figure it out."

"I want to help you," Noah called to Simmy, the roaring of the portal ringing in his ears.

"Help me by going back to your own timeline and defeating Garvan before he has a chance to befoul the Realm like he's done here," Simmy called back.

The portal was complete, and Ray was pulling Noah through it with surprising force. "I will!" Noah yelled. "I will beat him!"

Going through the portal felt like Noah was being forced through a very small tube. The pressure on all sides of his body made him feel nauseous.

And then, with a *pop*, he was free.

"Noah?" a voice called to him. "Noah, wake up!"

Opening his eyes with a groan, Noah looked around him.

Kneeling over him, shaking his shoulders, was Layla.

Chapter 48 - Layla

"Wake up, dammit. Wake up!" Layla pounded Noah's chest, knowing that it would bruise, but Noah didn't stir. If it wasn't for his shallow breaths, Layla would have thought him dead.

It had taken all of her strength to tug Noah up to the top of the hill and into the hut they'd shared with Aaron, and her arms were aching and bruised by the end of it. Nothing compared to the bruises on Noah's arms that were starting to appear, though. She'd gripped him with all her might, not letting him roll even an inch back down that hill.

Lifting a shaking hand, Layla tried to bring some blue healing powers to the surface, but only a sad emerald wisp flickered once before dissipating into nothing, and Layla let out a frustrated sob.

Noah was Realm knows where, Ray was missing too, Aaron had disappeared into thin air, and Nora and Tick were nowhere to be seen, which set Layla's teeth on edge, so she hadn't rested in the three days that Noah had been out of it.

The exhaustion was too much. Her energy was completely spent, and the terror of being attacked while she was so helpless had kept Layla awake this whole time. She'd only dared to allow herself a few twenty-minute power naps when she physically couldn't keep her eyes open any longer.

It was during her current power nap that Layla's usually dreamless sleep shifted, and she was standing in a pure white room filled with a white desk and white office chairs.

It looked like a corporate meeting room adorned with all white furniture.

"Uhh, hello?" Layla called out, stalking over to the table and running a finger along the smooth surface. "Did I have a meeting scheduled with someone?"

A deep chuckle sounded behind her, and Layla swivelled on her ankle to see who it was, so quickly that she almost sprained it.

"I see you haven't lost your sense of humour," Zion said to her gently, his eyes sad as he took in her haggard appearance.

Layla gritted her teeth, not interested in hearing what he had to say.

"I am sorry," Zion continued. "I know you're furious with me."

"You're damn right I am!" Layla stormed up to him, ignoring the sharp pain in her ankle. "Where were you? I've been stranded in that hut for three days! Noah's barely alive, nothing I do will wake him, and I can't access my energy enough to be able to heal him, or myself, or put up a shield around us so I can get some sleep! So, yeah, I suppose furious is a word that could be used to describe how I feel right now."

Zion didn't try to interrupt her as she ranted at him, which she was grateful for because if he had, she wasn't certain that she wouldn't pick up one of those squeaky-clean looking office chairs and throw it at his face.

"When Nora pulled Noah away, she also placed a barrier over you, stopping me from reaching you and the Realm

311

has also been blocking me from helping you. Noah must be working through a lesson," Zion said to her. A flicker of frustration sparked in his blue eyes for a moment.

"Doesn't that bother you?" Layla asked him, trying to keep her voice calm. When he didn't reply, she clarified. "That you've got all this power to help the people you care about, but the Realm stops you whenever it feels like without any warning."

Zion stared at her briefly before running a hand through his long, unbound, golden hair. "I am a creation of the Realm. I must do its bidding, regardless of what I believe to be the better choice. The paths that even us Celestials choose are not always in the best interest of the Realm's growth, and so it stops us from doing them before we get in too deep."

"You didn't answer my question," Layla replied.

Zion let out a sigh, stalked closer to her and laid a large hand surrounded in healing blue energy on her shoulder.

Instantly Layla felt brand new. Her energy levels had been replenished, and even the exhaustion had gone. It felt like she'd slept for the entire three days.

"Noah will be with you soon, and when he is, you need to go somewhere else." Zion placed his pointer finger on Layla's forehead, and an image of a very fancy looking treehouse was shown to her. "This is one of Aaron's more favourable dwellings. He's happy for you to stay there for as long as you need. The two of you need to rest and plan, and then come and find me when you're ready. There is still much to do. Garvan has completed his rebirth, so you're going to need to move quickly."

"What? He's awake already? Can't we just stay here and figure out what to do with you?" Layla called, but she wasn't with Zion anymore. She was back at the hut. "Bloody Realm dwellers," she gritted out through her teeth.

Before she could try to telepathically tell Zion exactly what she thought of this plan, she woke up when a low groan caught her attention. She quickly knelt over Noah, shaking him slightly, calling "Noah? Noah, wake up!" as his eyelids began to flutter open.

Chapter 49 - Noah

"Layla? Noah gasped, trying to move his stiff arms.

"Noah," Layla replied, trying to keep her voice calm. Pushing himself up, Noah shook his head to clear it. "What's wrong?"

"You were out for three days," Layla breathed. "Ray was gone, and I couldn't do anything except drag you back up to this hut after Nora attacked you."

A shiver ran down Noah's spine. "Three days?"

"Garvan's awake, Noah," she continued, looking him in the eye. "He's finished his rebirth."

"What?" Noah whispered.

Layla stood up and started packing the rations she'd been living off for the past few days, shoving them into a tattered old backpack. "We need to get out of here," she said to him, finishing her packing and pulling the backpack on. "We need to find somewhere else to hide until we can go up against him."

"Where are we going to go?" Noah replied, tentatively standing up. Even though Layla had said that his body had been in this hut for the past three days, he still felt tender from the energy he'd absorbed in that alternate timeline.

"Aaron's got a treehouse a little way away from here," Layla replied. "I think I can take us there."

"Let's go then," Noah said, unsteadily gripping Ray in one hand and taking Layla's in the other.

Both of them closed their eyes, and while Noah didn't know where they were going, he focused his energy on Layla, visualising that she had taken them to their new destination.

Layla used Ray to create a portal, and Noah opened his eyes just in time for Layla to pull him through it. "This is the place?" he asked, wincing as his back twinged.

"Yeah," she replied, pulling off the backpack. "I hope so, at least."

"Trust Aaron to enjoy living in a treehouse," Noah said, gripping the rope ladder tightly and testing that it would hold his weight.

Noah climbed to the top, and his mouth dropped at what he saw before him. He wouldn't call this place a treehouse so much as he would call it a tree mansion. It was huge! And very deceiving from the outside, where it looked like a modest wooden shack. There was a chandelier hanging from the ceiling, a large, comfortable looking couch in the living room and countless bedrooms.

Aaron had expensive taste.

If Layla was in awe of the house, she didn't show it. Placing the backpack on a table in the kitchen, she opened up a notebook and started to write.

"What are you writing?" Noah asked, walking over to her and sitting down.

"We need to make a plan," Layla replied. "We have to assume that Garvan has retained his memories from his previous life and that he's going to continue gaining power until he becomes the Master of the Realm."

315

Silently agreeing with her, Noah let Layla continue voicing her thoughts.

"There is no point in us storming in there while we still don't really know what we're doing," she continued. "We'd be killed in a second."

"Oh!" Noah said suddenly. "Right, Layla, give me your hand."

"This is no time to be cute," replied Layla, eyeing him off.

"I'm not trying to be cute," Noah huffed indignantly. "Just give me your hand."

Layla held out her hand, and Noah placed Ray on their two outstretched palms, focusing on splitting the energy he'd received in the alternate timeline between the two of them.

Letting out a quiet breath as the electricity flowed through her, Layla's eyes widened.

"Where did you get all this energy from?" she whispered when he'd finished.

Noah explained what had happened to him while he'd been knocked out for the three days, deciding to leave out the part where Ash was his girlfriend and emphasising his time with Simmy.

Layla's face was grim. "We can't allow that to happen here," she said solemnly.

"I know," Noah replied, "but we need to do something, and quickly, if we're going to have any chance of success."

"I was thinking…" Layla said slowly, tapping the tip of her pen on the paper in front of her.

"Yes?"

"We really need Zion's help with reaching our full potential. Do you reckon he would train us?"

The thought had never even crossed Noah's mind before.

"How would we get to him?"

"I don't know, but maybe we could get in touch with Aaron and ask?" Layla said.

Before Noah could respond, Ray shuddered violently in his hand, and he stood up so fast his chair toppled over.

"Someone's coming," he said quietly, pulling Layla away from the centre of the room and ducking underneath a window at the front of the house.

Peering over the window ledge, Noah saw a dark figure floating towards them before suddenly disappearing.

"I can see you," was whispered in his right ear.

Jumping in fright, Noah pulled Layla behind him and turned to face the voice.

It was Nora.

She was glaring at him maliciously as she held her staff in her hand. Her black mandala had been repaired, and it was even bigger than it had been before.

"I thought I told you that you didn't belong here," she hissed venomously, slamming the bottom of her staff into the ground and sending black shockwaves throughout the house.

Glass shattered everywhere as the windows exploded and the furniture toppled over.

Layla had managed to conjure a shield before the shock-waves had hit them, but even behind it, Noah could feel the intense power Nora wielded.

"I'm not going to let you take over the Realm!" Noah shouted to his sister, not even trying to reason with her this time around.

"And just what are you going to do about it?" Nora sneered, forcing even more power from her staff.

Noah handed Ray to Layla. "Keep the shield up."

"What are you going to do?" Layla asked, holding Ray out in front of her.

Noah gritted his teeth, not sure what he was going to do himself, until the broken windowsill he was standing next to caught his eye.

Roughly, Noah pulled a piece of wood from the windowsill, which had split apart from Nora's blast, and tore it into three strips, visualising them as arrows. Noah forced his amber energy into them, and they were instantly brought to life.

Plucking them out of the air, Noah threw them one at a time in Nora's direction, propelling them with the help of his energy since he didn't have enough time to make a bow.

Dodging them easily, Nora sneered. "Your aim's pretty pathetic."

Noah sneered back. "We'll see."

Glancing at the arrows that he had aimed at Nora and making sure that they were where he wanted them, Noah held his palm out in front of him and yelled "Yah!" closing his fist as he released the energy within the arrows he'd created, propelling them towards Nora at lighting speed.

Nora screamed in agony. The waves of energy she'd been blasting them with stopped abruptly. "How dare you?" she screamed at Noah, trying to pull out an arrow that had embedded itself in her ribs.

Ignoring her, Noah sprinted to the shattered windowsill, pulling off a larger piece of wood, this time visualising a spear as he forced his energy into it. Grabbing the spear, Noah threw it as hard as he could in Nora's direction.

His aim was truer this time around, piercing Nora right through her forehead.

Nora fell limply to the ground with a thud.

"Noah," Layla whispered, horrified at the sight before her. "You just killed your sister."

"Wait," Noah said to her, pointing at Nora lying limply before them. "Watch."

Both of them held their breath as the girl in front of them began to dissolve in front of their eyes. Her dark clothes turned to dust and scattered in the wind. When everything, even her staff, had disappeared, a small strand of dirty blonde hair fluttered to the floor.

"That wasn't Nora," Noah said, leaning against the wall of the treehouse.

Using Ray, Layla asked her to help repair the house, and Ray glowed emerald in her hands as the windows and furniture were restored.

Slumping to the ground, Noah sighed loudly, his body exhausted from everything it had been through these past few days.

Layla slumped next to him, and Noah put his arm around her shoulders, pulling her to his side.

"How did you know that wasn't Nora?" Layla asked after a short pause while the two of them got comfortable.

"I had to believe that Nora wouldn't try and force us out like that," Noah replied. "I mixed a drop of my blood with the spear I created, and if the Nora we fought today had a similar DNA to mine, the spear wouldn't have hurt her." Noah lifted his finger where a small trail of dried blood was smeared at the tip.

"That was a big risk to take," Layla replied, "and is really powerful energy. How did you know how to do that?"

Noah shrugged. "I just had a feeling that's what I needed to do. It was like something was guiding me. Maybe the energy

I got from the other Simmy had something to do with it."

"You're probably right," Layla said. "That shield I was holding up shouldn't have lasted as long as it did either. I wonder what else we can do now."

Noah shrugged again, exhausted, and he rested his head on top of Layla's, both of them too tired to move to a bed.

"Are we going to try and meet up with Zion?" Noah asked her sleepily.

"We have no choice. We need all the training we can get," Layla replied slowly, her voice thick as she held back a yawn.

Noah nodded absently.

They would need to be on their A-game if they had any hope of reclaiming the Realm and fulfilling their destiny of becoming fully-fledged Guardians.

But for now, sleep.

Chapter 50

HOW WILL NORA DEAL WITH GARVAN'S MIND GAMES? AND WHAT ARE NOAH AND LAYLA GOING TO DO NOW THAT THEIR MISSION TO RESCUE NORA HAS HIT A MASSIVE ROADBLOCK?

READ AHEAD FOR A SNEAK PEAK OF: THE MANDALA CHRONICLES: ALTERNATE TIMELINES

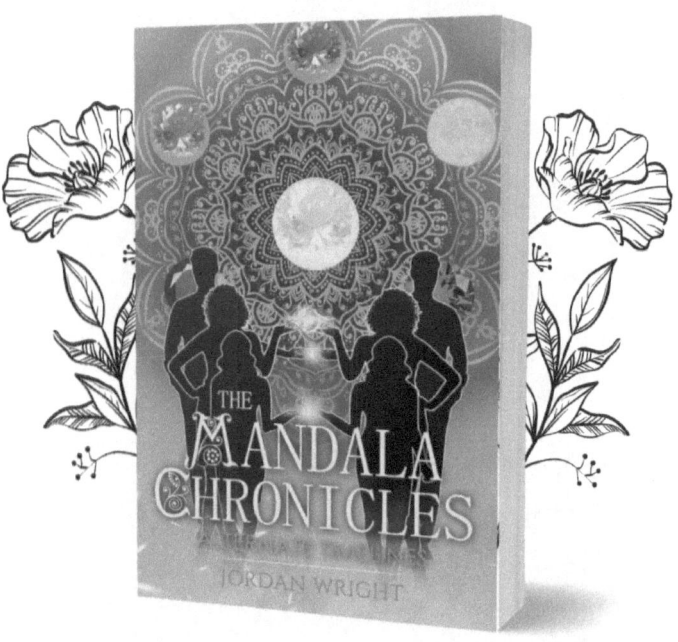

Chapter 1 - Nora

Nora's eyes snapped open at the soft scraping sound approaching the room she was still confined to. No one had been to see her since the duplicate she had sent to fight Noah and Layla had disappeared, so it disconcerted Nora that someone, or something, was coming for her now.

Slowly leaning up on one elbow, Nora squinted into her dimly lit room, trying to see what was making the noise. Her eyes struggled to adjust.

A shift in the air caused a shiver to run down her spine, and the red energy barrier locking her in the room slowly dissolved to reveal a shadowy figure in the doorway.

"Tick? What are you doing here?" Nora pushed herself up into a sitting position to better see the Shadow Being she had created when her Ego had been pulled out of her chest as she first arrived in the Realm.

Tick retracted her long, clawed fingers from the floor, and the scraping stopped. Nora raised her palm in the air and summoned a bright amber ball of light. She held it up, keeping her expression blank as she looked upon Tick's furious face, now an inch away from her own.

Tick's jagged teeth snapped as she took a step back, her

sharp, wispy features flickering in Nora's light. "Your little hair trick didn't work," she spat quietly. Tick knew better than to make too much noise while her master, Garvan, was recovering from his rebirth.

"Trick?" Nora replied innocently, tossing the amber ball of light in the air. She clicked her fingers, and it floated next to her head.

"You could have easily beaten your brother on your own, but you decided to stay here instead, hiding away in your room like a coward." Nora could feel Tick's simmering rage as the Shadow Being leant back and flicked her long hair behind her shoulder.

"I wasn't under any instructions to go on the mission *personally*. Why should I risk myself when my double did a fine job on its own?" Nora rebutted calmly.

Tick's teeth gnashed. "Fine job? *Fine job?* There's not a scrap of it left!"

"But I *did* find where Noah and Layla were hiding. We're playing the long game here, Tick. No need to rush." Nora absently inspected her fingernails, watching as Tick's shadows exploded around her in anger.

"Garvan should have sent me!" Tick screeched, all concerns about being too loud gone. "I wouldn't have let them go free!"

"Oh really?" Nora cooed. "Where's Aaron, then? Didn't you go in person to retrieve him? I don't see him here."

"He had help," Tick snarled, clenching and unclenching her fists.

"As did Noah." Nora lifted her chin defiantly as one of Tick's clawed fingers roughly stroked her cheek.

"You're getting too cocky. I'll be watching you," Tick whispered in her ear before floating backwards out the doorway, through the barrier.

"I'll be sure to put on a show," Nora purred in reply, letting the ball of light float back down to her palm, re-absorbing the energy into her body.

Once Tick was completely out of sight, Nora laid down again and sighed, resting her arm on her forehead.

She drew a circle in the air, and a small round mirror appeared in her hand, glinting as she looked into the glass. A gift from Aaron, although she'd been tempted to smash it into pieces when it had arrived three days prior.

There on the other side were Noah and Layla, resting after a long day of planning.

She ached to be with them, to jump through the glass and rejoin the mission she'd started, but she was stuck here. Aaron had rescued Noah instead, leaving her behind to fend for herself.

Nora ignored the burning sensation in her throat. She knew she could handle herself, but still, a small part of her wished she was the one being taken care of.

The mirror shimmered as her thoughts drifted to Aaron, and she was now looking at him, lying in his own bed, nursing a nasty scratch that ran down his chest.

Nora flinched at the sight of him and shook the mirror, trying to get it to show her Noah again, but the mirror ignored her.

Resigned, Nora couldn't help looking at the muscles rippling along Aaron's bare chest, rising and falling as he breathed deeply in his sleep.

Nora's cheeks grew warm as she tried to look away, but her treacherous eyes dragged themselves down to where his blanket lay loosely over his toned abdomen, ending just under the V of his hips.

"Enjoying the view?" Aaron purred from the other side of the mirror, one eye cracked open as if he could see her.

Nora's heart leapt out of her chest at being caught, but she gave a disgusted groan in response before throwing the mirror as hard as she could at the wall.

The last thing she heard before it disappeared into thin air was Aaron chuckling.

She drew the circle in the air again, trying to bring the mirror back so she could check on Noah, but nothing happened. Aaron had clearly taken his gift away since she was determined to smash it.

Scoffing, Nora rolled onto her side on her rock-hard bed, pulling the flimsy sheet over her shoulder mumbling, "Who even needs that many muscles?"

She could have sworn she heard Aaron laugh.

* * *

The next morning, after a restless night's sleep, Nora dragged herself out of bed to find a bag of fresh clothes and towels tossed into the room.

Garvan wanted to see her, it seemed.

Picking the bag up, Nora was instantly frozen in place. She let out a noiseless scream as Tick appeared out of nowhere. The Shadow Being hauled Nora's rigid body over her shoulder with ease, speeding her to the bathing room and unceremoniously throwing her inside.

"Garvan's picked up some new tricks," Nora muttered to

herself as she unfroze, rubbing her ribs where Tick had gripped her and held onto the wall to steady herself as her head reeled.

When she felt like she was able to stand without toppling over, she pulled off her filthy pants and top and turned on the hot water, watching the room fill up with steam before adding some cold water and stepping into the bath.

Sitting down, Nora ran her hands over her body and noticed a sensitive spot over her ankle. An old injury that hadn't properly healed. She called blue healing energy to her fingertips and gently pressed them to her skin, letting out a sigh of relief as the ache disappeared.

Keeping the healing energy activated, Nora ran her hands over the rest of her body, taking the time to mend anything else that felt sensitive. She then dunked her head under the water before scrubbing her body down with a floral-scented bar of soap, holding back a sigh of satisfaction as the grime coating her skin floated away.

She had forgotten what it felt like to be properly clean.

Sooner than she would have liked, someone banged loudly on the door, and the bath water magically disappeared, leaving Nora cold and wet as goosebumps pebbled her skin.

Exhaling loudly through her nose in frustration, Nora unwillingly pushed herself out of the empty tub before quickly drying herself. She pulled on a new pair of loose grey cotton pants and a matching shirt, which had been inside the bag she'd been given.

Strolling out of the bathing room barefoot, Nora was guided to Garvan's Throne Room by a see-through, floating Shadow Being. It looked old and frail as it wafted down the hallway.

Before Nora could ask its name, it pointed her towards a

pair of golden doors, which flung open as she looked at them.

Nora stepped inside, and her heart leapt into her chest. "What are you doing here?"

www.ingramcontent.com/pod-product-compliance
Lightning Source LLC
Chambersburg PA
CBHW030522120726
47904CB00005B/1575